The Autumn Collection

Paul John Hausleben

Cover photo by Paul John Hausleben

ISBN: 978-0-9886336-3-6

DEDICATION

To all the football games, turkeys, rakes, pumpkins, ghosts, red, yellow, and brown leaves, cranberry sauce, stuffing, and Thanksgiving Day parades, I have met along the way.

CONTENTS

"Autumn; it is when the world comes alive after stifling summer heat, when the warm sun reminds us that it is still there, and the cold winds foretell of the winter and snow to come."

Paul John Hausleben
September 2013

ACKNOWLEDGMENTS

Thank you once more to my friends, family, and all those readers that continue to read my drivel and assorted poppycock. I warmly appreciate your encouragement and compliments. In acknowledgement of my first story with ham radio featured in the storyline, I send a special thank you to WA2DIG (SK), "The Digger," Mr. Victor Ulrich, for starting me out on a lifelong journey of the mystery of wondering what will be on the other end of that radio dial. TNX ES 73 to you, Digger.

Preface from the Author

Autumn for me has always been a special time of the year. There are certain aspects of the character, Paul John Henson that indeed, actually does closely mirror this storyteller. One of them is the fact that I dislike summer heat and humidity. Autumn comes along, and the world takes a deep breath! It is a wonderful time of the year, and although the wintertime is my favorite season, those crisp, clear autumn days never fail to inspire me to new and different heights.

Although I stole some characters from Harry and Paul adventures, this book is the first book in which I have published that is not an actual Harry and Paul adventure. I can honestly say that the material was a long time in the making; for some reason, it took me forever to start and complete.

To some extent, I have always revolved around the seasons in my life. It was only a matter of time before I decided to select one of the seasons to provide a theme for a compilation, and then attempt to bind them together with storylines.

Perhaps it was the mood that I was in during this time period, or some type of other inspiration, but for some reason, I felt autumn presented a multitude of my own feelings that I would like to share with readers.

However, where should I start? That was always the question, as I would earnestly begin, and then shelve, another project.

After the success of the compilation, *The Time Bomb in The Cupboard, and Other Adventures of Harry and Paul,* I received a number of inquiries from readers asking if I would be planning a similar collection for the future. Based upon that input, I wanted to put together another book consisting of shorter stories or novelettes, similar in structure to *The Time Bomb in The Cupboard, and Other Adventures of Harry and Paul,* rather than another long novel. I had some extra work and materials hanging around, but nothing concrete and frankly, very good in quality. On top of that, only a few of the compositions were set in the autumn of the year.

After sometime struggling with how to create and find a common theme around the season of autumn, I found my inspiration for this book, by digging up a very old and strange story, which is included here with the title of *Eleven Sentences*. It was one of the few serious pieces that I had ever written, and it was a very convoluted, short story that I had created when I was about nineteen or so years of age. The story never seemed to go anywhere, but it had an autumn theme and setting, with a dramatic beginning and ending. I loosely based *Eleven Sentences,* upon an actual adventure that I had when I was very young and not very worldly at all.

Digging around on a day in late March, (hardly the time one is inspired to write stories about autumn) I found, and then read the original manuscript. I had tinkered with the original storyline a year or two earlier, but it never felt quite right. However, looking at it again, I felt that I had found the perfect vehicle for a Paul John Henson adventure. I knew that I could use this material to create a storyline, which would fill in some missing years when the character was on his own, away from his family, and his friends, while he was also pining, weepy-eyed for his long, lost, love; Ms. Binky Hobnobber.

I recently had received some inquiries about the subject of the missing years of Paul and Harry's lives between adventures; therefore, it was without hesitation that I put some material together to fill in some missing blanks in the chronology of the two characters. To my surprise, it all came together rather nicely. I rewrote the story, but kept the basic framework, and from that small start, the rest of the book came together too. I quickly wrote three or four new stories, which had been hanging around my mind for quite some time looking for an excuse to come to life, dug up some old poppycock, added a Halloween ghost or two, a few mysterious, as well as new characters, some words and it was finished.

Unlike much of what I have written, you will find some relatively serious storylines inside this collection, mixed with humor, wit, nostalgia, and even some touches of (yikes) romance. There are even some hapless and futile attempts at (cough, cough) poetry, or something that resembles (or barely resembles) poetry!

The Autumn Collection was an enjoyable piece of material to put together, and it may be a prelude to some more work based upon the seasons of the year.

Time and moods will tell.

The Autumn Collection, very much in my opinion, reflects the strong feelings that autumn invokes. To me, and in my olde tyme memory bank, autumn is about crisp mornings, with warm afternoon sun, followed by cold nights, around which we build the first fires of the year in fireplaces and wood stoves. In front of those first fires of the season, is where families gather around to chat, laugh, and enjoy good times. It is about family, breathtaking colors in the trees, friends, football games, pumpkins, and turkeys.

On a deeper note, autumn is truly about changes. This special season reflects changes in colors, changes in spirits as well as emotions, changes in moments in time, and changes in the air.

No matter what season it is that you are reading this book, it is my hope that these stories, words, and characters, all combine to help bring you closer to appreciate that very special moment in time, when all of us need to enjoy a little piece of autumn in our lives.

I enjoyed putting together this compilation, and it is my hope that you enjoy reading this book, as much as I enjoyed the experience of writing it. Thank you for reading it.

Paul John Hausleben
September 2013

The Autumn Collection

Cranberry Sauce and Stuffing

Featuring Paul John Henson and other characters from the Adventures of Harry and Paul

Eleven Sentences

Featuring Paul John Henson from the Adventures of Harry and Paul

Interlude on an Autumn Afternoon

Some words

The Hidden Valve

Featuring the brave and fearless, Walter P. Thrump

Red Wine and Autumn Memories

A short story featuring Paul John Henson and other characters from the Adventures of Harry and Paul

Love in a Pumpkin

A short story featuring Paul John Henson, Binky Hobnobber Henson, and other characters from the Adventures of Harry and Paul

Flickering Light on an Autumn Night

Some words

Prologue

The first smell of smoke from a wood fireplace, which drifts through the neighborhood on a cold autumn afternoon, announces loud and clear that autumn has arrived. The smoke escaping into the air smells so good, like warm apple pie cooling on a table, inviting you to join in the experience!

Autumn, in many ways, is the lonely stepchild to the other seasons, wedged between spring and the rebirth theme, summer fun, and winter festivities.

Yet, autumn has a very special uniqueness, a quality of freshness, and a sense of change that is in the air. The holidays are there, with Halloween fun, Thanksgiving food, parades, football, and family gatherings, but there is just a bit more to it than that.

Autumn brings to us what the other seasons fail to deliver; a sense of warmth and cold, a season of color, a season of wind, rain, and even an occasional touch of snow. In so many ways, it is as if the purpose of autumn is to shed nature's coat, then allow the world to lie naked until it can be dressed again.

It is so symbolic, because in our own lives, we sometimes need to shed who we are and lie naked too, until we can be changed or reborn.

In a strong sense, we are all part of autumn, within each of our own lives.

Cranberry Sauce and Stuffing

1

Flashback!

"Oh, twenty-seven, I am so sorry, but I have made a slight miscalculation for our huge family feast for tomorrow." My lovely wife Binky came into the living room and she looked at me as I sat in my easy chair in front of the fire. "I am afraid that I did not purchase enough cranberry sauce and stuffing for the amount of people that are visiting us for Thanksgiving dinner!" I took my headphones off my head, reached over, and shut off the music I was listening to this morning.

"Did you hear me, Paul?"

"I did hear a little, Binky. I was able to hear some of what you said over the top of the music. I can go to Foodworld for you to pick up what you need if you would like me to."

Binky immediately started with a famous Binky rapid head nod indicating that she would like me to go and pick up the missing items. I knew that I had a bit of time for her to nod, so while Binky was nodding, I set the footrest of the easy chair back in and stood up.

She had now completed the long, rapid head nod, and I asked her, "Now, what is it that you would like for me to pick up, dear Binky?"

"I need cranberry sauce and stuffing, twenty-seven. Let me write down the amounts for you. Please bring Paul William with you. He knows the store so well that you can get in and out very quickly. It will be jammed and you always are stuck in there forever. I usually advise you to wear your black suit and pastor's collar when you go out, since the statistics show that there is always a need for clergymen at the spur of the moment, but I think in this case, you should wear your No Way rock band tee shirt, and sneakers. Since time is of the essence, then being incognito will be the proper approach this time. I will be right back. I need to write this down, and in fact, I want to call Mother to see if she wants anything special."

I heard what Binky had said, and I just nodded my head slowly. But the truth of the matter was it was a blur after she had said, "Cranberry sauce and stuffing." As soon as I heard those words, my spine tingled, and my mind was heading back in time to another one of those déjà vu moments in my life that happen to me all the time.

I mumbled back to Binky, "All right dear, Binky. I will wait here for you." I knew that Binky never just came right back from anything. Once I heard that she had to make a telephone call to her mother, I knew that I had time to kill. I sat back down on the edge of the footstool, and my mind wandered as I waited.

I was returning in time to an almost identical situation. My little book of memories was once more flipping through the pages, back to a Thanksgiving a long time ago. I remembered a moment when my old man and I went on a similar mission for cranberry sauce and stuffing.

"Hellllooo Fluffy, Hellllooo Fluffy, Hellllooo."

My dear, beloved, Mother leaned her head two inches away from the cage of our pet parakeet, as she tried once more in vain to teach our pet bird, Fluffy, to say, "Hello." Mum had been working for a month or more now repeating the same long, drawn out hello every day for about fifteen minutes. At the sound of the first, hello, my old man who was sitting at the kitchen table reading his newspaper, looked over the top of his newspaper, moaned, and groaned.

"Hellllooooo Fluffy, Hellllooooo Fluffy, Hellllooooo."

"You know that stupid bird has not learned one stinkin' thing from you since you began this madness last month. I must have heard you say, hello Fluffy, twenty-two million times so far. He just stares at you and rings his stupid bell once in a while. Did you ever think he does not understand your English accent?" Mum just stared back at the old man and shook her head.

"I do speak English, you know, dear. I would think that your New Jersey accent would be questionable, unless, we would like to teach Fluffy to say youse guys, dawwwg, and cawwwfee! The book I bought here, tells you that you have to speak clearly, make hand motions to your parakeet, and sooner or later, he will speak simple words." Mum pointed to her Big Bob's guide to *How to Teach and Train your Pet Parakeet* book on the little shelf in the kitchen.

My sister, the old man, and I sat together at dinner time around our kitchen table. It was about one week before Thanksgiving Day, in or around 1974, and we had gathered in our house at 182 Belmont Avenue in good old Haledon, New Jersey. Neither my sister nor I said a word as we sat at the table and gauged the old man's reaction to our mother's comments. The old man just sat there, staring at Mum as she gave it another try.

"Hellllooooo Fluffy, Hellllooooo Fluffy, Hellllooooo."

Fluffy, the parakeet, just sat on his perch inside the cage and did not do a thing. In fact, Fluffy seldom did anything, except sit on his perch with his feathers all fluffed out and his head sunk down inside his body. He seemed to be the most uninteresting pet in the world!

"Are we going to eat tonight or what? That bird is the most useless pet of all time. All he does is sit there all fluffed out and stare at you. I will make a hand motion to him as soon as the kids are gone from the room." The old man had lost patience with the speaking lesson.

"Oh pooh, you are the most impatient man there ever was, and please do not give the children ideas that you make obscene gestures to our poor little bird." Mum waved her hand at the old man, turned away from the birdcage, and went over to the cooker. "I hope the stew has cooked enough. I would not want anyone to get sick, if it has not cooked long enough," Mum said as she stirred the stew in a big pot on top of the cooker. You could see the steam and heat rising from the pot as Mum stirred it around. Once again, the old man looked back over the top of his newspaper and he shook his head.

"When did you start simmering it?"

"This morning, at around eight or so."

"It is a wonder that it did not melt your spoon! How much longer ya want to cook it! It is like a volcano on the stove there, geezzzz!"

"Oh stop, I just am always worried that someone will get sick if you do not cook food long enough. Paulie, please go get your grandfather and tell him that it is time to eat, will you?" Looking back, our parents surely were the odd couple, a prim and proper English gal, who met and fell in love with a street tough guy from Paterson, New Jersey.

"Sure Mum," I said, as I jumped up from the table and ran across the first floor to the hallway to call my grandfather for dinner. I was about fourteen years old now, and I was full of speed, excitement, and energy.

"Gramps, time to eat!" I bellowed as I leaned into the upstairs hallway.

"Coming, Paulie boy. I hear you," my grandfather, or as we called him, "Gramps," acknowledged the call. I heard his apartment door open and his footsteps on the staircase.

Since our grandmother had passed away about five or six years ago, our grandfather lived alone upstairs from us in a small apartment. Gramps was my mother's father, and he had lived in England until after the big war, when he brought his young family over to America. Our grandparents had, until a few years ago, lived next door to us in a large apartment complex, and then moved into the apartment above us when my parents bought the house.

Shortly thereafter, our grandmother had become seriously ill, and she passed away. She was a wonderful woman, and we all missed her, but we felt very fortunate that Gramps was still with us.

"Do you want a Big Boulder or a Dingleberry beer, honey?" Mum asked the old man.

"Big Boulder, those Dingleberries are way too sweet." The old man folded his newspaper up and tossed it on a small table next to the kitchen table. "Why do we actually buy Dingleberry beer? No one ever drinks them!"

Mum looked at the old man with a puzzled look on her face. She began to answer, "Well, I am not. . .."

"Hello, hello, how is everyone tonight?" Gramps had arrived on the scene.

"Hello, Pop," Mum answered and gave her father a kiss on his cheek. "Here is your Big Boulder. I know you do not like those Dingleberries."

"Oh, those blood. . .." Gramps stopped in mid-word as he spotted Mum glare at him before he could get out the word. "Sorry love, I meant to say those wonderful beers are just a little too sweet for me." Gramps diverted attention as he had almost slipped up and used a word that dear Mum would classify as an "English bad word" in front of the children. The old man chuckled, and my sister and I got a little charge out of it.

We both had heard a lot worse than Gramp's colorful English vocabulary. During a single street hockey game that we played in over on Geyer Street, the neighborhood kids on our teams could cuss more than the old man and Gramps did in an entire year.

My sister was about three years older than I was, and she was firmly embroiled in the rebellious teenage phase of life, where she agreed upon nothing that our parents said or did. Most dinnertime meals around the kitchen table turned into adventures or debates over some rule or regulation that either Mum or the old man would pronounce or enforce.

This dinner was no different!

My sister struck the first salvo of the evening, "Can I please spend Thanksgiving Day over at Maureen's house? Her family is having baked ziti and meatballs and they invited me over."

"No, Dorothy, you will be spending Thanksgiving here with us. The whole family is coming over. You do not want to disappoint your family and Aunt Lois and Uncle Ed, now, would you?"

Mum pronounced her verdict while she shook her head and she dished out the stew to each of our plates. Dorothy was my sister's name; she received the name from some English relative or some character in a famous movie or something like that. I just called her Dottie or Dot.

"Oh but, please . . . I want to go over there. Her Cousin Jimmy is coming over, and he is soooo cute. It is always so boring over here."

The old man attempted to put a quick end to the debate, "You heard, Mum. You are not going over there and having Thanksgiving dinner with those pasta bombs, Zipperellis. Whoever heard of ziti for Thanksgiving?"

The old man was the ultimate traditionalist. Holidays came with an official set of the old man's stringent rules and regulations that everyone needed to adhere to in the strictest of manners. Otherwise, the risk was that the holiday was ruined. To the old man, it was simple and plain; Thanksgiving was about turkey, Fourth of July was about hot dogs, hamburgers, and fireworks, and Christmas came with a set of rules and regulations that made the old Roman Empire laws seem as if they were easy to follow. The old man would have no part of any foolishness of drifting away from generations of Henson family traditions.

That was it. My sister was now in silent mode, and she would do her best to fret from now, until next Thursday. Thanksgiving was still a week away, but you could bet that Thanksgiving dinner at Maureen's house would be mentioned by my sister at least twenty-two thousand more times. Maureen Zipperelli was my sister's best friend. She was a short, loud gal of Italian descent, who lived on the other side of the town of Haledon. She was kind of round and plump, as well as she was charismatic, outgoing, and very pretty.

She could also really talk a lot. I do mean talk a lot!

I was just coming into an age where I gave females just a little notice, and Maureen was of vague interest to me, even though she was a little less than three years older than I was. I could stand Maureen for about five minutes, and then I would take off to protect my ears.

I could see my sister already plotting how to work around the holiday boundary that our parents had set up. Her eyes darted back and forth, and she went into immediate shutdown mode to establish the battleground tactic of not speaking to them in protest. Her tactics would include wearing our parents down over a long period of time. The lack of the achievement of the desired results by the time that the actual event became closer or imminent, generally resulted in my sister adding a dose or two of all-out-sobbing-warfare.

I could hardly wait.

Mum dished my stew out into my bowl while she asked me, "Is Harry's family still going to Florida for the holiday, Paulie? Sit up now and keep your long hair out of your stew. Do you want a tie for all of that hair?" I always had long hair and most people called me a hippie.

"No, I am good, Mum. Yeah, yeah, yeah, they are all going down there next Tuesday. It stinks, cuz we have a big hockey game with the Buckley Park Bruisers planned on Friday, and we are a bunch of bums without Harry on defense. Harry don't want to go."

"Paulie boy, proper King's English, now. Harry would rather not travel to Florida, is much better sounding than that atrocious street New Jersey slang language, I hear creeping into your vocabulary." I nodded as Gramps provided me with some valuable, proper English language coaching.

"Maybe you can teach that stupid bird a word or two, Pop, your daughter, sure has not had any luck!"

The old man laughed at his own statement. Gramps ignored him as the old man shoveled in the stew. The old man always kept his mouth within an inch of his bowl and shoveled the food into his mouth like a mechanized shovel. He claimed he picked up the bad habit from his days in the military because they only gave you fifteen minutes to eat. The old man must have had an asbestos-lined mouth because he could shovel in the hottest food, and swallow it whole, even if the temperature of the food was high enough that it would melt steel.

Gramps, on the other hand, was a tough guy from England, but he was very proper in his table manners. He sat up straight and tall, and ate in an organized and orderly English fashion. Gramps stared in horror as he watched the old man shovel his food in his mouth, with gravy running down the old man's face, veggies and meat flying here and there, as though it was the last meal that he would ever eat.

Once Gramps could recover from the shoveling display, he looked at Fluffy and said, "I still say that bird is sick, the blood. . .. I mean, it just sits there all fluffed out and does not do anything. I would return it to the pet store. It is a mess."

The old man nodded his head in mid-shovel, "I agree, Pop. He is useless. At least Skippy is a real pet. Hey, where is ole Skip?"

I piped in, "The last I saw, he was asleep in my bedroom with his head under the radiator. He does that until the heat really comes on full blast and then he comes out. I think the heat eventually cooks his head."

My sister broke her protest silence, "That dog is mean and weird, all he does is chase Paulie and I around and growl at us. I wish we could get a nice, cuddly poodle like Maureen's cute, little, doggie. Her doggie's name is, Necklace."

Gramps was shaking his head in disagreement, "You would not want one of those dogs of French descent, Dorothy. The French have taught poodles too many bad habits. You want an English dog, however, the trouble with a terrier is that you need to show him who is boss, or he will run ramshackle over you and not listen. Please, watch."

Gramps leaned back and pulled his trusty English brass dog whistle out of his pocket, put it to his lips, and blew it. You could hear a low whistle come from the device, but it was just barely audible. Within nanoseconds, Skippy appeared next to our grandfather's chair, sat down, and looked at him for his next command.

"Good boy, Skippy, here is a bit of stew for you. Good dog," Gramps praised ole Skip as he spooned a blob of stew in a spare bowl and gave it to Skippy.

Skippy was a smooth hair, English fox terrier that Gramps had given to my sister and me as a present. He picked him up from an English breeder friend of his, while he proudly proclaimed, "Every child should have a terrier like I had in England!"

Looking back, ole Skippy was a rough one.

He only listened to the old man and Gramps. He would listen to me on very rare occasions. He totally ignored Dottie and Mum. He also loved my Uncle Ed, who was married to Mum's sister, my Aunt Lois. When Uncle Ed would visit, he would insist on calling Skippy, "Ralphie."

Skippy loved Uncle Ed, and he would run around the house as if his tail was on fire, playing, leaping, and having a blast the second that Uncle Ed would walk through the door.

Skippy's sole reason to exist seemed to be to hunt, terrorize, and kill things. His mortal enemies in life included every known species of squirrels, chipmunks, rats, mice, and other little animals, as well as Pussface, the cat who was a stray, orange colored, tabby cat that lived in our neighborhood.

Pussface was sort of everyone's cat. But he loved the old man for saving his life on a snowy Christmas Eve, but that is another story for another day.

He wandered all over the neighborhood, but as of late, it seemed as if he was more our cat than the rest of the neighborhood's stray cat. He would hang around the old man whenever he worked in the yard, or on our old 1964 Putter Classic model 200 car in our driveway. Pussface would just sit and watch the old man for hours. The old cat would also hang around our back porch when it was a cold night. The old man had sympathy for the old wreck of a cat, and the old man would let him sleep on our back porch on very cold nights when he was safely off Skippy's radar. Pussface would bring various gifts as payment offerings to the old man and Mum, such as dead mice, birds, and other things that he had killed or captured. The old man would feed him table scraps, milk, and oddly enough, the cat enjoyed a little beer in a bowl.

Pussface was the feline equivalent to a neighborhood hobo, mooching a warm bed and some alcohol wherever he could find it. He was old, battle scarred, and quite frankly, one ugly cat. His head was huge; it was three sizes too big for his body. His tail was almost gone from accidents with cars, as well as random attacks by Skippy and other dogs, but the old cat trudged on, fueled by beer and table scraps. You had to admire him.

Pussface the cat was the ultimate survivor, and a prime example of a true New Jersey, tough guy.

Another domestic target of Skippy's prowling included our neighbor's large Saint Bernard, named Barney. Barney lived in a house on the other side of a vacant lot that was between our house and the city of Paterson border. Our house was located about fifty feet or so outside the city of Paterson's gritty, northern border. Barney lived in a house right on the main drag and he often hung around on the porch of the home, watching life go by. When ole Skippy decided to take off and go on the prowl, which was pretty much every day, his main mission if he could not find Pussface, would be to harass a dog who was ten times bigger than he was. Skippy had the Napoleon Syndrome and poor Barney just wanted to go through life calm, relaxed, and dreaming of saving stranded people in snowstorms. Well . . . one time, he was lonely, and he ate our neighbor's living room sofa, but that is another story. Anyway, he mostly slept on the porch of the house, but he would run for the hills when he spotted Skippy on the horizon. He wanted nothing to do with Skippy's sharp front teeth!

Our family dog was a little bully.

"You see, Skippy is a great dog!" Gramps beamed proudly at his little English companion. Our meal was over, and my sister and I collected the empty bowls and helped Mum clean up the table.

"Did I receive any mail today, love?" Gramps asked Mum as she nodded, gathered up some envelopes, and handed them to Gramps.

"I will pour your tea in a second, Pop. Do you want tea or coffee, Paul?" The old man indicated that he wanted coffee. The only time that I ever knew the old man to drink tea was if he was sick. He said it mostly tasted like dishwater to him. There was, however, a natural inclination of the old man to resist my mother's side of the family's prim and proper English ways. Deep down, I think it was the old man's way of preserving his proud Paterson, New Jersey heritage. He sat back while he waited for his coffee and watched as Gramps opened his mail.

"Speaking of Florida, I think you received a letter from Aunt Alma in Florida," Mum said, as she poured the hot water into Gramp's teacup and then shifted into coffee mode.

The old man picked his coffee cup up by the handle and stared inside of it. Of course, in the typical old man fashion, he was being a little overly dramatic. He peered inside his still empty coffee cup and asked, "Who was speaking of Florida? I still need some coffee."

Mum did not even answer him.

Now, one of the things that annoyed the old man in life, more than it annoyed most people, was ordinary noises. It was very strange, but if you had a little nose sniffle, a little cough, you were prone to rustling a bag of potato chips as you munched on them while watching television, a car horn, you know; everyday noises, for some reason, it drove the old man wild!

If you sniffed once or twice, he would sit there stewing for a little while, until he finally blew his cork and would yell out, "Geez, go and blow your beak!" Other times, he would sit there steaming, and boiling over, listening to the little noise that was getting on his nerves, until he finally screamed out, "Just cut it the hell out!"

Keeping that in mind, Gramps had a habit of stirring his tea that got under the old man's skin and drove him bananas. After he added a touch of sugar, Gramps tapped the spoon against the side of the teacup, so it made an almost metallic, "clinking" noise. Gramps did not just stir his tea three or four times. He stirred it at least sixty-two thousand, four hundred, and twelve times.

The old man peered into the scene over the edge of his coffee cup in anxious anticipation as Gramps added the sugar.

Gramps then set the spoon inside the cup and opened up the letter from his sister Alma, who lived in Bloody Hot City, Florida. While Gramps perused the letter, he picked up the spoon and started to stir, "Clink, clink, clink, clink, clink." The old man's temples on the side of his head pounded in and out like little tom-tom drums.

"Oh good, Alma is coming up for Thanksgiving! She is going to fly into Newark and Pat will be coming down from upstate New York. My niece is going to pick her up from the airport and they will drive directly here. They both will be here in time for dinner and will be staying for a few days!" Gramps was reading the letter aloud, he was obviously excited about the acceptance of the invitation that Mum had extended to Aunt Alma and to Cousin Pat, a few months ago.

"Clink, clink, clink, clink, clink. . .."

As soon as the old man heard the name of Cousin Pat mentioned, his eyeballs popped out of his head, and he no longer focused upon the annoying stirring spoon noise. He looked over at me as I was stacking the clean plates in the cupboards, and gave me a quick head and hand signal to finish up and follow his lead to meet with him. His priorities had shifted from annoying noises to the pending visit of Cousin Pat.

"Well, let me go check the heat and see if that stupid furnace needs water or not. Thanks for supper. Paulie, let's go and check the water now."

The old man created a mission for us, to meet and to plan some type of Cousin Pat defense strategy. I jumped into action, eager to escape the boring dish and kitchen duty, as well as to hear what the old man's plan was to prepare for a visit from Cousin Pat.

Cousin Pat was a great woman, but she was very large. In fact, she was huge; she barely could fit through our doorways or into our chairs. She also was very loud. She always spoke as if she was screaming at you. Gramps said it was because she was deaf, but I was not so sure. I just think she was very loud. When she laughed, it was interesting, as she also snorted, choked, coughed, and her laughing was so loud that you had to hold your hands over your ears.

Cousin Pat was an adventure!

She also, in addition to being very large, was one of the clumsiest people that I had ever seen. The last time she visited us, which was about six months or so ago, she tripped on the top step of our porch steps, grabbed the handrail, and tore it right off the side of the porch. She fell, twisted her ankle, and ended up spending a week here, until it healed enough for her to go back to her home in upstate New York.

There also was the now famous Fourth of July barbeque incident during our annual cookout and picnic for the holiday. That incident is also a whole other story for another time and place.

She was always dropping pots, pans, food, dishes, drinks; almost everything was in her way. It took the old man a week after she had left to repair all the damage that Cousin Pat had inflicted on our household during her last visit.

This was unexpected news that Cousin Pat and Aunt Alma would be visiting us for the big Thanksgiving holiday. This was an unusual occurrence for both of them to visit at this time of the year. Aunt Alma was very English. She had not come across the pond until she was in her early sixties, and she married a chap who owned shoe stores in Florida. Florida was her primary residence, but Aunt Alma would come up to New Jersey in order to escape the heat in Florida in the summer, and she would usually stay with Gramps for a month or two. She then would spend the rest of the summer, and some of the autumn season, with her daughter in upstate New York.

We seldom saw them outside of that period.

I met the old man in the living room and we huddled up.

"Oh geezzzz, Cousin Pat is coming! I did not actually think they would show up when your mother invited them. Look, you have to help me reinforce the bottom of our old sofa with some plywood and wood braces. The sofa is on the last roundup as it is, and if that giant blimp sits on it, she will collapse it for sure!" The old man was never very worried about how he classified people; he just stuck to the cold, hard facts.

"She is really nice, though, Dad. I like Cousin Pat." I came to her defense.

"Yeah, yeah, yeah, I like her too. I just cannot afford to spend two weeks rebuilding the house after she leaves. It will be Christmas and we have to set all the decorations up, you know!" I nodded in acknowledgement of the poor timing of her visit.

"We have to wait until Gramps finishes stirring his tea, drinks it, and then goes back upstairs. We can then turn the sofa over and jam some wood in there to prop it all up. The sofa is the likely spot for her to sit since she cannot fit her huge ass in any of the other chairs."

"Clink, clink, clink, clink. . .." I could hear the stirring was still going on. The old man grew impatient as he heard the echo of the spoon hitting the teacup.

"Geezzzz, what kind of sugar is in that tea? Does it ever dissolve? Run down and get my tape measure. We will take some quick measurements and finish it up once he leaves." The old man motioned for me to run down to the basement and obtain the tape measure from his workshop.

My primary function in these types of missions was for emotional support, tool fetching, and on rare occasions, I actually provided manpower. Once in a while, the old man allowed me to do some actual work on my own.

Slowly, my best buddy Harry M. Redmond Jr., under

the guidance of his old man, could also perform some actual work. Little did we realize where it would take all of us! Once again, that is a whole other story.

Gramps finally finished drinking his tea, said goodnight, and he returned upstairs to his apartment. As soon as the coast was clear, the old man and I flipped over the sofa, and he took some measurements. The old man was feverishly measuring and drawing a sketch on a pad when we heard Mum shriek out a terrible, bloodcurdling scream. We dropped our tools and ran into the kitchen, along with Dottie and Skippy. We found poor Mum running around in circles as she slammed the back door shut.

"What? Are you, okay? What the hell is wrong?" The old man yelled as we watched Mum run to the kitchen table, pull out a chair, and jump up on it.

Poor Mum was beside herself as she explained, "Oh that, Pussface! It is cold out there tonight, so he was meowing at the back door to come in for the night. I poured a little leftover beer in a dish for him. I checked to make sure Skippy was with you two preparing for Cousin Pat's visit, and when I opened the door to let him in, he dropped a dead mouse at my feet! Ohhhhhhh! That cat!"

Skippy was now beside himself with excitement. He was snarling and running around the house, preparing for battle. The old man shook his head. He made sure Skippy was off in the other room sharpening his teeth, and then he opened the back door. Sure enough, there was the gift on the floor. Pussface looked at the old man and meowed at him. The beer was gone from the bowl, so Pussface was happy for tonight.

Our northern New Jersey neighborhood had everything, from mobsters to a beer-loving tomcat.

The old man picked up the dead mouse and chucked it out into the yard.

"He just wanted to show you that he loves you, honey!" The old man was laughing, but Mum did not find it funny in the least. We went back to our Cousin Pat preparations and reinforcements of the forward Henson defense front. Mum cleaned up the kitchen and covered up her precious Fluffy for the night.

We heard, dear Mum opening up a quick last minute, teaching lesson, as she began saying, "Goodnighttttttt Fluffy, goodnighttttttt. . .." from the depths of the kitchen.

We completed our task, and the old man made me jump up and down on the sofa to test it. He stood in front of me with his hands on his hips, nodding in satisfaction with a smile on his face.

"Good, good, that should hold her, even after she sucks down half of our Thanksgiving turkey. It is a good thing the shop is giving away big turkeys this year. I put in for a twenty-five pounder. We will need it with all of these folks coming over this year. We will need to go up to the Rickel Home Improvement Store on Saturday and pick up some longer lag bolts for the front railing, a few tubes of epoxy, and some all-purpose glue for when Cousin Pat breaks stuff, but I think we are all set."

Everything was quiet in the Henson household at 182 Belmont Avenue once more, as the night drew quietly to a close, and our Thanksgiving preparations were now well underway.

On the other hand . . . I thought it was going to be quiet.

"Daddy, I will ask you again. Daddy, can I pleaseeeee go to Maureen's house for Thanksgiving?"

"NO!"

Oh boy, this was going to be a loud one! I was out of here. The way this debate is shaking out, it may be still going on next Thanksgiving. I think that I will go and stick my head under the radiator and hang out next to Skippy.

2

The Great Fluffy Incident

The Saturday before Thanksgiving started out with a clear sky and an unusually cold chill in the air. We usually had a street hockey game planned with the guys over on Geyer Street every Saturday afternoon; however, since it was the weekend before Thanksgiving, and we were playing the Buckley Park Bruisers on Friday, we decided to cancel the regular game. Today, I had promised the old man that I would help him around the house with some more preparations for the arrival of Cousin Pat and the big Thanksgiving Day gathering.

Even back then, I realized that Thanksgiving was a special day. First off, in those days, it was the official kickoff to the great Christmas season. This is in stark contrast to how the world is nowadays when the Christmas kickoff occurs right around the Fourth of July. Growing up, Thanksgiving was my favorite holiday.

In fact, it still is!

Thanksgiving has no pressure, no gifts, and no shopping lines. It is a special day of hanging with family, friends, enjoying a big meal, watching or playing football, and just sharing good times. It does not really get much better than taking a step back, taking a deep breath, and thanking God for all that you really have. Even Pussface the cat, homeless on the streets, could be thankful for a warm porch on a cold night, a few scraps of meat, and some beer.

Life is really good. No matter how badly you think that you may have it, if you really stop and think you can find someone worse off than you are. All of us have something to be thankful for. Sometimes, you just have to probe a bit deeper to find it.

I pulled up my window shade and gazed out into the morning. I rubbed my eyes and tried hard to shake off the sleep of the night. I glanced at the clock on my little shelf, and it told me that I was up even earlier than the old man was. On the weekends, the old man had a rule of when he was up; the whole house had to wake up too. He would help my mother cook breakfast on the weekends, and do his best to bang dishes, pots, pans, and make as much noise as he possibly could, in order to wake us all up.

I laid there in my bed for a long time, staring at the ceiling. I turned on the transistor radio that I kept propped up behind my pillow to listen to the hockey games late at night. I tuned it into the top forty radio station on the A.M. radio band, and I think I actually started to drift off back to sleep . . . when it happened.

At first, I heard some water running and the sound of some pots and pans coming from the kitchen. I could barely make out my father and mother talking in a low muffle in the early morning shuffle. Then, a bloodcurdling scream tore apart the quiet calm of the early morning! I jumped out of my bed and tore out of my room towards the kitchen. Skippy was sleeping at the foot of my bed; he popped up and tore off with me.

We arrived in the kitchen a few seconds before Dottie, and we both found Mum staring into the birdcage covering her eyes with one hand, while holding the cage cover with her other hand. The old man was next to her, peering into the cage as well.

The scream had reached all the way to the top of the house, as Gramps had arrived on the scene, holding a wooden rolling pin in his hand, just in case hand-to-hand combat was required.

After all, Gramps had gone through the big war in

England and he was always prepared.

Dottie took one look in the cage and she screamed, too. My father made waving motions to me to pull Mum and Dottie away as he reached into the cage. I grabbed Mum and my sister while looking over my shoulder at the horrific scene inside the cage. There, upside down in the bottom of the cage, with his feathers all fluffed out, his wings tucked in, and his little feet sticking straight up in the air, was Fluffy the parakeet!

It was quite obvious that Fluffy was not feeling very well at the moment.

I offered up an optimistic angle. After all, it might not be as bad as it initially seemed.

"Maybe, he is just sleeping funny," I said as I looked at everyone.

Hey, it was a nice thought.

Gramps put his rolling pin down on the table and watched as the old man reached inside the cage and scooped up the sad remains.

Gramps provided some in-depth commentary on the current status of Fluffy, "Bloody well, dead as a doornail, I am afraid. I told you there was a reason he just sat there all fluffed up. Oh, quite sorry, about saying the word bloody in front of the children!"

Gramps called it as he saw it.

Mum screamed and burst into tears, as did my sister. I tried hard to console them, but it was a bad scene.

The old man had scooped up poor Fluffy and held him in his hands. "Nah, he must have croaked last night. He is as stiff as a board."

Poor Mum was heartbroken.

The old man continued with his cold-hearted analysis of the situation, "All that hard work at trying to teach him to talk, and all he did was keel over and croak. Poor old Fluffy, he was a bomb of a bird." Mum and my sister were now waving their hands in the air for the old man to stop his in-depth description of the demise of poor Fluffy. They both sobbed their eyes out as they sat around the kitchen table.

The old man carried poor Fluffy the parakeet out to the back porch, and he turned and looked at Skippy, who had been carefully watching the scene unfold.

He pointed at ole Skip and said, "Let this be a lesson to you and your evil ways there, Skippy. Pets do not last forever you know." The old man pointed his finger and nodded his head at Skippy, who sat down and whimpered a little at the loss of his fellow Henson pet friend.

Mum sobbed out some instructions, "Please bury poor Fluffy in a nice spot, Paul. He was such a good birdie."

Mum struggled to convey her love for poor Fluffy through tears of sorrow. I was not exactly sure if she was actually sobbing over Fluffy checking out, or over the fact that she had said, "Hello" well over two million times for naught. Gramps picked up his rolling pin, gave Mum and Dottie a kiss to console them, and he returned upstairs to his apartment.

"Do you have an old shoe box? I will chuck the Fluffster in there to plant him, but first, I want to bring him back to the pet store and get a new bird. After all, he cost me four bucks, not to mention the cage, food, clippers, and that stupid book. I will bury him when I bring him back. I promise that I will. I am sure he had a warranty for croaking after only one month," the old man said as he stood there, still holding the body.

I was not sure that pet shops actually had warranties on birds, but I was sure that I would go with the old man on this adventure to find out.

Dottie jumped up from the table and ran into her room, yelling the entire way, "Now, I *have* to go to Maureen's house for Thanksgiving, I cannot stand to be around pets that keel over and die right and left!"

I spotted the old man and Mum, both quickly glance

over at Skippy to check him, but ole Skip was still sitting watching the sad scene evolve. They both realized it was just an early morning ploy by Dottie to gain a slight, sympathetic advantage in the ongoing Maureen Zipperelli, Thanksgiving campaign.

Mum rose up from her chair, blew her nose with a tissue that she always stuffed up the sleeve of her arm, and looked at the old man.

She continued to pour out her heart for the demise of the Fluffster, "Make sure you bury poor Fluffy, and please do not just toss him in a waste can somewhere. I will go find a box, and the sales receipt. Oh, my, oh my! I cannot stand to think about getting another birdie. Fluffy was such a great pet."

Mum staggered off towards my parent's bedroom. I looked at the old man and shrugged my shoulders. The only real memory that I had of Fluffy, other than him sprawled on the bottom of his cage with his feet stuck up in the air, was of him sitting on his perch all fluffed out, with his head sunk down deep into his body. I saw him ring his bell once, but that was about all. I guess Mum had grown attached to him, but I was not exactly sure why.

Mum returned with an old shoe box and the store receipt. She instructed him as she handed the items to the old man, "Please, take Fluffy out on the porch. I cannot even look at him again!"

The old man placed the stiff body of Fluffy in the shoe box and put it out on the shelf on the back porch.

We shared quite a somber breakfast, as the passing of Fluffy so close to the holiday, as well as the horrific vision of Fluffy on the bottom of the cage with his feet sticking straight up in the air, had greatly saddened poor Mum. She pushed her scrambled eggs around on her plate and picked at her food. The old man made a little bit of small talk, but Mum was still upset. Dottie was also playing the sad card, but since I knew she did not really think that poor Fluffy was all too swift of a pet, I think she was just weighing the moment strategically in order to slip in another visit to Maureen's house salvo. You know . . . to prey upon the situation and catch our parents at a weak moment. It was all part of a kid's evil strategy to get what you wanted.

I tried to brighten up Mum's spirits by telling her that we will pick out a new parakeet for her. But the old man demonstrated some cutting motions across his neck when he saw that it was not going over so well.

Skippy was nowhere around at the moment. I think he was lying low, because he saw what had happened to poor, old, Fluffy, and he thought that today just might not be a good day for Henson family pets.

We cleaned up after breakfast. The old man told Mum that we were off to the pet store as well as to the Rickel Home Improvement Store, and we were off.

"We will be right back honey, we will bring you back something special," the old man proclaimed as he bent down to give Mum a kiss goodbye. "C'mon Paulie, tie all of that mop of hair back and let's go!"

Mum weakly waved back to us and she attempted a feeble smile. The pain of the loss of Fluffy was huge, but I think Mum's spirits were a little brighter now, knowing that a replacement Fluffy was on the horizon.

Now, I knew that with any Henson adventure, a trip to a store, a walk around the block, or other random wandering of any sort, the term, "we will be right back," was usually a fallacy. Something always happened and I do mean always. We never came; right back from anything. Even a trip to the mailbox was risking some weird, strange, or unusual encounter. I was sure that this adventure was not going to be any different. The old man grabbed the shoe box containing the sad remains of Fluffy, and he waved for me to follow him.

Out the back door, we went. Off to who knows what this time around?

The old man and I climbed into his beloved 1964 Putter Classic model 200, and the old man turned the key. Now, it had dropped down into the thirty-degree range overnight, and any night that it was not, at least eighty-five degrees could cause the starting of the engine on the 1964 Putter Classic model 200 to be an adventure. We rebuilt the Putter's engine twelve times from the pistons up. It had more than three hundred thousand miles on it, and the entire vehicle barely held together with some tape, sheet metal screws, and epoxy.

The old man loved epoxy. He used it to repair everything. He bought tubes and tubes of it. The 1964 Putter Classic model 200 started to rust about five years ago, so the old man stuck all sorts of body putty in the holes and had the car painted by one of those companies that paint any car for fifty bucks.

He picked out a weird blue color, but when the rust popped up again here and there, he could never match the original shade of blue. Even the guy who painted it said he did not know what color he used. Therefore, the old man just used any shade of blue that was close. The result was that the Putter looked like a multicolor paint chart of different shades of blue. Recently, the old man had given up on the body putty, and just reverted to holding the rusty fenders on with epoxy and sheet metal screws.

The color no longer mattered.

Thankfully, the old Putter spit, coughed, choked, and wobbled to life, so we were over one hurdle. A quick push of the automatic transmission button on the dashboard, a fiddle or two with the manual choke knob, and we were off.

Now, I could tell that the old man was irritated. He was ready for battle. There was nothing that he enjoyed more than going toe to toe with some store clerk, supervisor, manager, or other authority figure in a retail environment when he felt that he had been short-changed on a deal. His eyes went back and forth in his head a little; he hunched over the steering wheel and licked his lips. The ritual for battle preparation was usually the same. Part of it was always a life lesson for me, as the old man was always sure to include a lecture and a dissertation on the evil world, and the error of your ways for following the normal ways of the world. The old man was a keen observer of how the retail establishment "roped" you in and took advantage of poor people such as we were.

This trip was no different.

I looked over at the old man as he started his speech, "You know, Paulie, this here, croaking Fluffster incident, just shows you the way the world is these days!"

Yup, here it comes.

The old man pulled his New York Bugs baseball cap off his head and scratched the top of his head.

"This here guy . . . here at the Scruffy's pet store, he knew that Fluffy was a bomb. How could he not know? You see, he saw poor Mum come in, and he took advantage of her trusting, kind, loving nature. She liked the stupid bird because he was all fluffy like that. Poor Mum thought it was cute! All the time, he had some kind of rare jungle bird disease, some kind of . . . crud! The guy sold Mum a defective bird, anyway! Let that be a lesson to you, these pet store guys, they just care about money only, not birds, or breaking the heart of your mother. He only wanted his lousy four bucks. These guys nowadays, all they care about is money, money, money. It is never about quality!" The old man looked over at me to make sure that I was paying attention. I nodded my head rapidly to show my agreement with his assessment of evil pet store owners.

I felt as if I had to offer up some kind of response, so I sputtered in with a stupid and lame reply, "I sure hope all of his birds do not have rare jungle bird diseases!"

We turned onto the Hamburger Turnpike and headed for Wayne Township, where the pet store and the Rickel

Home Improvement Store were both located. The old man had been gaining speed because he knew that very shortly; the Hamburger Turnpike would turn into a long, steep hill that went on for a mile or so. The speed that the Putter gained on the flat stretch of the road quickly faded, and we slowed down considerably, as the incline loomed ahead of us. An old man walking his dog on the side of the road stared over at us as he heard the Putter's engine whining and moaning at the steepness of the hill.

The Putter struggled to make it up the long hill that led us to the shopping center location, and shortly, a line of cars, miles upon miles long, backed up behind the powerless Putter. Horns blared, while drivers behind us shook their fists in the air at the old man. My father fought back with typical New Jersey road rage mannerisms as he screamed out the window to them, declaring that he was going as fast as he could.

Actually . . . I cleaned that part up quite a bit. He did a little more than scream at the other drivers. There were some hand and finger gestures and other words involved, too.

Indeed, the old man was standing on the gas pedal, but the Putter had negative horsepower, so the long hill was a formidable opponent.

Thankfully, the road widened to two lanes, and allowed the old man to steer the Putter over to the granny lane, as four hundred thousand cars zoomed by the 1964 Putter Classic model 200. Each and every driver that passed was yelling obscenities out the window at us, including one car driven by a priest with four nuns in the backseat.

The old man fought back in vain, and shook his fist in the air at his critics, but even my father recognized that there was not much defense left, when the old man walking his dog on the sidewalk had already beaten us to the top of the hill.

After what seemed as if it were two lifetimes, we finally

made it to the shopping center, pulled the 1964 Putter Classic model 200 into a parking spot, grabbed the shoe box with the body of our beloved expired pet inside, and made our way to the front door of Scruffy's Pet Store.

The entire walk towards the front door of the store was riddled with the old man spouting off one of his better speeches, "I can tell. I just know this manager guy will give us a hard time. Mum told me how he forced some special birdseed that was twice the price of the regular seed down her throat when she bought the stupid bird. He must have planted some type of bug in the seed, and that is why the Fluffster keeled over. It is part of a plan to sell more birds!"

The old man and his endless conspiracy theories were something that we all were accustomed to and accepted. Each month, he would read his new copy of his favorite magazine, called *Dark Secrets*. The magazine outlined the latest in wild conspiracy theories, Cold War trepidation, retail rip-offs, shifty government hankering, and on and on. The old man loved it, and he sucked it all in like a vacuum cleaner.

Growing up on the gritty north side of Paterson and lower Haledon Borough, I was used to the old man identifying evil, shadowy figures that prowled our streets and took advantage of unsuspecting people. I just pushed all of my long, blonde hair out of my eyes and tucked it back inside of my vest, while I nodded my head in agreement with the old man's theories.

A short, baldheaded man of about sixty years of age, who smiled at us, immediately greeted the two of us when we walked in the front door of Scruffy's Pet Center. He stood behind the counter, and he was writing something on a pad and clipboard. He wore eyeglasses, and when he looked up at us, he put the clipboard aside and perched his glasses up on top of his head. His outward appearance made me feel relaxed, since he seemed as though he was quite a friendly chap.

"Welcome to Scruffy's," the store clerk loudly proclaimed. The old man would have none of this happy banter because he was loaded for hunting bear. There was no way he trusted this guy.

"Yeah, yeah, yeah, are you, Scruffy?" The old man answered back as we approached the counter and he placed the shoe box on the counter.

"No sir, actually, there is no real Scruffy, that is just a sort of made-up title that we came up with for the name of our store."

"Ah hah! More, flim-flam! I knew you were a rip-off joint, even the name of your store is phony baloney!"

The old man was laying the groundwork for his battle. There was an older couple in the store, who were looking at some fish food on a shelf right next to the counter. They both turned and stared at the evolving scene.

"How can I help you, sir?" The previously cheerful store clerk's demeanor changed, as he now realized that this was not going to be a happy shopping episode. "I am the owner of the store. My name is, Mr. Rupple."

The old man stared back at the owner, put on his best tough guys' stance and said, "Rupple, look here, inside this shoe box and you will see my trouble." The old man lifted the lid of the shoe box and the owner of the store stared into it. The older couple also came over, as they were now interested in what had caused such an unhappy situation in a pet store.

"Oh, my! The poor budgie!" Mr. Rupple cried out as he quickly closed the lid.

The older couple did not have a chance to see what was inside, so the older man tapped me on the shoulder and asked, "What was in there, hippie kid?"

"Well, sir, it is, or actually was, Fluffy, my mum's parakeet. He died today, and he was only a month old."

The older couple nodded, and the man asked me, "So, your mother's bird croaked and it is the store's fault?"

My father whirled, looked at the older man, and angrily shot back, "Hey buzz off you, old crow, if you had a wife at home who found her beloved bird croaked with his feet up in the air you would be back here too. Mind your own ass and go buy some old age tonic or something, will ya!"

The old crow man's wife tugged at her husband's shirt. She pulled him away, and they retreated to the fish food aisle.

The old man turned back to Mr. Rupple and fired back at him, "Budgie, budgie, Rupple, you do not even know what you sold here! This is a parakeet. He was a bomb. All he did was sit his ass on his perch, all fluffed out with his head sunk down inside his body. He did not do a thing, and my wife yakked at him a million times trying to teach him to talk. I was losing my mind. You sold us a sick bird with some rare jungle disease! I know all about these diseases, you see. My 'Dark Secrets' magazine had an article all about it a few months back. Here is the receipt!" The old man whipped out the sales receipt and showed it to Mr. Rupple.

Mr. Rupple pulled his glasses off the top of his head and placed them over his eyes. He then stared at the sales receipt and shook his head. Apprehensively, he placed the receipt down on the counter.

He looked at us and said, "I am so sorry about the loss of your Budgerigar. That is the actual name of your parakeet. I used the nickname which is budgie. I feel terrible. Perhaps, he just caught a cold and could not shake it. Did you have him next to a window?"

The old man waved his hand in the air to discount the theory, "Nah, nah, nah, he was in the kitchen away from any windows. He lived better than the homeless guy who lives in a box over on Geyer Street, and Pussface the cat. My wife treated him like a king! She fed him, talked to him. He had the best of everything!"

"Well, I am afraid to ask about what a Pussface the cat

is, and remind me to stay away from Geyer Street, wherever on Earth that may be, but I am glad to hear how much your wife loved the little birdie. I am also glad to hear that Fluffy had such luxurious accommodations during his life. I am sorry to see that the poor budgie passed away. I love animals and all kinds of pets, so the last thing I like to see, is when any pet passes on."

Mr. Rupple seemed as though he was a very kind man, and I looked at the old man, and then back at Mr. Rupple. He nodded his head to both of us in what appeared to be a display of utmost sincerity at the demise of poor little Fluffy.

Just as it seemed as if he was a softie, he opened his mouth and struck the fatal blow, "But, I do not give out any guarantees on my birds. There is just so much that could happen that is out of my control, sir. But I am willing to. . .."

That was all it took to set off the old man. His eyeballs spun around in his head, his temples started to pound like little tom-tom drums, and his mouth was off to the races!

"I knew it! I just knew it! Another, money grubbing, rip-off, pet store operation! I just knew it, Paulie! I told you!" The old man poked at my chest with his pointer finger. He was upset and quite excited. I stood there and nodded my head as this was rapidly turning into a bad scene.

When Mr. Rupple tried to speak, the old man continually cut him off in mid-sentence. He gave it another shot, "Sir, please sir, I was just about to say. . .."

"Oh, boy! Four hard earned bucks gone! Down the drain, all because of some rare jungle bird disease!"

"Sir, if you would please stop saying that about jungle bird diseases, there is no such. . .."

The old man cut him off once more, and he rambled on and on about, charlatans, rip-offs, conniving schemes, jungle bird diseases, and other assorted wild descriptions of the evil plots of retail stores against the common man.

The old man was on a classic roll now; he was spinning around tighter than a go-go dancer in her dress was on a Friday night.

Mr. Rupple gave up, put his glasses back on top of his head, folded his arms across his chest, and leaned on the wall behind the counter.

Mr. Rupple looked at me and pointed his finger as if he was appealing to me for intervention. He spoke up loudly, "If your father would just shut up, son, I am trying very hard to tell him that I will work out a deal for him."

I was just going to tap the old man on the arm, when my father heard the word, "deal."

That was all it took! It was as if he stuffed a sock into the old man's mouth. He hit the brakes on his long-winded speech and turned first towards me, and then to Mr. Rupple and asked, "A deal? Did you just say that you would work a deal?"

Now, the old man was a legendary dealmaker. He was not unlike most residents of northern New Jersey who lived and breathed, making deals every day of their lives. Deal making was a hobby where I grew up. No one ever paid retail for anything; the price tag was merely a suggestion.

In fact, in our neighborhood, we never paid for some things at all. In our neighborhood, we had an old timer, a chap named Wesley Whipamore.

Wesley used to tell all of us neighborhood kids, "I am in the moving business, youse dopey kids. And the good part is, folks do not even have to be home for me and my boys to show up and clean your joint out."

It was not until years later, when I heard that Wesley went off to the clinker to do some time for breaking and entering that we realized what type of business Wesley was actually "employed." In fact, that too, is a whole other story, for another time and place.

"Yes, yes, Mr. ah, ah. . .."

Mr. Rupple picked up the sales receipt and looked at our name.

"Mr. Henson, if by the grace and intervention of God, and if it is actually possible, I would like to make you a happy customer, so I would like to give you a major discount on a replacement parakeet for Mrs. Henson. I just could not get a word in edgewise, with you flapping your jaws on and on with evil, storekeeper theories."

The old man screwed his face up and folded his arms at the very strategic comeback by Mr. Rupple.

"What kind of deal there, Rupple? I am from Paterson, you know, the north end. You are not going to pull the wool over my eyes!"

Mr. Rupple picked up the sales receipt once more and looked at it, while commenting, "For four bucks, Mr. Henson, or am I in need of new glasses, and this is really four hundred dollars?"

Oh boy, Mr. Rupple only looked as if he was a meek, kind, mellow storekeeper who loved little birdies. He actually was going toe to toe with the old man! The old man was a little uncomfortable and shifted his feet, then looked over at me. The older couple who had scampered off when the old man attacked had now mustered up enough courage to return, as they had been secretly watching from the fish food aisle, and their curiosity could no longer hold them back. They had to come over for a ringside seat.

"Well, what is the deal? You know the four bucks, is not the point, Rupple! It is the utter despair that my wife and the boy's dear mum have suffered. She is English ya know, and they all love their birdies ya know! It is much more than just four bucks. This is about broken hearts, Rupple."

The old man in his classic tradition had rebounded nicely and pulled it out in the end with a drama filled and heart wrenching speech.

The old crow man crept in closer to the counter and his

wife leaned in next to her husband. The old crow man put his can of fish food on the counter and spoke up, "Yeah, yeah, yeah, Rupple, think about the poor woman. She is English after all. They were on our side in the big war, ya know. I was over there with them." Now, the older couple and the old man all nodded their heads in agreement, and the former adversaries had joined forces in the effort to milk poor Mr. Rupple.

Mr. Rupple shook his head and mumbled, "I should have been a Methodist minister like my mother told me to be."

He took his glasses off his head, placed them down on the counter, and waved for us to follow him. He came out from behind the counter and made his way over to the side of the store where there were hundreds of birdcages.

"Come over here and I will show you what I have in mind."

The four of us followed him over to the birdcages and we walked by what seemed as though it was an entire jungle of squawking, shouting, and hollering birds of all sorts. There were little finches darting back and forth in cages, canaries singing, and rows upon rows of parakeets, and larger birds that hollered at us as we walked by. I stopped and looked at a huge cage with a brightly colored parrot sitting in there. He was huge, and when he spotted me, he walked over on his perch and opened his beak at me. I guess he thought I was going to give him a treat of some sort.

"Don't get your hair caught in that cage, hippie Henson kid. Toodles the parrot is strong and he will give you a good pull," Mr. Rupple warned me.

I moved away from Toodles, pulled a hair tie out of my pocket, and tied all of my hair behind my head.

Mr. Rupple stopped in front of a cage and pointed while he explained, "This is, Fritzie the parakeet. He was a very young bird that I sold about one month ago, to a young man here in town. The man then unexpectedly transferred to a job in another state and he asked me to take Fritzie back in, and I did. He is a great bird, very active. He speaks and knows his name."

The old man's ears perked up when he heard that Fritzie already could speak. He immediately turned to me and said, "Say, this bird can talk already. Maybe that will save us from listening to your mother saying hello five million times!"

I nodded my head and pushed some strands of hair that I missed tying up out of my eyes, while agreeing, "I think so, Dad, and look. He sure has a lot more energy than Fluffy did.

The old man nodded his head and said, "Well, that is not saying much, Paulie. If you look in that shoe box, it is really hard to tell the difference from when the Fluffster was alive and how he looks now."

I agreed and pointed in the cage as Fritzie the parakeet ran back and forth on his perch and rang his bell numerous times. He was jumping and running back and forth on his perch, playing with his bell and some plastic whirlybird thing that he jumped and landed in as it spun around.

The wife of the old crow man looked in the cage and said, "He sure is pretty, and he has a lot of spunk." Her husband nodded in approval. Fritzie was also a good-looking bird. He had the same green and yellow color scheme as Fluffy did, but he had real feathers and looked normal. Actually, other than his colors, he did not look anything at all, as Fluffy did, both when he was alive and when he was dead.

"I like him, Rupple, but that name Fritzie, well, it sounds German. I will need to change his name. I am afraid bringing some German bird into our house will not go over well with my father-in-law. He had a little rough time with them folks over in England during the big war."

The old crow man now jumped back into the fray, when

the old man mentioned the big war, "Yeah, Rupple . . . that will not go over so well!"

Mr. Rupple looked at the older couple and asked, "Who are you people? Can I check your fish food out now?"

"Nah, nah, nah, now let them be, Rupple. They are my . . . consultants," the old man rushed in for defense. The old couple both smiled, since they were now part of the team.

This sure was one weird adventure. Even as far as Henson adventures go, it was turning out to be highly ranked on the all-time, weird list.

Mr. Rupple recovered, "I would advise against changing his name. It would confuse the bird at this point. I would just tell your wife and father-in-law that all parakeets come from Australia. That should work. After all, they are part of the British Empire."

Mr. Rupple had realized that this was a bit of a strange encounter and that in order to make the sale to us oddballs; he needed to lockstep with us, and appeal to us on our nutcase level.

The old man rubbed his chin and said, "That will work, Rupple, but what about this price tag here! Ten bucks for a lousy bird. Big deal if he can speak! Pussface talks to us too."

"I am still not going to ask what a Pussface is, despite my now, rather intense curiosity. Now, now, please do not get all worked up there, Mr. Henson. Let me tell you what I will do here before you blast off in your spaceship there. I will give you the credit for the first bird and take another dollar off. You can have Fritzie here for five dollars."

"That seems like a good deal!" The older couple's wife happily piped in.

The old man seemed swayed, but not sold. He pulled his New York Bugs cap off and scratched the top of his head. "Well, it does seem fair. He is a lively bird, but it seems that I should get a little more for the Fluffster keeling over there, Rupple. The shock of the scene was terrible! Will ya throw in for free a bag of that fancy seed that you roped my wife into buying?"

"Sure, sure, sure, it is a deal. Anything, to move on with this day, Mr. Henson. I will pray tonight for Fritzie's long-term health. I will give you this transport cage, too. I usually charge a deposit, until a customer returns the cage, but I will throw it in for free. You do not have to return it to me, Mr. Henson. Let me tell you that you can buy this Big Bob's Special Australian Outback seed blend, down in Sal Zucchini's store in the riverside section of Paterson. That will save you a trip to Wayne Township and from bugging . . . oh . . . I mean, from shopping here."

It seemed as though; Mr. Rupple was working very hard at convincing the old man not to visit his store anymore.

He added, "Please, also note that Fritzie here has not had his wings clipped. He is quite a capable flyer, so please be careful when you exercise him. You may want to bring him back here . . . I mean . . . find a pet store closer to Haledon that will clip his wings for you."

"No kidding, Rupple, I thought Sal only sold tools and pools, but I see he is branching out in efforts to hide his true organization from prying eyeballs. I am not worried about that wing-clipping thing. I read the book my wife picked up here that you ripped her off on, and it shows you how to do it. You also ripped her off on the clippers that you sold her, so we are all set."

Mr. Rupple just stood there, rolled his eyes, and did not say a word.

"This is great. We have to go over to the Rickel and pick up a few things, and we will be right back to pick up the bird. I do not mind bringing the transport cage back to your store here, Rupple. I am here at the Rickel most every weekend. Our old house in Haledon is falling down, so I always need to buy something to repair things."

"No, no, no, that is fine. I will throw it in with the deal to get rid of you, Mr. Henson." Mr. Rupple finally decided to stop beating around the bush and call it as he felt it!

The old man smiled and shook hands with Mr. Rupple and the older couple. He thanked the old couple for their combined efforts at shaking down Mr. Rupple, "Thanks for the support on working the deal there, old timer. Good luck with your fish food. I hope your fish do not croak like our bird did. Be careful of rare tropical fish diseases. They can be tricky."

The old crow looked at me and asked, "All of that hair there, sonny, are you a hippie or something like that?"

"Well sir, I was. . .." The old man pulled me away and out the front door of the store.

"Mr. Henson, please do not forget your shoe box with Fluffy's sad remains in it. You need to give him a proper burial, of course." Mr. Rupple held out the shoe box with Fluffy's stiff remains inside.

"Can ya chuck him in the dumpster, Rupple, or flush him down the toilet?"

"Dad, you promised Mum that you would bury him in the backyard!" I protested the old man's cold-hearted request.

Mr. Rupple was horrified, "Mr. Henson! You should be ashamed of yourself! The hippie kid is quite correct. A faithful pet that stood side by side with you and gave you his unfaltering love and companionship, deserves more than being flushed down a toilet upon his demise!"

"Oh, all right, Rupple. Calm down and keep your feathers on. Give me the shoe box. I will plant him in the backyard. We will be right back."

We walked out the front door of Scruffy's Pet Center, dropped the shoe box in the backseat of the 1964 Putter Classic model 200, and then headed over to my old man's favorite place in the entire world.

Well, next to his easy chair in the living room, that is.

The old man loved the Rickel Home Improvement Store. It was a virtual cornucopia of household repair lust for the old man, as he wandered through rows upon rows of tools, bolts, paint, screws, plumbing parts, cement, wood, garden accessories, and anything else that you could ever use or imagine for your home projects. His heart rate increased just when he looked at the front door alone.

Now, I knew that we were never right back from anything in our lives, so I buckled my chinstrap up for the next phase of this mission. I just knew that something would happen as we entered the front door of Rickel.

It just had to be.

During the entire walk across the shopping center parking lot over to Rickel, I learned another life lesson from the old man on wheeling and dealing with cold-hearted storekeepers. He seemed as though he was quite satisfied with the deal that he had worked out for Fritzie. I had to admit that it all had turned out very well. I could have done without the pesky older couple nosing around, Toodles the strong beaked parrot, the hippie comments, and the drama; however, for the most part, it was another valuable lesson in weirdness and in life from the old man. I chose not to bring up the fact that Mr. Rupple was a very nice guy who was also very fair. Why test the waters? The old man was happy, so I was happy.

We walked into the Rickel and headed for the bolts and screws aisles. The old man scanned the selections and picked out a few six-inch long lag bolts that he studied carefully.

"This should hold the porch railing in place, despite Cousin Pat's tonnage and her tuggin' on it. I am afraid the four-inch lags that I put in there after her last visit, did not hit enough meat behind them." The old man handed me the bolts, "Here, hold these, Paulie. Let's head for the epoxy aisle. I need some glue and some more epoxy. The last time I checked, I was down to about ten tubes of epoxy, and that is not enough in reserve to sustain a visit from Cousin Pat."

I held the lag bolts and followed the old man as he headed for the glue and epoxy aisle. As he settled in and scanned the shelves and selections for the type of epoxy that he wanted, I stood there holding the lag bolts. I knew this would be a long process, as my father was a true connoisseur of epoxy. This was the equivalent to a fine wine tasting event, as the old man read the labels, compared prices, and other virtues of the various epoxies, which were for sale.

As I stood there, I became vaguely aware of a man who was looking over his shoulder towards us. He then would look back at the merchandise, pick up random items, and pretend to read the labels. I watched him, and I then looked away. When I turned back to look at him, he turned away quickly and went off to pick up another random item on the shelf. He was obviously spying on us, and he seemed, even in our world, to be a little strange.

I huddled in close to the old man and whispered to him, "Say, Dad, there is this guy over here watching our every move. He seems like he is a whacko."

The old man glanced over his shoulder, and sure enough, the man turned away quickly, and made believe that he was looking at a tube of glue.

"Oh, that guy is the store detective. He is the worst undercover detective that I have ever seen. You can pick him out from a mile away. He thinks he is that British movie secret agent guy, Ian Leadfoot. For some reason, he follows me whenever I come in here. He must think that I am a crook. Watch this."

The old man shuffled his hands around quickly and pretended that he was putting something in his pockets. He then tugged at my shirt and pulled me quickly into the next aisle. Sure enough, the store detective jumped into action, and he almost ran behind us. The old man was going to have some fun with him. We arrived in the next aisle and the old man unexpectedly turned around as the store detective almost ran into the back of us.

"Hey, there, Ian Leadfoot, on the trail of some hot criminal spy case I see!"

The poor detective was flustered that his cover was blown.

"Well sir, I was . . . just, ah. . .."

"You were just what? Trailing us? Can I ask you why you follow me every single time I come into this store?"

"Well sir, I am not actually the store detective, I am, just a shopper, or I mean, ah. . .."

"Oh, c'mon! You've got to be kiddin' me! You are the worst undercover guy I have ever seen. Now, who is being dishonest there, chief!"

Realizing that we had detected him, the store detective put his head down and sulked a bit.

"Well sir, I spotted the long-haired, hippie, young man here and saw him carrying the bolts and. . .."

Now, he has worked me up! I was the actual target of his investigation! I decided to defend my long-haired honor. I looked up at his little, shiny, baldhead, and I watched as his eyes followed mine.

"I never put the bolts in my pocket. I held them here in my hand the entire time. I am not a thief, you big dope."

I showed him the bolts still in my closed fist. I was mad, because I was an honest kid, and I was going to let this jerk know just how mad that I was.

I decided to blast him where it hurts, so I blurted out, "Say baldy, at least I have hair!"

I shocked even the old man with my fervent defense because I usually did not have much to say in these types of situations. This time, I was getting just a little sick and tired of the hippie classifications.

"Atta boy, Paulie, go get him! I cannot add much more to it than he did already. It looks like you picked on a feisty fourteen-year-old there, secret agent man. The kid is a tough one, ya better watch out. It takes him a long time to get angry, but when he does, he can clean some clocks. He might put some hair back on your head." The old man's fist pumped a little in the air. The store detective touched the top of his head as though it might have been a sudden revelation that he was bald.

"I am sorry, sir, and I apologize to you, young man, for judging you upon your appearance. I am just doing my job, but I can see that you still have the bolts in your hand. Let me give you a little store discount for the inconvenience and embarrassment of the situation. I would appreciate you not giving away my undercover status here in exchange for a little store discount card."

"Well, being honest there, Ian Leadfoot, ya have to work on your technique. I can always spot you when I come in here. I can tell you are the store detective from a mile away. Ya stand out like a tuba player in a symphony orchestra!"

The store detective frowned at the old man's observation of his skills, reached into his pocket, and pulled out a little card and a pen, as he said, "Here, please give this to the cashier, and she will apply a little discount for the items that you purchase today."

"Thanks, chief! Have a great day hunting down criminals. Look for us next time, we can play a little cat and mouse for a few aisles, you can try to insult the boy here, and then you can give me another one of these cards!"

The store detective shook his head and went the other way down the aisle. I am sure he wanted to get as far away from us as quickly as he could. Between him and Mr. Rupple, we had developed quite a little fan club today. The old man was ecstatic at his good fortune for receiving the discount card.

"Good work there, Paulie! That is the way to speak up and defend your honor. I am proud of you. You do not have to take that nonsense from anyone. I can see that wild game of hockey has made you a tough guy, that is for sure. I knew that long hair would come in handy one day. I think I will pick up another tube or two of epoxy since I have this discount card to use!"

The old man put his arm around me and pulled me closer. I took his comments to heart; after all, it is not every day that my hippie appearance could lead to a reward and justification.

We paid for our supplies at the Rickel check out, and the old man was thrilled at the thirty-five cents he saved, because of my long-haired appearance. We then headed over to Scruffy's Pet Center, paid Mr. Rupple the five dollars, and picked up Fritzie and the free birdseed. Soon, we were on our way back down the Hamburger Turnpike with the 1964 Putter Classic model 200, barely rolling along and now, with a backup of cars for miles and miles, behind the powerless Putter.

It is always a bad sign when the traffic report on the radio is talking about a major traffic jam, and you are the cause of the traffic jam.

It did not bother the old man as he happily tooled down the road, occasionally shaking his fist at a passing car, or insulting driver, but for the most part, it did not bother him. In the tumultuous world of the old man, this had been a successful trip. He had worked what he perceived to be a major deal, received a discount on his Cousin Pat defensive supplies, evened the score with the store detective, and now he was heading home with a replacement bird for dear Mum. He whistled his favorite melodies from his favorite Harvey Crooner songs, and Fritzie the bird whistled back at him, as the little bird sat next to me inside the transport cage on the front seat of the Putter.

Everything was well in the world; I just hoped that Mum would like Fritzie!

"We are home! Look, at what we got you, honey!" The old man and I burst through the back door and into the kitchen, carrying our little transport cage with Fritzie inside. Gramps, Mum, and Dottie were sitting around the table, enjoying cups of tea. We set the cage down upon the kitchen table and the old man stood back and beamed. Fritzie jumped, hopped, and skipped from the little perch in the transport cage to the floor of the cage.

"Oh, honey! He is beautiful! He even has the same colors as Fluffy did! I love him, thank you dear." Mum was thrilled. She stood up and gave the old man a big kiss. "Thank you, Paulie. I am sure you helped pick him out!"

Mum gave me a hug and kiss. I already towered over my mother, so she had to pop up on her tippy toes to reach my cheek as I bent down a bit.

"I did, Mum. His name is Fritzie! The guy in the pet store told us he already can say his name."

"Fritzie, eh?" Gramps leaned over and peered at the little parakeet as he jumped around. "Sounds, German! He is not one of those German birds, now, is he? Let me go upstairs and obtain my rolling pin!" Gramps leaned back, screwed his face up, and clenched his fists.

The old man stepped in to diffuse the volatile situation, "Nah, nah, relax, Pop, it is just his name. The pet store guy told us Fritzie is from Australia!"

"Australia! Now that is more like it. No wonder, the little lad has such spunk. He is part of the British Empire. I dare say Paul and Paulie boy, you two have picked out a champ of a bird here!" Gramps was thrilled that Fritzie was part of the bloodline!

Skippy appeared and sat down next to Gramps to check out what the excitement was. He then stood on his back paws and put his front paws on the table, to get a good look at the replacement Fluffy, until Gramps yelled at him for touching the kitchen table.

"I cleaned out Fluffy's cage, and swabbed it down, just in case there was some kind of rare jungle disease that caused poor Fluffy to conk out. I changed the paper in the bottom and washed all his dishes out really well. I was so hoping that you would bring me a new birdie!" Mum was apparently a subscriber to the rare jungle bird disease theories as well as an occasional reader of *Dark Secrets* magazine too. She was now standing next to the cage, and she was signaling for us to bring Fritzie over to put him inside the big cage. My father picked up Fritzie and married the open door of the transport cage to the open door of the big cage. The bird danced, jumped, spotted the open door, and he scooted in the big cage and flew onto the big perch. He spotted the bell, ran right over to it, and gave it a ring.

Dottie was thrilled, too. She circled in now and smiled as she watched Fritzie jumping around. "Wow, he sure is a happy, little thing! I like him. He is so much better than that dead Fluffy."

Mum put her face up against the cage and said, "Hellllooooo Fritzie, Hellllooooo Fritzie, Hellllooooo Fritzie."

"Oh, geez, here we go already! Give him a few minutes to get used to his new cage before you go right up there with your big, moon head trying to get him to speak!" The old man rolled his eyes as Mum waved her hand back at the old man.

"Oh, pooh! Do you want some coffee?"

"Yeah, yeah, yeah, some coffee. So, you like, Fritzie?"

"Oh yes, he is very nice. He is so happy. You said he could say his name. Have you heard him speak yet?"

"Nah, nah, nah, not yet. He needs to settle down a little. That rip-off store owner of the pet shop assured us he could speak, so we will see. I had to go toe to toe with him to get our dough back. It was a fierce battle, dear."

"Oh my, I knew you would win, dear, and receive your four dollars back. You were gone so long. I just knew that you had a fight on your hands."

I did not say a word, as I had learned a long time ago not to interrupt my father's exaggerated stories of gallant battles and all out warfare with storekeepers, repairmen, policemen, and other assorted characters, who crossed swords with him during the many adventures within the Henson family history.

Gramps stood up and walked over to the cage. He looked in and said, "Well, I guess I will go back upstairs. Thank you for the tea and crumpets. He is a nice bird, bloody well a lot more exciting than that dead thing."

Gramps then turned to look at Mum when he realized that he had let the big, "b" word slip, when Fritzie suddenly shouted out in a loud and clear voice, "Bloody well!"

The old man spit out his coffee, and Dottie and I started laughing.

"I guess he can speak!" The old man yelled out.

"Pop! Now look, what you have done. My little birdie now knows the big, b word!" Mum was now standing next to her father with her hands on her hips.

"Oh sorry, love. I guess he is an Aussie bloke all right!" Gramps was smiling now as he looked at his little fellow loyal to the crown supporter, jumping from perch to perch.

"Acckkkkk! Acckkkkk! Bloody well! Fritzie! Fritzie!" Fritzie the parakeet was hopping around and spouting off inside his cage as Gramps did his best to stop him from talking by waving his hands at him.

"Shh, now Fritzie. Please be quiet! That is enough now, little lad!" Gramps was turning red as Mum stood next to him. The old man, Dottie, and I did our best not to fall on the floor laughing as we potentially faced the wrath of Mum, but it was difficult to hold back. Gramps gave up, apologized once more, and retreated to the safety of his apartment.

My mother was a dear, sweet person, but she could be a tough gal when she became angry. As Mum stood there next to the cage, speaking slowly to Fritzie, my sister also retreated and headed for her room, as she tried to hide the fact that she was red-faced from laughing. The old man signaled me to cut it out, and then he waved to me. Our mission was not over yet.

"Oh Fritzie, you sweet little birdie, please do not say that nasty word."

"Acckkkkk! Acckkkkk! Bloody well!" Fritzie shrieked as he spoke the newly acquired, colorful language. He jumped from perch to perch, looking at himself in the mirror, ringing his bell, and jumping on the plastic swing.

The old man and I were about to burst the veins in our heads as we struggled to hold our laughter inside. The old man finally mustered up enough superhuman strength to say, "We have to go outside and bury Fluffy, we . . . will be right back."

Mum turned around and said, "Oh please, pick a nice spot next to the garden. Fluffy did not do much, but at least he did not say bad words."

We nodded our heads and darted outside. Once safely outside, the two of us held onto each other and we laughed so hard that we had tears in our eyes.

"Thank goodness that Gramps taught him those words. If I had done that, I would be sleeping inside the Putter Classic from now on." I could not argue with the old man on that one for sure.

I turned my attention back to the task at hand, "Say, Dad, how are you going to bury Fluffy? The ground is already frozen solid."

The old man was in the garden shed poking around for his shovel and he stuck his head out, "It sure is frozen. The days sure have been cold already. It was a short autumn season this year. This winter is going to be a rough one. Well, we might find a soft spot in the garden where the sun hits it, plant the Fluffster there, and mark it with a stone. If the weather warms up, we can move the Fluffster. If not, he will be dust by springtime. Hey, go get the shoe box will ya?"

"Sure, Dad."

I went to the back seat of the Putter, grabbed the shoe

box, and came back to find the old man beating and poking the ground in the garden. The old man tried many spots, but to no avail. The recent cold spell had made a rock out of the ground. The old man was always a little short in the old patience department, and he quickly grew weary of the same result, no matter where he tried to poke the shovel point in the ground. Hmmm . . . not too much longer, I thought in my head, T-Minus ten seconds and counting until he blows.

"Oh, forget this bullshit!"

I had only made it to T-Minus five.

The old man angrily tossed the shovel aside and picked a little corner of the garden next to the shed. He bashed at the ground with his boot heel, grabbed the shoe box, and dumped old rigor mortis, Fluffster in the little belly, which he had made in the ground. He then grabbed what little loose dirt he could find with the shovel and dumped it over the top of Fluffy. He then covered him with a bunch of leaves. He stood back and before I could say it, the old man noticed the brightly colored wing poking out from under the makeshift Fluffster mound. The old man pushed the surrounding leaves some more and found a few little stones to drop on top to hold it all in place.

"There! C'mon Paulie, we have to put those bolts in the railing before lunch! Remind me to check and tighten the mounting bolts for the toilet too, in case she sits on there, and she has some ass troubles and wiggles around. I also have to make sure the fire extinguisher is put up in the kitchen, just in case, Cousin Pat starts another fire."

I almost said that it did not seem like a good burial for poor Fluffy, but I decided to pass on my input. It had been a long morning and my stomach was growling now. Sometimes, you had to pick the proper time for comments with the old man, and now was just not the time to risk it. We worked on the rail, drove the longer and stronger lag bolts in the mounts, checked the toilet mounts, did a bunch of other odd jobs, and then we ate lunch.

Mum seemed to be over the shock of Fritzie's newly acquired slang, and Fritzie was actually quiet during the afternoon, as he was eating a bunch of seeds violently in his dish and tossing the seed hulls all over the place. Fritzie was a different type of bird for sure.

The old man and I had completed the advance fortification tasks for Cousin Pat's visit. The final preparations were complete.

It was now time to relax.

The old man was off sitting in his easy chair listening to his Harvey Crooner records on his Victrola. I had most of the afternoon to myself, and without a hockey game going on, and my best buddy Harry already off for his holiday, there was not too much going on. I grabbed my trusty wooden Victoriaville shooting stick for hockey, which being a goaltender, I did not use very often, and Skippy and I went into the backyard. The two of us passed the time together as I shot a lightweight rubber ball with my stick, which Skippy would fetch and retrieve for hours.

It had grown colder, increasingly overcast, and a few dark clouds floated overhead here and there. It looked as if it would snow a number of times, but other than some occasional snowflakes that spit out of the passing clouds, not very much really came out of the sky. The wind was picking up, the dried leaves spun and danced around our backyard as they blew from corner to corner. It now was really starting to become the week before Thanksgiving, and the weather had turned more towards being a prelude to winter.

Skippy was a tough little dog, and the cold did not bother him. He and I were from the same mold. There was nothing that I enjoyed more than a cold, blustery day, and it was, in my opinion, a perfect setting for this time of the year.

The afternoon waned and soon it was growing dark.

Mum stuck her head out the back door and called for both of us to come in for dinner. Skippy and I headed inside, I washed up, and we all gathered for dinner. Mum had made a large pot of soup and some slices of ham and baked potatoes. After being outside all afternoon, the warm meal sure tasted good! It was a pleasant meal. My sister dropped a few more hints on the visit to Maureen's house for the holiday, but she made no significant progress, due to receiving a quick retort and shutdown from the old man.

I am sure that she was ramping up for the final blows in the next few days before Thanksgiving. She was just strategically waiting in the weeds for the big move.

Gramps and the old man were well into a few Big Boulder beers, and Mum had a big glass of her special Saturday night red wine. Once the two of them knew that Mum had a bit of the wine floating around in her, they risked a tease or two on the vocabulary of her now much beloved, Fritzie the Aussie talking machine. Mum laughed and dismissed them. She faked that she was still angry at Gramps, but then she got a good chuckle out of the situation, when Fritzie let a few more of the big, "b" words fly in the background.

I asked the old man if I could watch the New York Rovers hockey game on channel nine later that night, and he agreed. We only had one television, which was a nineteen-inch screen black and white set in our living room. It did not receive all the channels very clearly, and we always had to climb on the roof and fiddle with the antenna. Channel nine was one channel that came in fairly strongly without a lot of snow, ghosts, and fading, so we could watch the game. The old man was not a big hockey fan, but he would watch a game or two here and there with me. If he had a few Big Boulder beers, he would be sound asleep by the second period, anyway. My sister was going to go over to Maureen's house to listen to records and watch Maureen's television in her bedroom.

That fact reminded me of another legendary Henson family battle, when Maureen got a new television for her room. My sister cried the blues for weeks as she pounded our parents for her own television set. A few weeks ago, Gramps actually gave her an old, used black and white television for her room, but it required repairs and did not work yet. The old man said he would bring the broken set to the television and radio repair shop once he saved up enough extra money. That would be another escapade, as the old man always fought with the television repair guy, so I was looking forward to that adventure and more . . . life lessons.

The battles with the television and radio repair guy were legendary in the annals of Henson family history.

Mr. Zipperelli was going to pick up my sister and bring her back home, so we all cleared the table and helped Mum with the dishes. Dinner was over, the night approached, and Gramps took off for his apartment. Dottie was off when she heard the honk of the Zipperelli's car in the driveway, and the old man and I settled in to watch the game.

The old man and I could hear Mum in the kitchen practicing new words with Fritzie. We both listened as from the kitchen; we could hear the long, English lesson finally end with, "Goodnighttttttt . . . Fritzie, Goodnighttttttt . . . Fritzie."

Mum then clicked the light off in the kitchen and joined us in the living room. Mum was reading her *Ladies House, Home, and Happy* magazine in her rocking chair while we watched the game. Skippy wandered in, curled up in front of the steam radiator, and he was asleep in a minute. All those endless trips of fetching the hockey ball this afternoon had finally worn old Skippy out. Everything was calm and quiet in the Henson household once more.

It was a peaceful family setting before the big Thanksgiving celebration.

The referee just dropped the puck for the second period, and the old man was already asleep in his chair, snoring his brains out, when we both heard Pussface meowing at the back door. Neither Skippy nor the old man even moved a muscle as I looked at my mother in her chair. It was a cold night out there, and Pussface was looking for a dish of beer and a warm place to sleep for the night.

Mum asked me, "Is there any beer left in your father's bottle there, Paul?" I walked over and picked it out of the old man's hand and he did not move a muscle.

"A little bit is left, Mum," I answered her, "do you want me to let Pussface in and give him the beer?"

"No, no, sit and enjoy your game. I want to make a cup of tea, and make sure that Pussface did not frighten, poor Fritzie. I covered his cage for the night, but I am not sure he went to sleep yet. A strange cat meowing could have made him very upset."

I handed Mum the beer, and she headed off towards the kitchen. I sat back down and watched the game. I looked up for a second when I saw her click on the kitchen light. I heard the back door open, and then the porch door.

A few seconds later, Mum let out with another bloodcurdling scream shattering the quiet, placid, cuddly, Henson evening! Oh no! Oh no! Not again! This was becoming an everyday occurrence!

I jumped into action, as did the bleary-eyed, now startled, old man followed by poor, startled Skippy. The three of us dashed into the kitchen and arrived to find poor Mum holding her chest and covering her eyes. She had slammed the back door violently behind her as she ran away from the porch. Mum then ran over to the old man and hugged him.

Poor Mum could barely speak but she managed to squeak out, "Oh, it is so horrible! That crazy, Pussface! He has gathered up the worst gift this time!"

Gramps arrived on the scene with his trusty rolling pin,

and the old man signaled for him to grab Skippy so that we would not have World War Three in our kitchen. The old man and I cracked the door open to see Pussface, who meowed loudly at the appearance of the old man. There, on the floor in front of him, was the cause of the horror.

The stiff, frozen body of Fluffy the parakeet was sprawled out there on the floor, in his full, rigid, glory on the floor of the porch!

"Oh geezzzz, Pussface!" The old man moaned as he scooped up poor Fluffy.

This parakeet was the gift that just kept coming back.

We could hear Skippy barking and growling, and Fritzie the bird had awoken under his cover and he was dropping the "b" bomb in the background. Once more, the Henson household was anything but normal.

Pussface earned his dish of beer. After all, he was just being well, Pussface. It took a long time for Mum to calm down. Gramps even gave her a shot of his special, high-octane, Canadian rye whiskey that he kept hidden deep in the recess of his cupboard. You see, all of us in our neighborhood kept time bombs hidden in our cupboards for occasions such as these.

The next day, before church, the old man and I took turns bashing the ground with a pickaxe and shovel. We finally broke the ground and buried the Fluffster deep enough that even Pussface could not find him. The old man lugged a big flat stone and dropped it on top of the poor bird's grave.

In the annals of Henson family history, we now forever in perpetuity knew this incident as, "The Great Fluffy Incident." Looking back, even though the Fluffster just sat on his perch and did not really do anything, he was Mum's dear little birdie. All in all, the Fluffster was not such a bad guy. So, all of us, in the world of Henson, remembered poor Fluffy the parakeet forever more. A tear or two was shed, a glass was raised in his honor once or twice a year, a laugh here and there, but poor Fluffy the parakeet will never, ever, be forgotten.

3

The Mission

"Oh no! I am afraid that I do not have enough cranberry sauce and stuffing!"

We were all sitting around the kitchen table having our breakfast, and upon hearing the drastic statement from Mum on the level of critically low Thanksgiving Day meal supplies, the old man looked up from his *Paterson Morning Call* newspaper and frowned. He took a sip of coffee, looked over at Dottie, and then towards me. He then looked at Mum and asked, "Yeah, so what?"

"Well, dear, I do think I have made a mistake. I did not buy enough of either item for the amount of people that we have visiting for dinner, so we will not have enough for Thanksgiving, unless we go to the Foodworld and pick up some more. I know that you love your stuffing and Aunt Alma, just loves cranberry. . .."

"Oh, geezzzz! I get it! You need me to go to the Foodworld for cranberry sauce and stuffing! You do realize it is the Wednesday before Thanksgiving and that dump will be a madhouse?"

The old man had taken the day off from work, so he was going to whip up a huge guilt trip for Mum's store shopping request. He had taken a very rare vacation day to relax and prepare for the big holiday. I knew that the last place he wanted to go was the Foodworld. The old man was not a big fan of Foodworld anyway, so for him to venture out on one of the biggest food shopping days of the year was not going to be very high on his fun list. The old man sighed deeply to exaggerate the boldness of Mum's request, and then he looked at me. I knew once more that I would be part of this mission. My sister always seemed to get off the hook, because in this case, the old man knew that she would just bug him to go over to Maureen's house.

"I will go!" The old man shouted as he spun around in his chair, looked at Mum, and did his best to emphasize the level of the tragedy of such an audacious request.

"Oh, thank you, dear! Please bring Paulie with you. He knows the store so well. You two can get in and out and be right back."

There were those fateful words once more. Those untrue, cold words that never panned out. "Right back," never failed to send shivers down my spine!

"What time does that joint open? If we can get there early, it will be better," the old man said while he was staring at his watch.

"Well, I do not know, but I would think they may open up early because of the holiday rush, dear."

The old man jumped up from the table as if his pants were now on fire. "Let's go, Paulie!" he shouted and nearly blew all the Big Bob's Sugar Fizzly Whizzly cereal out of my bowl. I looked at the clock on the wall of the kitchen and it was not even six thirty in the morning yet.

"I do not think they will be open yet, Dad."

"Nah, nah, nah, let's go. They will be open soon. I will get my coat and warm up the Putter. Swallow those sugar, flake, blob, things and get your backside out here! I do not know how you eat those sugar blobs, anyway!" The old man stood there with his hands on his hips, waving his hands over my cereal bowl. "Now that you are a hockey player, ya should be eating Big Bob's Muscle Wheat Flake-A-Ma-Bobs! They are not loaded with sugar like those things you eat. Besides, the box we bought last week has Jim Beaver from the New York Bugs on the cover!"

The old man was an avid collector of the cereal box covers from his Big Bob's cereal, which always had endorsements of famous athletes on the covers. He would cut out the pictures of his favorite players and staple them to the wooden beams above his workbench in the basement. The wheat cereal was always soggy within ten seconds of pouring milk on it, and it was disgusting. In addition to tasting better than the soggy wheat flakes, the Big Bob's Sugar Fizzly Whizzly cereal always had some junky, cheap, plastic toy inside the box.

Since this sudden mission was food and appetite related, my sister thought it might be a good time to slip in a Maureen's house sales pitch that would appeal to the old man's voracious appetite.

Dottie struck quickly, "Dad, Maureen will have some extra ziti that I could bring home for you for Thanksgiving if you let me go over there!" Dottie smiled as she had shifted gears from the crying and sobbing approach, to the more refined and appealing, "Daddy's little girl style."

The old man still had his hands on his hips as he now blasted my sister's suggestion, "Are you kidding me? You must be kidding me. No one ever has ziti for Thanksgiving! Finish your cereal, Paulie!"

Nice try, Dottie, but the same results. I did have to admit that she had earned bonus points for not only creativity, but also for her sheer persistence.

I shoveled in the cereal, washed my hands, grabbed my vest, and I was out the door. The old man was already sitting in the Putter and he was turning the ignition key. The old car protested, but it started up. He jammed the 1964 Putter Classic model 200 in gear. It coughed, and spit up a giant cloud of blue and black smoke. He shook his head and fiddled with the manual choke knob on the dashboard until the Putter started to smooth out.

"Stupid ass Putter, I swear if it ain't July and a hundred degrees out, this hunk of junk will not run!"

The old man leaned into the dashboard, hunched over with a death grip on the steering wheel of the Putter. We pulled out onto Belmont Avenue, and the old man gunned the engine. We gradually increased our speed up to about fifteen miles per hour, bucking and spitting blue bombs of smoke out of the tailpipe, and immediately a line of traffic sixty-two miles long pulled up behind us, honking their horns. We rolled up the road and lucky for us, and all the cars behind the 1964 Putter Classic model 200, the Foodworld store was only less than a half of a mile or so up the road. We pulled into the parking lot, and it was mostly empty, except for a handful of cars off in one corner of the lot.

"I do not think they are open yet, Dad. It is way too early."

"Nah, this jerk who runs this store is a money-grubbing dope. He will open up early to squeeze all the money he can out of people. That is all Thanksgiving has become, a money-grubbing holiday to extract more money out of your wallet for food!"

Wow! I had to admit that this was the first time I had heard this unusual conspiracy theory from my father! Poor Thanksgiving, which had remained unmentioned until now in the old man's extensive menu of conspiracy theories, had now officially been lumped in the same old man categories as most of the other holidays.

The two of us jumped out of the Putter, locked the doors, and made our way towards the front door. There was not another soul in sight. We made it to the front door and the old man tugged on the handle.

Sure enough, the store was not open.

"You have got to be kidding me? This place is a dump!" My father stood with his arms folded across his chest while he stared in through the door glass.

I did not say a word. I knew better. We stood there for a few moments, when to our surprise, a chap who had longer hair than even I did came along, spun a key in the door lock, and then walked away.

The old man looked at his watch, smiled, and announced to me, "See, I told you these bananas would open up early."

"This is great. We can shoot in here before anyone else and be home in a flash. Well, maybe not in a flash with the Putter, but we will be home soon for sure."

The old man nodded. We walked in the store, picked up a little basket, and headed into the aisles. I knew the store well, so I led the way as we navigated first towards the cranberry sauce, and then we would head for the stuffing. Since it was early, the old man walked at a leisurely pace, and he gathered up a few little extra items that he would never have even considered if the store had been jammed. He tossed a little bag of Big Bob's famous, chocolate covered, peanut chewers in the basket, and then a jar of Big Bob's famous pickled onions. It was very strange as there was not another person in sight in the entire store. Even the boring, canned music that usually played over the speaker system was not on.

It was quite odd indeed.

The old man picked up the jar of pickled onions and told me, "You know, Big Bob used to make these in a store over in Paterson, about a block or so from Ryerson Avenue where we all grew up. That was when Big Bob was first starting out. Now, look at him. He is rolling in dough and makes everything!" I had heard the Big Bob story a few kijillion times before, and while it had changed over the years a little here and there, for the most part, it was the same story.

We turned into the aisle that had the cranberry sauce, and immediately, two very large and angry police officers met us and screamed at us, "ON THE FLOOR, YOU TWO! ON THE FLOOR! DON'T MOVE A MUSCLE!"

The old man yelled, threw his basket in the air, and

signaled for me to hit the floor. We hit the floor, sprawled across the tile, and did not move a muscle. The pickled onions landed in a loud crash on the floor, and the glass shattered and pickled onions flew in all directions into the air. There now was a distinct odor of pickled onion juice in the air.

"Don't move, Paulie! Just lay there!" The old man shouted. We both stayed down as the police officers rushed in and looked over the top of us.

Another man rushed over and stood by us too, while he shouted, "That is them, officers! I have no idea how they got in here, or how long they have been in the store!"

My father and I dared not to move a muscle as we were both sprawled across the floor of the Foodworld supermarket, shaking in our boots, as the police officers hovered over us and drilled us for answers.

"What are youse guys doing in here? How did you break in?"

The old man looked up from the floor and then looked over at me. He then replied in an astounded delivery, "Break in? Are you kidding me? We are shopping for cranberry sauce and stuffing! Who do you think we are, Santie Claus, and my son here is one of his elves, and we came down the chimney?"

"Ah, a smart guy, huh!" One of the officers scowled at us, as they now had their guns drawn and trained down upon us. Even for a Henson adventure, this one was a good one, and the old man was digging us deeper into trouble.

In a last-ditch effort to save us, I decided to intervene on our behalf. I rolled on my side and raised my hand in the air very slowly, "Mr. Police Officer, sir, I am just a kid. I am only fourteen years old. A long-haired guy with hair longer than mine, came to the front door, unlocked it, and we walked in. What my father told you is the truth! We are here for cranberry sauce and stuffing. My mother sent us for an early morning mission for Thanksgiving dinner."

The police officers looked at each other and then they looked at the man who had rushed over.

One of the officers asked me, "You are only a kid? You are awfully tall and hairy for just being a kid."

"He is just a kid. He is really big and tall for his age. What he tells you is the truth. The kid does not lie. He is an honest kid, sometimes too honest. He gets me in trouble all the time with my wife, because he spills his guts, and I cannot cover up a thing. That is the truth that he is telling you!"

The old man rolled around on his belly and looked up at the two officers. He was starting to become a little red-faced as he continued to tell our sad tale, "Some long-haired dope opened the door and we walked in. This is nuts! I am a Korean War veteran! I shop here all the time, and this is the thanks that I get for being a loyal Foodworld shopper, and defending our country! From now on, I am going to that new, Hippity Dippity Food Market, up the street!" The old man was now sitting up on his backside, looking at the police officers.

The officers waved at the old man to stop talking, and turned towards the man, whom I now presumed to be the store manager.

One of the officers asked, "So, do you have a long-haired dope who works here or what? You are the manager here. You should know when you unlock the front door! You called us, ya know! We were right next-door grabbing coffee and donuts, so we sped right over, but you better be right about these two guys that we have apprehended here!"

Apprehended? This was really getting wild now.

The manager stammered and started to speak, and then he stopped.

His eyes nervously went back and forth in his head while the manager said, "I do have an employee . . . Larry . . . he has very long hair. I will need to call him. I do not know what to say."

I now felt secure enough to roll over and sit up next to the old man. Just as I sat up, I spotted the long-haired guy who let us in, walking past the front of the aisle.

I yelled out, "There he is! That is the chap who unlocked the door." The long-haired guy stopped, looked at the scene in front of him, and his eyes almost popped out of his head.

"Larry! Get over here!"

Larry walked over slowly to the scene of the crime. He knew this was a bad scene for him.

"Ah yes, Mr. Orsini."

"Did you unlock the front door already?"

Larry looked at us sitting on the floor, then to the police officers, and then back to his boss.

He pushed all of his hair out of his eyes and stammered, "Well yeah, like, man, you told me to unlock the front door at six thirty. I was a little late, and I did not open it until almost seven, man. I forgot, man. I am like sorry that these police had to come because I was late. Like, am I being arrested for a late door opening or something?" The police officers were shaking their heads and putting away their guns.

"Larry, you long-haired, space cadet! I told you to unlock the front door of the loading dock, you nitwit! Not the front door of the store! LIKE MAN! Learn how to speak! Now, get a mop and clean up that broken jar of Big Bob's pickled onions, then go in the back and sort the oranges. I will deal with you later. Oh, and lock the front door, you idiot. We do not open until eight in the morning." Larry nodded and stumbled off, still in dreamland.

One of the police officers extended his hand out to help pull the old man up, and the other officer waved to me to stand up now and get off the floor.

"Wow! You are a big kid, fourteen years old!" The

officer said as he scanned me up and down from close up. "You play basketball there, longhair?"

"No sir, hockey. I am a goalie."

"Bet it is hard to score on you. You must cover the whole net, kid."

The old man was on his feet now and he was spitting nails, "So Mr. Manager Orsini guy, who exactly is the head nitwit around here? You or like man, hairball, Larry?"

"Oh, sir, I am so sorry. I sincerely apologize for this unfortunate incident." The manager was a tall man who was very skinny, and you could tell that he was a nervous wreck. He wore thick eyeglasses and had jet-black hair, in which he neatly combed in a classic, comb-over style. All of us, including the police officers, circled around the manager and put our hands on our hips, waiting for his answer.

"I saw two strange men walking around and one with long hair. I guess I just panicked. This is going to be a busy day for us. Maybe the busiest day of the year, and I am under such pressure to make my numbers for this Foodworld store number x four dash two. The corporate office is rough on me, and the pressure is horrible."

"Ah, clamp the jaw flapping, Orsini! I don't have time for another crybaby story from some half-blind, Foodworld store manager. The world is full of them these days. You are acting like a scared, little, rabbit. You look like ya can't see anything, anyway. How you spotted us is a miracle. We are becoming a nation of winky, dinky, doos. Man, up and just say ya blew it. Tell it like it is, ya bum. The whole world has a sob story. We all have numbers to meet. Stop crying about it and get to work to make those numbers. If you never get in the batter's box, ya never are going to hit the ball. All of us guys here do not have time to listen to another guy crying like a boo-boo about something."

Somehow, the old man had shared some of his own unique variety of inspirational advice to Mr. Orsini. As the years went on, I realized that my old man was a very smart man.

One of the police officers nodded his head in agreement with the old man.

"C'mon Paulie, let's go to the Hippity Dippity Food Market! I am done with this dump! You meet whacko space cadets, and dopey, blind, managers who try to get you arrested. This place is a torture chamber, not a food store!"

The old man waved his arm and then he looked at the police officers. He offered up, "Youse guys, coming? I will spring for some coffee and donuts for you." The officers nodded their heads, and the four of us started to walk out the front door.

Mr. Orsini chased after us, "Wait, please, I have everything here for you. Please, please, do not shop at my competition! Please! I am so sorry. Foodworld will make it up to you. Please, I will have Larry bring you a free case of Big Bob's cranberry sauce, the pickled onions, your peanut chewers, and your Big Bob's stuffing. Please, officers, I have donuts and coffee here. Young man, please pick out anything you want for free. Please, I am so sorry. Everything is for free!"

As soon as the old man heard the word "free" he stopped dead in his tracks.

"Well, now! That is more like it there, Mr. Manager Orsini guy. Say, can I get a whole case of those Big Bob's pickled onions? I grew up right next door to the joint where Big Bob started making them. I need to tell you the story sometime there, Orsini."

The manager nodded his head. He led us to a back room inside the front offices of Foodworld and we all sat around a big table. The manager had an older woman bring us coffee and donuts, and we all sat around laughing and relaxing. It was easy to laugh about the incident now, but it sure was wild for a few minutes!

Soon the old man had made some new friends, and he was in classic form telling everyone wild stories of the old neighborhood, hand-to-hand combat with Paterson mobsters and criminals, and a million other, old man type stories. Mr. Orsini appeared with another man who had a two-wheeled hand truck loaded with our supplies. I guess Larry had not made the cut.

Mr. Orsini looked at me and asked, "What would you like, son?"

"Can I please pick out a bone for my dog and maybe a seed snack for Mum's bird? She just got a new parakeet to replace the one who croaked, and I bet he would like a snack."

"Sure, please go get it, son. That is nice to take care of your mother. You look like a hippie kid, but you are very nice and kind."

The police officers nodded and one of them said, "He is a nice kid, very polite, and well spoken. He speaks clear and straightforward. Not like Larry. I am going to give him one of our P.B.A cooperative citizen's cards. One for you Henson and one card for your son too." The officer reached in his pocket, grabbed a couple of official looking cards, filled them out with his pen, and then handed them to the old man.

"Hey, thanks, youse guys!" The old man beamed.

The old man was on cloud nine. This was a dream come true for him. Free stuff, a humble store manager, it was unreal.

I went off and picked out the items for Fritzie and Skippy. We all shook hands, said our goodbyes, and we followed the man with the hand truck out to the Putter. The old man unlocked the trunk, and we loaded the supplies in the Putter. The poor Putter sank about a foot off of the ground, and you could hear the springs creak and a groan from the weight of the supplies. This was another classic Henson adventure and the words, "right back" never seemed as misleading as they did today. It was past eight now. The store was officially open, and the lot was filling up fast.

We were about to climb in the Putter, when I looked out across the lot, and saw a little man open the hood of his car and a big cloud of steam escaped out from under the hood.

I recognized the car and the little man.

"Hey, Dad. That looks like Mr. Zipperelli over there. It looks as though he has some kind of car troubles."

The Zipperellis were almost as famous as we were for having junk automobiles. In fact, my best buddy Harry M. Redmond Jr. and the Redmond family, as well as the Porters, the Lens, the Headys, the Clipclocks, and the rest of the neighborhood families, had junk cars too. There was not a decent vehicle among all of us. I pointed over towards the broken-down car and the old man looked up.

"Yeah, yeah, yeah, I think you are right. He must have some kind of trouble there with all that steam coming out from under the hood. Let's go!"

Now, the old man was one of the greatest driveway and backyard mechanics in all of Haledon and Paterson combined. There was nothing that he enjoyed more than fixing the Putter's latest malfunction in the driveway on a freezing cold or a stifling hot day. The Putter never broke down in fair weather or a day with sunshine and a gentle breeze. The car only broke down when it was a one-hundred-degree day with a blazing sun and stifling humidity, or when relentless sleet, snow, and blizzard conditions were pelting us.

To my old man, fixing junk cars was better than obtaining free stuff, returning things to stores, or arguing with a store manager. It was what made him tick! We jumped in the Putter. The old man kicked it, and after some sputtering, we rolled over to Mr. Zipperelli.

The old man pulled next to him, rolled down the window and yelled out, "Hey there, Zipperelli! Ya got troubles?"

The little Italian man looked up and smiled as he waved his hands in the air. He began explaining the situation as best he could in northern New Jersey Italian dialect.

Luckily, the old man and I spoke it fluently.

"Paula, I ama soa glada toa seea youa! My cara it is ona fireinnia! Alla I dida, wasa coma downa herea fora morea ziti for Thanksagivinga and looka whata happeninia! I tolda mya wifea I woulda be right backinia!"

I knew those words, well sort of those words, without all the Italian overlays. As soon as he uttered those words, then that was the stake in the heart of his luck, and his dire fate was sealed.

The old man put the 1964 Putter Classic model 200 in park and shut the engine off. He leaned out the window, waved his hands at Mr. Zipperelli, and tried his best to calm him down, "All right, all right, relax there, you people are so excitable. I think that I followed most of that, Zipperelli. Keep your meatballs and sauce on your plate and relax. I have my tools in the trunk here, let's look, and see what is going on. By the way, you should be having turkey for Thanksgiving, not some pile of ziti. Whoever heard of ziti and meatballs for Thanksgiving there, Zipperelli?"

We both jumped out of the Putter and the old man unlocked the trunk and pulled out his trusty Substantial Industries Whiz Bang tool set.

Keeping a tool chest in the trunk of your car, as well as a rolling stock of common auto repair parts and supplies, was a regular way of life in our neighborhood. It was just not worth the risk of leaving home without your tools and supplies, because the sides of the road repairs were normal. Without your repair kit, it was a huge risk that you were taking by venturing out in your heap of junk car more than fifty feet, or at least what you felt was a comfortable range for pushing your car back to the front of your house would be.

The old man waved some steam away from his eyes, and the three of us peered under the hood to see what was going on there.

"Whata youa seea Paula?"

The old man mumbled that he could not see anything yet. He pointed to me to open his tool kit, as he asked, "What kind of crazy car is this pile of junk, Zipperelli? It must be one of those Italian, foreign, pasta bomb cars!"

The old man was not a fan of foreign cars.

"Ita isa nineteena sixta foura Italiano Puccininia Zucchinia Tena cara Paula. Ia justa bought ita froma Italiano buddinini of minea for fiftio buckas," Mr. Zipperelli explained.

The old man screwed his mouth up and frowned as Mr. Zipperelli explained about his car.

The old man responded with his frank opinion of the automobile, "Yeah, yeah, yeah, whatever there, Zipperelli. This car is a pile of junk. It looks like he is not much of a buddinia or whatever ya called him. Ya should get your dough back. Hand me that flashlight, Paulie."

I grabbed the light and the old man leaned in over the front of the car near the radiator and pushed some things out of the way.

"Ah, this is no big deal, Zipperelli. You just blew an upper hose here. We can wrap it up with some Big Bob's Death Grip Tape, fill it with some water, and you can make it back home. This is easy to replace, just two clamps and a new hose. Even you should be able to handle this one, Zipperelli. Here slip on in here and take a look." Mr. Zipperelli smiled and looked at what the old man was showing him.

"I seea the holea Paula! Looka the water comma outa of the hosea!"

The old man stood up and frowned. "Yeah, yeah, yeah, I think you got it now there, Zipperelli. Boy, you smell like you swallowed a pound of garlic there, Zipperelli. Your breath must have melted the hose."

"Whata?"

"Forget it. Here, take that glass jug from the trunk of my car, go to the Foodworld, and ask for Orsini, the manager of the store. He is a paesano and he will understand you. Tell him that Henson sent ya. He will do anything for ya once he hears my name. Ask Orsini to fill it up with regular water for you. While you go in there, Paulie and I will tape up your hose and seal the leak, so we can fill the radiator back up."

Mr. Zipperelli nodded, grabbed the jug, and he was off. We pulled the special tape out of the repair kit, and the old man tightly wrapped the split in the hose to repair it. Mr. Zipperelli returned with the water. We poured it into the top of the radiator, and started the car.

Everything was well once more!

"Now, you and your garlic breath need to get home right away there, Zipperelli. Buy a new hose before the auto parts stores close for Thanksgiving, slap it on, and you will be good to go."

"Oha Paula, I canna nota thanka ya enuffa! I make surea that we cooka youa a bigga meal and bringa you somea winea we makea in our basementinia for a fixa mya xplodinia cara!"

"Yeah, yeah, yeah, calm down there, Zipperelli, that is all good, whatever you said there. Hey, get on home there before the tape pops off there, and we have to rescue your pasta butt again."

Mr. Zipperelli jumped in his car, started it, and put his transmission in gear. He tore off in his car a million miles per hour, cut off about ten cars as he waved out the window, and he was gone.

"The guy drives like a maniac," the old man said as we watched Mr. Zipperelli racing off into the main drag.

We both shook our heads. We put all the tools and the

glass jug back in the trunk, started the Putter, and we were off for home. The old man had the cars lined up for miles as the Putter crawled up the road from the added weight of the supplies stored in the trunk.

He jumped back to life, as he thought of his good fortune, "What a day off from work, Paulie! Free stuff, we shut up that rat fink Orsini, and fixed that pile of Italian junk for that garlic breathing Zipperelli. What a day!"

Yes, it was. Just as an added bonus, we now had enough cranberry sauce and stuffing to last us for at least ten years.

4

A Henson Family Thanksgiving with a Little Twist

I rolled around in bed, and Skippy jumped off the foot of my bed. He sat on the floor and looked at me with pleading eyes. I peered over the edge and looked at him. "I guess you have to go outside, eh, Skip?"

Skippy jumped up, put his paws on the edge of the bed, and wagged his tail. He was always nice to me when he wanted something. If he did not need something, he could not be bothered with us, or would chase Dottie and me around growling at us.

It was early, just around six in the morning, and it was finally Thanksgiving Day. I got dressed, washed up quickly, grabbed my vest, and took Skippy out to the backyard to do what doggies do. The day was clear, windy, and cold. In my mind, I thought this was the perfect Thanksgiving Day weather. The wind pushed the leaves around and swirled them at our feet. Skippy ran around for a while and then he looked at me as though he wanted to go back inside. I think he was hungry, and come to think of it, so was I.

Skippy and I walked into the kitchen and the old man was already up and sitting at the table, drinking his coffee. Mum had prepared the turkey, and it was in the oven already cooking.

"Hello, wow, it smells good already. Good morning and happy Thanksgiving, to everyone," I said, as I sat down at the table. The old man growled a few words back, and Mum came over and gave me a kiss. "You guys are up really early. Is Dottie up yet?"

The old man was not in a holiday mood, "I hope not, all she will do is whine about going over to the Zipperelli's house and drive me nuts! Yeah, yeah, yeah, your mother insisted on putting the turkey in at three in the morning. She wants to cook it until it is a thousand degrees! I will have to wear a spacesuit to carve it."

At first, my mother did not say a word. She just stood there with her hands on her hips, shaking her head back and forth.

She then replied to the observation of her cooking time, "Well, the last thing that I want is for someone to get sick from under-cooking the turkey. Everyone will be here by noon and we plan to eat by three or four, so I need to make sure it is cooked well."

"Fritzie, Fritzie!" Fritzie was jumping around in his uncovered cage, yelling out his name.

The old man shook his head. As now, of course, the parakeet was annoying him because he could talk. "I think I liked the Fluffster better. In fact, when the Fluffster was upside down on the bottom of his cage with his feet sticking up in the air, was the best of all! Fritzie has not been saying the, b word as of late. I guess he became sick of saying it. That was all he said for three days straight."

Mum once again did not answer him, but she instead asked me if I wanted some cereal.

"Sure, Mum. Thank you. Hey, I bet it will be windy for the big Crumbley's Department Store parade. I wonder if those parade guys will tangle up one of the balloons on the top of a tree. I think I will watch it this year."

The old man smiled as he recalled a fond memory, "The best year was the parade when Santie Claus lost his pants after the parade had ended. He was running into the front of the store, when he turned around to wave to the kiddies, and his pants fell down to his ankles! I loved that!" The old man never forgot his favorite parade, which was the year of the now famous Santa Claus incident. This story was not an old man exaggeration, but it was indeed correct, as we were both watching it together. The old man roared with laughter for hours after that. It was a holiday highlight for him, even years later.

We enjoyed breakfast, Dottie woke up, and we listened to some occasional moaning and groaning from my sister on the continued lack of an approved visit to Maureen's house. Dottie seemed to have conceded defeat on the subject, or she was actually looking forward to the holiday because her protests were short-lived and not very creative. I had a feeling that she may be holding back and would deliver the final attack as the day wore on, but time would tell.

Gramps came down for breakfast and tea. We all sat around and enjoyed some small talk. And of course, Gramps had to stir his tea a million times for good measure, but that was normal. We cleaned up, and Dottie and I watched the parade on the television. Mum and the old man would dart in and out, but for the most part, they were busy in the kitchen preparing for the arrival of our family. The old man went outside to the porch and tugged on the railing to check it once or twice. He then sat on the sofa and bounced up and down on it to check it, and he double-checked his supply of epoxy and Big Bob's Death Grip Tape, but he seemed content that he had fortified the house enough for the arrival of Cousin Pat.

The parade ended at noon, without any malfunctions of Santa Claus's pants. The old man kept checking with us on the status, and he seemed disappointed that it was uneventful this year. We did get the usual speech from him, on how every year the parade gets worse, because, it is, "One big commercial for Crumbley's rip-offs!"

Mum had the house set up nicely for the holiday, and she set out a dish of assorted nuts, some little sugared fruits, dates, and chocolate-covered mints on the living room table for snacks. I knew what was coming, as I just knew that Mum would warn Dottie and me not to scatter what she called, "fuds, bits, or bobs, all about the rug."

She stood in the front of the little dish as she refilled it with snacks and sure enough, she reminded us once more as she said, "Now, I just cleaned in here. I do not mind if you watch the television, but please, I do not want to see any fuds, bits, or bobs around from you eating here in the living room.

My sister and I both nodded our heads in acknowledgement of the instructions. Now fuds, bits, and bobs were a classification that our mother used for small items of an undetermined nature that landed here and there on your clothes, in your hair, or on the rug, or floor.

Mum was a continuous cleaning machine, and she waged an eternal war against dust, dirt, and performed general house cleaning on an ongoing basis. There was a definite range of classification of these unknown items that seemed to stem from the actual size of them. From the best that I could tell, and interpret the English lingo, a fud was a little larger than a bob, and quite often, you could find them on your clothes. For example, Mum would reach over and pick a little item off the old man's suit jacket in church, and whisper to him that he had a fud on it. A bob was bigger than a bit, but smaller than a fud. You could find bits and bobs, most often on the rug or the floor. Mum would often be sitting in her chair in the living room, and she would spring into cleaning action, when she spotted bits and bobs, "Scattered about."

My sister and I were used to the strange terminology. The old man would mostly just roll his eyes and say something such as, "Do ya mean those damn crumbs on the floor from the cookies the kids were eating?"

The old man was our link to regular New Jersey speak, as well as exceptionally poor grammar! I just knew that I had to be careful when I cracked the shells of the walnuts or pecans, because they could produce a multitude of fuds, bits, and bobs, and I would be in deep trouble with dear Mum!

I was big and strong for my age, so it became my job to carry up the extra section of our dining room table that we kept in storage in the basement. We placed the expanded section into the dining room table to seat the additional guests, and the old man checked the chair where he was going to have Cousin Pat sit. In a last-minute fortification effort, he had added some small metal braces and a wooden brace on it. The plan was to make sure that she only sat in that chair. The old man worked out an intricate plan with me, of how to make sure that Cousin Pat sat in only the reinforced sofa, and in this particular chair, but I was not quite sure it would work.

The wonderful smell of the turkey cooking floated throughout the house, with the enticing aroma drifting in every nook and cranny of our home. My clothes would smell like roast turkey for days, and the house would take a month or so to air out, when it would be just about time for our Christmas turkey to renew the holiday odor once again.

The doorbell rang, and the old man greeted my Aunt Lois and Uncle Ed as the first guests to arrive. Aunt Lois was my Mum's kid sister, so Gramps was very happy to see them and have family members for the big gathering.

As soon as Skippy heard Uncle Ed's voice, he came tearing into the living room to greet him.

He ran around like a racecar, from one end of the house to the other while Uncle Ed yelled out, "Hey there, Ralphie! Atta boy Ralphie, go get 'em." Skippy finally rested, sat next to Uncle Ed, and allowed Uncle Ed to pet him. It was peculiar behavior from our bizarre family dog. Skippy seemed to accept the fact that his name was Skippy to everyone else in the world, except for Uncle Ed. He even would respond to "Ralphie" when Uncle Ed called him by that name! Uncle Ed smiled and simply said, "He sure is excitable."

Uncle Ed was a tall man who had a kind face, a calm and friendly demeanor, and was just a plain, old-fashioned, nice guy. He was a regular old Paterson, New Jersey guy, having been born and raised in the city.

Aunt Lois had the same kind, friendly demeanor as Uncle Ed. She was short, a little shorter than Mum was, with short hair and a beautiful face. She was very soft-spoken, with a light English accent, but she had an easy laugh and a nice smile. They both had great senses of humor, and I always was very close to them and enjoyed their company.

After some small talk, the old man cracked open the first few Big Boulder beers of the day and he shared some cold ones with Uncle Ed and Gramps. Aunt Lois and Mum enjoyed a glass of wine, and we all sat around talking and sharing some family time. The big holiday was finally here, and the celebration had begun.

The old man took everyone into the kitchen to show them Fritzie, and despite his best efforts, he could not get him to utter the "b" word. Mum was pleased since it seemed as if Fritzie had forgotten that particular word and he had moved towards learning other words for his limited vocabulary. The old man was putting it on really thick today for our guests, as he wove an intricate tale of how he wheeled and outmaneuvered Mr. Rupple in the pet store to come away with his prize bird at such a bargain price. When we all returned to the living room to sit around and talk, he then wove another magical tale of the now famous Foodworld incident, and that story had now graduated to include agents who descended upon us from the FBI!

The old man was a magical storyteller, and once he had a few beers floating around in him, then he could really spin a few expanded versions of his yarns.

We heard the doorbell ring and Gramps looked at his

watch, "That should be Pat and my sister Alma now. It is right about when I expected them."

The old man looked at me and his eyes darted back and forth in his head, as I knew he wanted to go and watch in order to make sure the handrail on the side of the front steps held.

We both jumped up from our chairs as the old man shouted out, "I will get them in!" We raced to the front hallway, then out to the porch and sure enough, there were Aunt Alma and Cousin Pat standing on the front steps. They were both smiling and waving at us.

The old man flung the door wide open, and they both shouted out to us, "Happy Thanksgiving, Paul! Happy Thanksgiving, Paulie boy! It is so nice to see you both!"

Oh boy! They are so loud! We both returned the greetings as the old man scanned the porch and steps for residual Cousin Pat damage.

So far, so good.

Aunt Alma walked up the last step first, and she gave my father a hug and a kiss. She then turned her attention to me.

"Oh my, you are getting so big, Paulie boy. You must have grown a foot since I last saw you in the summer! My, my, and so handsome too with all that long hair. What is that I see, but a little beard on the end of your chin or what? Oh my, you are going to have an awful lot of young ladies chasing after you very shortly, eh." She hugged me and gave me a kiss on the cheek.

"Hiya, Aunt Alma, it is nice to see you," I managed to squeeze out a compliment between hugs. Next, Cousin Pat made her way up the final steps as the porch creaked and cracked. Her final step resulted in a long, low moan and a groan from the old wood, as the enormous weight of Cousin Pat landed full force upon it. The old man looked down at her feet, and I saw him cross his fingers as Cousin Pat landed with a little "thud" on the flat part of the porch.

She had made it!

"Hello, Paul and Paulie boy! I made it safely to the porch this year! Last time that I visited, it was not so good!"

Cousin Pat nearly blew out our eardrums with her volume. She had a big smile on her face a mile or so wide. I noticed that she had something in her hand, and when she reached the final resting spot, she reached out and handed it to the old man.

The old man's eyes bugged out as he realized that it was our mailbox that had, until a minute or two ago, been mounted on the side of the porch right next to the first step.

"Oh, Paul, I am so sorry about your mailbox. Here." Cousin Pat handed my father the twisted remains. "I slipped just a little on that first step. It is a tricky one down there. When I reached up, I grabbed the mailbox, and it just fell right off the wall. You should really have mounted it better, Paul. You needed longer screws."

Cousin Pat then snorted and laughed and turned her attention towards me, "Oh, Paulie boy, Mum is so right. You are quite the handsome young man. Oh boy, you are going to have many girlfriends soon! Look at that hair. I would die for hair like that! You are so tall now too!" Cousin Pat gave me a hug and a kiss. She was snorting and laughing, and she gave out what seemed as if it was a belch or two along with her snorts. I held onto the porch wall just in case she crashed into me and sent me toppling over.

The old man took what formerly used to be our mailbox, nodded his head, and mumbled a low faint, "Yeah, yeah, yeah, right, thanks Pat."

"Oh, that little girl of mine, she is a wee bit on the clumsy side, eh!" Aunt Alma was laughing and waving her hand at the scene. Aunt Alma and her sense of humor got quite the kick out of how Cousin Pat could easily dismantle our family home. We all walked into the house and the big greeting was on. Gramps was thrilled to see his sister and his niece, as were the rest of the family.

The old man stood there holding his mailbox in his hand as he tried to bend it back into shape. He gave up and disappeared down into the basement. I assumed that he went to put it on his workbench for a future repair effort. My guess was that this weekend would require another trip to the Rickel Home Improvement Store.

Aunt Alma was a wonderful person. She was full of life and adventure. She was tall, very pretty, and outgoing. She had flaming red hair, big horn-rimmed glasses, and she always wore brightly colored dresses. Usually, she wore red, green, or bright blue dresses, with a string of white pearls around her neck. She had a very thick English accent, and she spoke a little Welsh at times mixed in with her English words. I loved her and being around her. She was a ton of fun and laughs, with a great dry sense of humor.

She had married a chap who lived in Florida part-time and in England, the other half of the time. They owned shoe stores in Florida and England and were successful at the businesses. Her husband had passed away a few years back and Aunt Alma sold all the stores. Now that she was a widow, she traveled all the time. After Gramps had retired, she was always working hard to drag Gramps all around the globe on her travels, but her brother would have none of it. The most he would do was to stay with his sister in Florida for a month or so in the winter. He did visit her once in the summer, and all we heard for two months was how terribly hot and humid it was.

Much to the chagrin of Mum, he continually used the dreadful "b" word to describe the level of heat that the weather inflicted upon him during his Florida stay.

Cousin Pat was a charismatic gal. In many ways, she was a much larger version of Aunt Alma, as she also was very pretty, had red hair, and she laughed (and snorted) all the time. She joked about her legendary habit of being clumsy, her unique penchant that she had for breaking things, and her large size. Cousin Pat lived on a small farm in upstate New York.

Her husband had passed away a few years ago. I had only met her husband once or twice, when I was only eight or nine years old, so I only had some vague memories of him. He was also a large man, but I did remember how he was a very funny guy. I could remember how hard he made Dottie and me laugh. He was a great guy, full of life and fun, and I was saddened to hear that he had passed away at such an early age.

Even at a young age, I wondered why God took all the nice young folks at such an early age, and the old crabs stuck around forever. Later in my life, I would find some answers that I was looking for, but that was a whole other story.

"Oh, Cousin Joanie, Cousin Lois, Eddie, and little Dottie! Dot, you look so much like your Mum! You're so beautiful."

The greetings were on in full force and I stood on the sideline, watching. We did not get together very much, but I had to admit it sure was nice to see and hear all of these folks. You cannot pick your relatives in this life, but you sure could love them! I knew that we all would be speaking New Jersey twang laced with English accents and Welsh words for a few weeks after this visit.

Uncle Ed went to sit down on the sofa, after all the hugs and greetings were over, and the old man jumped into action, "Say, Ed, would you like another Big Boulder, ladies, some drinks? Pop, do you want another beer?"

Uncle Ed stopped before he sat down and said, "Sure Paul, yeah, yeah, yeah, let me help you." The old man took a count of the drinks and refills as he nodded my way.

The window of opportunity came my way, so I did my part to save our furniture, "Here, Aunt Alma and Cousin Pat, sit here on the sofa, I will take your coats and hats and hang them up for you." They both handed me their coats and hats.

"Oh, Paulie boy, you are such a young gentleman!"

Aunt Alma was thrilled at my polite behavior, as she was unaware of my part of being a mere pawn in the old man's diversion plan. My father and I watched as Cousin Pat slowly descended onto the reinforced sofa. She landed safely, and the sofa creaked a little, but as we held our breath for a moment . . . it held!

I went to hang the attire up, and as I walked out of the room, I heard Aunt Alma say, "My, what a sturdy sofa! Dottie, what are you up to these days? Why you look just like Cousin Emily back home in Nottingham."

"Oh, Aunt Alma, I so want to go over to my friend Maureen's house after dinner!" My sister was deploying the last resort tactic of bringing the visiting relatives in on her side to sway and influence our parents.

Very impressive!

In the kitchen, the old man was preparing the drinks and the beers with Uncle Ed, and secretly celebrating our making it over the sofa hurdle.

It was quite the time, as I sat on the floor listening to a true mixture of accents, backgrounds, personalities, and a lifetime of experiences. It is these times of our lives that we always cherish the most, the times when families and friends gathered together, sharing their love, their lives, and their thoughts. I learned even then at a young age that I should always try hard to remember these moments and rewind the hands of time on occasion. Then, we all could visit with one another again, and my life would always be enriched forever more.

"Let me tell you about the time, the Rapp brothers and I shot the rubber band arrow with a flaming end on it, off the top of Preakness Mountain one night after Thanksgiving!"

My father had enough beer in him now to tell a good one.

"You see, the Rapp boys . . . there was, let me remember

now . . . Johnny, Joey, and Bobby Rapp. They were three brothers in our neighborhood and they were, how shall we say, not a good influence on me. Well, the day after Thanksgiving, they stole some leftover beer and wine from their old man, and we all snuck up on the top of Preakness Mountain to drink it. Well, it went straight to our heads, we were not used to drinking, ya see, and us guys were only fifteen to sixteen years old."

Gramps and Aunt Alma shook their heads at his classic, New Jersey laden, butchering of the English language.

The old man turned to my sister and me and said, "Do not get any ideas, you two birds!" He then continued his tale of childhood adventure.

"It was getting darker now, and we found this old truck tire on top of the mountain. We took the inner tube out of it and cut the rubber into two long strips with our pocket knives. Johnny Rapp, he was a criminal, but he was very smart. He attached it to a fork in a tree there that was open to the side of the mountain. You see, us guys had made a big slingshot! So, us guys took an old shirt, a long stick, tied the shirt on the end of the stick, dipped the shirt in gasoline, and lit it with a match. Then we put it in the slingshot and we all pulled it back with all of our strength and let it go. Zoom! It flew out into the air, through the night sky, and down the side of the mountain. Lord only knows how we did not burn a house down, but lucky for us, it landed in the middle of Preakness Ave and not on some house rooftop. We all took off and ran home as the police and fire engines were all over the place. The next day, the 'Paterson Morning Call' newspaper had a big headline, describing how the local police and fire precincts were flooded with calls about a fireball in the sky over the mountain. The article went on to tell that the flaming fireball that lit up the night sky was the work of local pranksters! The Rapp's old man and my father knew it was us, and boy oh boy, did all of us guys get a beating!"

The old man received a good round of laughs, and my sister and I heard a story that we had not heard before. I guess, as we grew older, the old man allowed more and more of his childhood tales from his more mischievous side to come out!

Aunt Alma shared a story of her trips to New Zealand and Australia. She visited with some long-lost uncle or cousin who had received land from the queen to relocate and develop sheep farms there. She told of the fantastic adventures of visiting such far-off countries. She told of stopping off in Hawaii and Guam to visit there as well as California. It was wonderful storytelling from a woman who had truly experienced a full life, traveled, and lived all over the globe.

Mum kept checking the progress of the turkey, and soon the fateful and long-awaited moment had finally arrived. Mum proclaimed the turkey finally, fully cooked! The thermometer stuck in the turkey's backside had finally reached forty thousand degrees! That was not some trivial fact, because it seemed as if it had been cooking for half of my lifetime.

"Oh, that is great news. It smells so wonderful and we are so hungry!" Cousin Pat shouted, clapped her hands together, and proceeded in her excitement to knock the entire bowl of assorted nuts all over the rug in the living room. "Oh my, I have made a mess of fuds all over. I am so sorry, Joanie." Cousin Pat was obviously able to classify the objects correctly. Dottie went into action to clean the misplaced fuds up, while the entire clan moved towards the kitchen to inspect the glorious turkey.

The old man was already in position, next to the table and his cutting board, as he had laid out his Super Deluxe, Substantial Industries, Carving Set that he picked up for Christmas last year.

The old man loved them.

For six months, he had told us endlessly about the

television commercial where a Japanese man demonstrated by cutting through a brick with a carving knife. After the old man had dropped fifteen million hints, Gramps finally could not stand it anymore, and he finally bought the knives for a Christmas present for the old man.

"Stand back, everyone! Stand back! This turkey is just four degrees cooler than a volcano is after it has erupted," the old man yelled, as he lowered the door to the cooker and peered into the oven cavity with his oven mitts on. He yanked and pulled under the guidance of Mum, and he pulled the turkey free from the oven cavity. The steam billowed off the bird like a smokestack, and the old man struggled to avoid the intense heat that was practically melting the hair right off his head. He rushed the turkey to the table, and sat it down, as the crowd of relatives clapped and cheered at the sight of the fantastic turkey.

"Oh, goodness. I do hope I cooked it well enough." Mum wrung her hands and fretted. "I do not want anyone getting sick if I have not cooked it enough."

All of us, just stared at the turkey sitting there with steam pouring out of it, watching the paint peel off the kitchen walls from the heat of the turkey, while the old man struggled to regain his breath, ran to the sink, and he put a cold dishcloth on his neck.

Gramps finally piped in with a simple observation, "Looks done to me, love. Anymore cooking and it might have melted the bloomin' steel pan, eh?"

Mum nodded, but she still looked concerned as she gave the old man some direction, "Well dear, let it cool a bit so it carves up nice." The old man was still gasping for air as he nodded in acknowledgement.

"Oh my, what a pretty budgie!" Aunt Alma had spotted Fritzie, who the entire time seemed to be eyeing the crowd as well as the cooked bird on the table.

I think he secretly was wondering what terrible fate had befallen a fellow winged friend.

Skippy also made a guest appearance, as the aroma of the turkey became a little too much for him to withstand anymore. He sat down and stared at the turkey on the table while he secretly wished that he had longer legs and a pair of hands.

"Oh, how I wish I still had my two pretty budgies! I miss Zippy and Flippy so much! You do remember my two birdies now don't you, Pat?"

"I sure do, Mum," Cousin Pat answered.

The old man asked Aunt Alma, "Did ya find them on the bottom of their cage with their feet sticking up in the air?"

Cousin Pat nodded and said, "Why yes, Paul, we did as a matter of fact. How did you know?"

"Lucky guess, Pat."

"Flippy and Zippy used to love treats. Do you like treats? What is your name, pretty bird?" Cousin Pat pushed a fig and a date that she had been munching on into the cage.

"ACCCKKK! Fritzie! Fritzie!" Fritzie flew down from his perch to the bottom of the cage and started to tear the dates and figs into bits and devour them.

"Oh my, he talks so nice. Fritzie, eh? But it sounds German!" Cousin Pat and Aunt Alma both whirled around quickly and stared at Mum.

"Oh no, it is just a name. He is from Australia," Mum assured them. As soon as Aunt Alma heard Australia, she was happy, and they went back to throwing another date in the cage.

Fritzie was eating the fruits as quickly as Cousin Pat and Aunt Alma could toss them into his cage. Fritzie was in fig and date heaven. He consumed all the fruits thrown into his cage, and flew back on his perch.

We all watched as he sat on his perch, wiggled his tail a bit, and yelled out, "Bloody well!"

"Oh, my!" Aunt Alma sprung back from the cage and

she and Cousin Pat turned to look at Gramps. "John, did you teach this lovely bird to say that?" Aunt Alma questioned her brother. Aunt Alma knew already who the teacher had been.

"Well, Alma, it was an unfortunate error on my part. I do feel terrible. It just slipped out one day. The budgie is smart. In my futile defense, the little lad picks up things quite quickly. Joanie has already scolded me."

Uncle Ed and the old man loved it, but Mum was frowning. I think she really thought that her dear Fritzie had forgotten the word. Perhaps all the English accents had led Fritzie to some epiphany of his background and true native tongue.

You know, disasters or accidents can strike at any time, sometimes in a flash of an eye, things can change without a moment's notice. I guess that in looking back, it was just inevitable that Cousin Pat would collide with something other than our mailbox, and a mere dish of table treats. No one could ever have imagined that such a simple thing could have led to such severe and far-reaching consequences. In the world of Cousin Pat, this was a relatively gentle collision and accident. Gentle, in relative terms to what she was usually able to do.

As Cousin Pat turned back towards the cage to look at Fritzie, her giant elbow and arm struck the birdcage, and it swung hard on its stand and hook.

The cage rocked side to side violently as Mum gasped, and Aunt Alma let out with a loud, "Oh no!"

Fritzie screamed, and he flew around the cage, his water dumped, and his seed cup fell to the bottom of the cage. Aunt Alma and Cousin Pat struggled to control the swinging cage as Fritzie frantically flew around, trying to maintain his stability.

Then, it happened!

The hard blow to the side of the cage had jolted the little door to the cage wide open, and Fritzie flew out into the wild blue yonder!

As Fritzie took to the air, I vaguely remembered Mr. Rupple saying something about having his wings clipped soon, "Because he was quite the capable flyer!"

Oh no! The old man never had his wings clipped and Fritzie was off to the races!

"Fritzie! Come back here, Fritzie!" Poor mum was off chasing her beloved bird. Fritzie was enjoying his newly found freedom, and he swooped from room to room, swirled, turned, and spun and flew from one end of the living room to the far end of the house, and then back again. We all chased after him and ducked when he came close to our heads. Skippy was chasing him and barking his brains out until Gramps scooped him up and hustled him out on the back porch. That was good thinking. I am sure, Skippy would not have treated poor Fritzie quite fairly if he had landed within his reach!

"DON'T CHASE HIM! LET HIM SIT! JUST LET FRITZIE LAND AND WE WILL CAPTURE HIM!" The old man bellowed out instructions.

We all froze in position and watched as Fritzie swooped, banked, dove, and then finally landed on top of the kitchen cabinets above the sink.

"Acckkkkk! Fritzie! Fritzie! Ackkk!" The little bird rested on the top of the cabinets and peered down at us all. Mr. Rupple was indeed correct. Fritzie could really fly.

The old man grabbed the step stool from the kitchen, set it up in front of the sink and slowly climbed up, "Nice Fritzie, stay Fritzie, stay there."

The old man closed in with his outreached hands and was within a few inches of Fritzie when bang! Off he flew into the wild blue yonder once more! He was not going back into the cage easily. He flew off into the living room, turned, banked, and landed on top of the dining room china cabinet. This time, Uncle Ed closed within inches of him, when off he went again.

"Oh, my poor Fritzie, we have to capture, Fritzie!" Poor Mum was now getting upset, and Aunt Alma and Cousin Pat fretted that they had allowed him to escape. Fritzie flew, circled, and landed once more on the top of the kitchen cabinets, as we now tried to lure him with more dates and figs, but to no avail.

Freedom was more fun than fruits were tasty.

Off he flew, but this time, he chose an unusual landing spot. As he banked in the kitchen, he flew over and sat directly down on top of a remarkable landing position. You see, Fritzie decided to land directly on top of our fantastic, luscious, wonderful, Thanksgiving turkey. Fritzie was perched atop the beloved centerpiece of our holiday celebration as the turkey sat there, waiting to be carved into juicy, tender, heavenly slices, for our once-a-year feast!

"No one moves! I got him now!" The old man closed in.

Then it happened. One of the greatest events in all of Henson family history, as the newest member of the Henson family decided to, how shall I say, or describe this scene but, Fritzie, decided to provide a contribution to our Thanksgiving celebration in his own little birdie way.

Fritzie wiggled his tail, gave a loud squawk, bellowed out, "Bloody well," and proceeded to drop his "recycled" figs and dates all over the top of our turkey!

The old man froze in mid-lunge and yelled out, "Geeeeez, our damn turkey just got shit-bombed on! We all stood there dumbfounded and in dismay, as Fritzie wiggled his tail, loaded the cannon, and let poor, defenseless Mr. Turkey have round two!

"Bloody well!"

Kaboooom!

I had no idea a little bird could—I am not sure how to explain—but how a little bird could explode quite so much. Another large bomb dropped in celebration of all the good things we received all year and were so thankful for in our lives.

It was as if we all froze in place. Our mouths were open in horror, as we watched our prize turkey christened by Fritzie, the date and fig-eating machine.

It was also very obvious that figs and dates did not quite agree with his digestive system.

I was a hockey goaltender and known, even at my young age, for my fast reflexes. I was not going to stand around much longer and allow any additional inflamed bowel abuse of our poor turkey. Fritzie wiggled his tail once more, and while he prepared for round three, I dove in, grabbed him, and scooped him up tightly in my hands.

"ACKKKK! ACKKKK!" Fritzie screamed. Aunt Lois was next to the cage, and she opened the cage door as I ran to the cage with Fritzie held tightly in my grasp. He, of course, let me know his displeasure at his capture, as I felt his revenge dripping down my arm. I placed him in the cage, and Aunt Lois slammed the door shut. He flew up on his perch, rang his bell, and screamed, "Fritzie! Fritzie!"

I was washing my hands and arms off, when I heard Mum sobbing as she held her hands over her face, "All that work! Our turkey is ruined!"

We all turned and watched in revulsion, as recycled figs and dates dripped, and ran down the side of our precious turkey. It gave a new meaning to turkey dressing.

"Nonsense," the old man said, as he took a wet dishcloth and wiped down the top of the turkey. "He only hit the top of it, you see. Well, youse guys, maybe some dripped down here too, and some over . . . here. Hey, youse guys, look, it is not that much. In the military, we had the five-second rule for food. If food dropped on the ground, it was still okay to eat it, if you picked it up within five seconds." The old man turned around and smiled at everyone. "See, good as new!"

"I am so sorry, Joanie," was all Cousin Pat could muster up.

The old man's optimistic smile faded as Dottie burst into

tears and ran out of the kitchen, screaming, "Yuck! Ewww! I am not eating that! If only, I could have eaten at Maureen's house! Thanksgiving is ruined!"

Gramps offered up his wise sage-like advice as he cleared his throat and said in his deepest English accent, "Well, I must say that Fluffy old boy was a tad bit uninteresting, but at least he bloody well had more respect for turkeys! Are you sure that this Fritzie character is not German?"

"No, Pop, he is Australian, all budgies are," Aunt Lois shook her head at her father while she reinforced the recycled date and fig machine's bloodline.

"I would then suggest that you discontinue figs and dates from his diet immediately!"

We all stared at the turkey and the general opinion was that, despite the old man's best efforts, we all had lost our appetite for this turkey. I let poor Skippy back in from his exile, and he circled around the turkey, looking for the current status of the meal. A little bird dropping or two did not deter old Skippy! He still felt that turkey was going to be a big part of his Thanksgiving celebration. As we all recovered from the shock, Mum and Aunt Lois did their best to put a positive spin on the situation.

"Well, after all, we still have mashed potatoes, gravy, green beans, turnips, cranberry sauce, and stuffing, too!" Aunt Lois explained as the two sisters held up all the fantastic side dishes and desserts to entice the disappointed crowd.

"We have lots of cranberry sauce, Big Bob's pickled onions, and stuffing, youse guys, and a lot more in the cupboard if we need it," the old man pointed to the cupboard. I could also vouch for how much of those items we had.

Uncle Ed gazed over longingly at the turkey and said, "That is nice, but it sure would have been nice to have a little turkey. Maybe Paul is correct. I think he didn't hit one of the legs there on the side. Well, it did get hit . . . but at least it did not have a lot of stuff land on it." No one was buying Uncle Ed's best efforts.

"We have homemade apple pie, we have cherry pie, and some more beer and wine. I might even have some bologna in the refrigerator. Let's move on now, and not let this little bump in the road spoil our wonderful Thanksgiving Day," Mum had recovered, and she was perking up the troops as she hustled everyone into the dining room to gather around the table.

We all shuffled sadly into the dining room, while glancing over our shoulders at the turkey, still sitting there in the midst of golden brown, oven baked goodness. Maybe the old man was correct. After all, it was only a little bird dropping or two. We could close our eyes as we ate it and pretend that it never happened!

As we arrived in the dining room, and the old man led Cousin Pat to the reinforced chair, the doorbell rang.

"Well, who could that be on Thanksgiving Day?" Mum asked.

"I dunno. C'mon, Paulie, let's go."

My father and I both headed for the front door. When we opened it, there, to our surprise, stood Mr. Zipperelli and a bunch of other folks behind him!

I recognized Mrs. Zipperelli, Maureen, Maureen's brother Frank, along with three other people, whom I did not know. All of the family were holding and carrying brown bags in their hands.

"Paula and youngini Pauliea! Happy Thanksagivinga!" Mr. Zipperelli shouted out when he spotted us, and he smiled widely.

"Zipperelli! Yeah, yeah, yeah, happy Thanksgiving. What are you doing here?" The old man asked.

"Paula, Ia bringa mya wholea family to say thankyoua on Thanksagivinga to the mana and young mana who savea me and my cara! This is mya wifea Gina, youa knowa my beautifula daughtera Maureena alreadya. Thisa isa my sona Frankini. This isa my brothera Tony, his sona Jimmy, and my sistahalawa Antoinette! We bringa you gifts fora being such nicea yooseaa guysa!"

Hmm . . . Mr. Zipperelli had picked up a little authentic New Jersey slang in his mixed bag of languages.

"Well, c'mon in the house here you big, old, pile of spaghetti, Zipperelli, bring your whole family in, get off the porch, you're letting all the heat out of my house," The old man waved them all inside, while I held the door wide open as they clamored by.

"Hi Paulie, you're such a cutie. I love that hair," Maureen said as she wiggled by me. I did not say a word. I just smiled at her.

"Heya do youa knowa youra mailaboxa isa missini?"

The entire Zipperelli clan stomped into our house, and the old man introduced them to our whole family as we all stood there in the living room together. Our house was not small, but it was not huge either. It was getting smaller by the minute.

As the holiday greetings ended, the old man stepped in and said, "Zipperelli, please, we must take your coats and please put all your bags down. Here, here, let us help you. Paulie, go get your blubber gushing sister, out of her bedroom and tell her that the Zipperellis are here." I was off in a flash because Dottie was not going to believe this one!

"Mrs. Hensonina, ifa we cana put thisa alla ina kitchenini," Mr. Zipperelli was motioning at all the bags that his family and he were carrying. Mum nodded her head as she tried hard to understand Mr. Zipperelli. She finally understood him and motioned for everyone to follow her to the kitchen.

Dottie and I were back in a second or two. As soon as she heard the news that cute Cousin Jimmy had come along, she suddenly, magically recovered from the trauma of the now famous turkey incident. We gathered in the kitchen as Mum pushed the now polluted turkey aside, and all the Zipperellis placed the bags on the table.

Mrs. Zipperelli did not say very much. She just smiled, reached into the bags, and began to pull items out. It was clear that aside from Mr. Zipperelli being able to speak English, or an unreasonable facsimile of English; Maureen, her brother, and Cousin Jimmy seemed to be the only true English speakers.

The rest of the clan just stood there, smiling.

Maureen translated as her mother spoke in Italian, "This is homemade baked ziti with homemade sausage, meatballs, gravy, and melted mozzarella cheese."

Mrs. Zipperelli pulled out the bags, three enormous, flat baking pans covered in tin foil, and Mum placed them in a row upon the table.

She then pulled out some more items as Maureen continued, "We have antipasto, Parmesan cheese balls, diced tomatoes and peppers in homemade gravy, jars and jars of my mother's special gravy, or what you would call sauce, and homemade calzones, stuffed with mozzarella cheese, salami, and baked ham. We also have some homemade desserts, some Italian pastries called, biscotti, and cannoli."

The food all sat there on our table, calling out all of our names! I swear the ziti was waving at us. It was an out of this world display of homemade Italian cooking! A drool-fest, a heavenly delight of taste bud mania!

Mr. Zipperelli waved his arms and hands over the top of the display as he said, "Alla fora youa Paula and youa wonderfula familya! Youa my how do youa saya . . . mya heroini!"

My family circled around the wonderful array of food and drooled as we gazed forlornly at the turkey. And then to the pieces of Heaven brought straight from Mrs. Zipperelli's kitchen.

"Oha, we alsoa havea alla thisa homeamadea wine that Tony and Ia madea in the basementinia!" Tony handed his brother glass jugs filled with both red and white wines. They both smiled and set them down on the kitchen counter.

"Happy Thanksagivinga!" Mr. Zipperelli was animated and his hands waved over his head, and he was jumping up and down in excitement.

The old man stepped back and surveyed the situation. His eyes darted back and forth while he . . . gazed first at the turkey, and then towards the mountains of fantastic, steaming hot meatballs, smothered in tomato sauce, and cheese, all piled high upon layers upon layers of heavenly ziti.

It was right then and there, on Thanksgiving Day, that my father made a monumental decision. It turned out to be a decision that shook the very foundations of Henson family traditions, and the old man's now legendary holiday rules and regulations. Looking back, critics or outsiders could say that hunger drove the old man to the fateful decision. On the other hand, perhaps, very "unusual" circumstances caused the radical change. However, I chose to believe that in the old man's heart, the display of friendship that Mr. Zipperelli and his family displayed, and the true spirit of Thanksgiving Day, was the actual cause of the old man's change of heart!

The old man put his arm around his little Italian friend, and pulled him in tightly as he told him, "Ya know, Zipperelli, I think we are going to push aside that big, old, turkey, and instead we are all going to have ziti and Italian food for Thanksagivinga this year! And I want you and all the Zipperellis to join us in a huge celebration. Between both of our families, we have enough food here to feed an army now!"

The old man leaned in close to Mr. Zipperelli and spoke very softly to him as he said, "But, we are not going to have the turkey. I will explain it to you someday!"

"Whya Paula, wea woulda lovea thata!"

"Ya know, Zipperelli, I really do not understand most of what ya say, and you reek of garlic and wine, but ya are one helluva nice guy."

Mr. Zipperelli grabbed the old man by his shoulders and gave him two kisses on opposite cheeks! "Paula, youa the besto!"

The Pilgrims and the Indians had nothin' on us.

Gramps tugged at his belt and shouted, "Well, this is more like it! Now, let us all bloody well eat! I am starving!"

"ACKKK! Bloody well!" Fritzie chimed in his support for the situation. All the women worked in the kitchen to prepare the food, except for Cousin Pat, who the old man led to her special reinforced chair, gave her a glass of Zipperelli wine and told her to stay put. The old man, Uncle Ed, and I gathered up extra tables and chairs out of the basement. We cleaned them off, and as best that we could, we made a table arrangement that all of us could fit around. It spread out from the dining room to the living room, but we did not care.

Dottie was thrilled as she maneuvered to sit next to Cousin Jimmy, and in the end, her plan, while not exactly as Dottie had originally envisioned it, did eventually come together rather nicely. Maureen ended up next to me. She was talking my ears off my head already.

Soon the food was all set out. We sat down in our makeshift seats, and we were finally set to go. What a feast it was that had been set out in front of us.

"Paulie, you are really good at all those prayer things. Please, can you say a little word for us?" The old man pointed at me.

Everyone bowed their heads as I nodded and said, "Lord, thank you for the friends and family that we have around this table. Thank you for the food, thank you for this special time, our blessings, and for everyone here today, as we praise you and thank you for all we have. Please, we ask you to bless the food to us, and us to thy service. We truly are thankful for all that you have given us." I stopped and could not resist as I added, "Even for Fritzie the bird. In Jesus' name, we pray. Amen."

A resounding "Amen" was the answer as we all dug into the food.

"Pauliea youa shoulda becomea a priesta! Youa speaka fantastico prayerinia!" Mr. Zipperelli complimented me.

I heard Maureen whisper low, just loud enough that I could hear, "I surely, hope not. That would be a real waste of a glorious hunk of man."

I was just old enough to realize that Maureen was flirting with me.

We ate, and we ate, in fact, we ate for hours. We laughed and told stories of times both now and in the past. We heard stories about places in Italy, England, New Zealand, Florida, and Paterson, New Jersey. We enjoyed the main courses, Big Bob's pickled onions, and the veggies that Mum and Aunt Lois had made. Of course, we had cranberry sauce, and stuffing too. We dove into desserts, both Italian and English, and we consumed an awful lot of wine and beer. I even snuck a sip or two.

It was a magical time for all of us to remember, and I am sure we all would never forget.

All these different folks from literally all corners of God's great creation, gathered around, enjoying simple things, and one another. Despite the language barriers, somehow, we all understood one another. In fact, I never heard Gramps say, "Eh," more times than when he had a comical conversation with Mr. and Mrs. Zipperelli.

Somehow, they managed to make it through it though!

Once he had spent an afternoon conversing with the Zipperellis, let me tell you that Gramps was now more willing to accept the Henson side of the family and our native New Jersey tongues.

We even managed to sneak through the rest of the day without another major Cousin Pat incident. She did tip over her wine glass, and broke her teacup. But in the grand scheme of things, those were minor fatalities in the world of Cousin Pat.

After dinner was finished, we cleared the table, washed the dishes, and cleaned up the kitchen. Then some more fun began. We moved some furniture aside in the living room, and the old man put on his Harvey Crooner and big band records on his Victrola. What a scene it was, as the Zipperellis, Alcotts, and Hensons all took turns dancing and singing to the music. We all held on tight, as Cousin Pat jumped around out there. As the walls shook, the floor joists rattled, and Fritzie's birdcage swung, while Mum's teacups in the cupboards danced in time to the rhythms.

The old man ran down into the basement to check the floorboards and for any leaky pipes, due to the extreme house rattling that was occurring because of the dancing. Dottie was thrilled when she shared a dance with Cousin Jimmy. I hid and narrowly avoided a dance with Maureen!

What happened to the turkey, in case you wondered? Well, it did not go to waste, as the old man, who was still itching to give his new knife set a workout, sliced it up, and all the neighborhood pets and strays shared in the delights and culinary wonders of the bird dropping, coated turkey.

Even Skippy, in the spirit of Thanksgiving, shared his turkey with Pussface, and he even walked nicely with the old man and me, as we delivered a helping to Barney. Perhaps, in a bit of optimistic thinking, old Skippy had undergone a reformation, and he had seen the error of his previous ways.

As the afternoon waned and evening was approaching, this wonderful day started to come to a close. I grabbed my vest and Skippy's leash, and hitched him up for a walk. As I walked out the back porch and into the early evening air, Maureen Zipperelli suddenly joined up with me, as she came down the back steps calling out to me as she put on her coat and hat.

"Hey, Paulie! Do you mind if I join you and Skippy for a walk?" I turned around and looked. Oh no! Maureen was coming along. I did not want to be rude, and she was very pretty. It was just that she was such a blabbermouth.

"Sure, sure, come on along, Maureen." She ran a little and caught up with us.

"Wow. It was such a great day! All of that food, I will not have to eat for a week! I really had a great Thanksgiving. Didn't you, Paulie?"

"Yeah, yeah, yeah, I did. I had a greata Thanksagivinga!"

She chuckled at my fake Italian accent and told me, "You have a nice laugh and a dry sense of humor, Paulie. You are a lot of fun, and a really nice guy. You are such a cutie! You send ripples down my spine!"

I did not comment.

I was not awkward around young women. In fact, I was not awkward around anyone.

As we walked, I primarily listened. I did not have any real experience with gals yet, but I could sense it was coming very soon. The wind had died down, and we walked along, kicking some dry, brown leaves out of our way. I could see the warm breath from our mouths as it hit the cold air when we spoke. The streets were brightly lit up now, and the lights inside the houses glowed with the flash of televisions tuned to football games, and the many family celebrations going on inside of them.

It was one of my first real encounters with a young woman, and as I looked over at Maureen, I could see that she was indeed very pretty. Her long brown hair flowed behind her, and she had a nice smile. She was nice. I could do without her talking so much, but she was nice.

"Are you not cold? All you have is that little vest on. I am freezing. It is so much colder than it was earlier."

"Nah., I like it cold. In fact, the colder the better. I usually just wear this vest."

"You could put your arm around me and keep me warm."

I smiled and gently did so. Maureen leaned into my body and I had to admit that her softness felt wonderful.

Skippy tugged and pulled as we turned up Cook Street. I usually always walked the same route all the way around the block. Old Skippy and I could walk it blindfolded.

"You know, Paulie. We are not really that far apart in age. I am a little younger than your sister is. When I am still nineteen, you will just have turned seventeen." I did not know exactly what she was hinting at, but I decided to stay away from that subject.

"Say Maureen, do you like hockey? I have a big game tomorrow, and if you want to, you can come and watch it."

"I do not think I ever watched hockey, Paulie, but Dottie tells me that you are a very good player. I think I will like it. I will be there to cheer you on! The sport is very much like soccer, and I watch soccer with my dad all the time." Maureen cranked it up, and soon she was talking a mile a minute. The walk around the block was never as long as this particular one was. I think if Skippy could have covered his ears, he would have.

When we arrived back at 182 Belmont Avenue, the tearful goodbyes were underway. We said goodnight to Uncle Ed and Aunt Lois as well as the Zipperellis. I endured a kiss on the cheek from Maureen while turning ten shades of red. Aunt Alma and Cousin Pat were going to stay for a few days and visit with Gramps and leave next Monday.

Soon, our house was quiet once more. Mum had gone off to take a shower and get ready for bed, Dottie was in her room dreaming of Cousin Jimmy, and playing her rock-and-roll records. Skippy had packed it in, and he was asleep with his head under the steam radiator in my bedroom. The old man had let Pussface onto the back porch for the night, given him a dish of beer, and some more turkey, so he was good for the night too. I wandered into the kitchen and found the old man reading Mum's parakeet book. I sighed and sat down at the table; it had been a long day.

He was having one last Big Boulder beer, and he looked up at me, marked the spot in the book, and placed it on the table. Our kitchen still smelled of the very strange combination of Italian food and oven baked turkey.

"I put the extra tables and chairs back down in the basement, Dad."

"Oh good, thanks."

"Are you reading how to clip Fritzie's wings?"

"Yeah, yeah, yeah, that's right."

"Say, get a little glass. I will pour you just a taste of beer. Three fingers high . . . that is all you will get."

I picked a small glass out of the cupboard and set it on the table. The old man placed his fingers upright next to the glass to measure the beer. He poured about three fingers of beer in the glass and pushed it back over to where I was sitting.

"Here, don't tell, Mum."

I nodded and took a little sip. It tasted really cold and good.

"Say, I think Maureen has her eyes on you there, Paulie. What do you think about that?"

"I dunno . . . she is kind of nice."

"She is very pretty too," the old man said as he took a sip of beer and looked at me over the beer mug.

"Yeah, she is, Dad. She smells a little like garlic and talks an awful lot though."

The old man nodded and smiled at me.

I decided to change the subject and offered up a positive note, "At least the furniture held up."

"Yeah, it did. Big street hockey game tomorrow, against

the team from over at Buckley Park. Is that, right? No, Harry though. Right?"

"Yup, we gotta play the Buckley Park Bruisers, without Harry. We got Jeff Porter though. He is a good defenseman too. They are tough guys too. A big center man who loves to take headshots at me." I took a sip of my beer and it was just about gone.

"Well, get some sleep. You will hang in there. You are a tough guy. Bet you will come home with some blood and cuts though."

"Yeah, yeah, yeah. Hey, Maureen said she was going to come and watch the game."

"No kiddin! She likes hockey?"

"She told me that she had never watched a game, so I dunno."

The old man sat back in his chair and chuckled. He waved his hand in the air and said, "She is not interested in the game there, Paulie boy. She just wants to see you. Say, we need a new mailbox. Ya up for a trip to the Rickel on Saturday?"

"Sure, Dad. Maybe, we can have some more fun with that dopey store detective." I stood up, took my glass to the sink, and washed it out. "Goodnight, Dad."

"Goodnight, Paulie. Happy Thanksagivinga."

I washed up and climbed into bed. What a week it had been! What a great holiday! I sat upright in my bed, while propped up on the pillow for a few minutes, and stared at the ceiling. I thought about how great it was to have times like this in our lives. It was so simple, yet it brought more joy than anyone could ever buy or even imagine. I discovered at an early age that I had a tendency to build memories in my life upon simple yet wonderful times, amazing people, and plain joy. Sometimes, you do not have to spend a ton of money, or purchase expensive gifts, or plan elaborate gatherings. So often in our lives, it is the simple things that give you the most pleasure. A laugh, a touch, a kind gesture, or special words. Upon those simple things is the foundation, in which the greatest of our memories will come from, forever until the end of our life . . . they make the most impact.

Besides, forever more, I would associate ziti, Italian food, parakeets, pickled onions, cranberry sauce, and stuffing with Thanksagivinga.

I drifted off to sleep to the faint voice of Mum as she said from the deep recesses of the kitchen, "Goodnighttttttt Fritzie, goodnighttttttt."

"Oh, I am so sorry, twenty-seven, but I was quite a bit longer on the telephone with dear Mother than I had originally planned. I have added a few more things to the list."

I shook my head and came back to reality. I stood up from the footstool and smiled at my wife as she approached me.

Binky walked back into the living room and she handed me the shopping list, as she explained, "Here it is. I need just a few things. You should be out of there very quickly. If you go now—I am sure, they are open. The day before Thanksgiving could be a madhouse there."

"I agree dear, it could be jammed. I sure hope they are open early though."

Binky nodded, and called for Paul William, who magically appeared with his coat and hat on already.

"It is cold out there now, you two. Please wear your coat twenty-seven, not that light vest. You need to stay warm. You are not twenty years old anymore."

I went to the closet, took out my coat, and put it on. I disliked heavy coats, but there was no escape from Binky on this subject.

"And your hat, Paul!"

I pulled my wool hat out of my pocket. I pulled it over all of my long hair, kissed Binky, and out the door, I went. Paul William gave his mother a kiss, and he was right behind me. We climbed in my old jeep and I started it. It sputtered a bit and coughed in the cold air, but it wobbled to life rather quickly.

"Do you have the list, dear Father?"

I dug around while reaching deeply into my pocket, and after fumbling a bit, I finally found the list and handed it to Paul William. He took it and held it in his hand as I reached to put the jeep in reverse. I started to push the clutch in and then I stopped.

"Say, Paul William, please, open up the glove box, hand me the pen in there, and then give me the shopping list back."

"Sure thing, Father." He handed me the items and watched me as he asked, "Do you want to add something to the list, dear Father?"

"Yes, Paul William, I do." I took the list and the pen, and directly underneath where Binky had written, "Cranberry sauce and stuffing," I wrote in, "two boxes of ziti, meatballs, and tomato sauce." I then handed the pen and list back to Paul William, who carefully studied it.

I put the jeep in gear and backed out of the driveway as I said, "This year, Paul William, I think we will celebrate Thanksagivinga."

THE END

Eleven Sentences

1

An Old Pub

I think that at one time or another, in all of our lives, certain unusual situations come along that at first glimpse, you just cannot understand. They seem at first glance to be normal, or a chance coincidence, and then upon further examination or study, we cannot explain them. Occasional instances occur during all of our lives that contain a mystery, an unexplained twist of fate, an encounter with strange or different people, or a bizarre or unexplained turn of events. It is something that I am very sure all of us have experienced, and when you take the time to look back upon it, you have sometimes wondered from where it all came.

I am no exception.

I had just finished an ice hockey game in Concord, New Hampshire. Concord was one of my favorite places on Earth, a clean New England city that most areas of the country would consider a town. I enjoyed it for the people, for the climate, and the general atmosphere. I may have been born and raised in northern New Jersey, but I really enjoyed visiting and playing professional ice hockey in New England quite a bit. While you could never remove my New Jersey accent, my poor grammar, street slang, and other elements of New Jersey from me, I think I was becoming an adopted New Englander.

We had won a hard-fought battle in a late Saturday

afternoon hockey game, with a team from New Hampshire. They did not have a good record, but they certainly were no pushovers. They had battled my team; the Albany Flying Dutchman, tooth and nail, and in the end, we pulled out a three to one victory.

I was physically a little worn from the game, some bumps and some bruises, but I was used to that. It was still early in the season, and by the end of the year, I would be a lot more beat up than I was right now. I had escaped this game without any cuts or stitches, which for a hockey goaltender was always a bonus.

The actual source of my pain and trouble was that I just did not emotionally feel very good right now. Playing a hockey game always lifted my spirits up. It let me forget some recent past and dulled the little ache that was inside of me all the time these days. An ache caused by a common issue for young guys such as I was. I was missing a gal . . . not an ordinary gal, but in my heart, she was the only gal.

Yet, there was just something about being an ice hockey goaltender that lifted me up. It was the challenge; it was the exhilaration; it was the thrill of a save, and it was the sweat running off my mask. It made me forget the loneliness and the pain. It made me forget her face, her smile, and her beauty. The trouble was that after the game ended, it all came back.

As I dressed in my civilian clothes after the game and after taking a shower, I replayed the one goal that I had allowed in my mind over and over. Ordinarily, I did not dwell upon goals that I had allowed, but as of late, I had placed some demanding standards upon my performance. The goal that I allowed started out as a hard slap shot from the point through a screen, which an opposition player then tipped about halfway to the goal. I had gotten down low on the ice when I heard the shot take off, and despite the tip, I had tracked it. When the player tipped the puck in front of the net, it changed direction. But I had come out just past the top of the crease to cut down the angle. I had followed the flight of the shot, and watched as the puck hit me just above my right elbow, and glanced off my shoulder pad. The force of the shot caused the puck to flip and flop, and it spun off my body and leaped towards the net. I spun around, because; I knew that the puck was heading for a goal, and despite my last second lunge, it had just enough momentum to trickle across the goal line.

It would have been a spectacular save, but it was a save that I had made a million times before. I swept the puck out of the net in disgust at my performance as my teammates provided encouragement.

"C'mon Paul John Henson, number twenty-seven, for the Albany Flying Dutchman!" I screamed at myself.

As I said, I always shook off goals scored on me rather quickly, but this one, for some unknown reason, really bothered me. I was mad at myself. I had just made a close game closer, and I should have made the save. Then again, you cannot make all the saves all the time.

I had learned that.

It was the first day of November in 1980; All Saint's Day, to us Lutherans, to many others; it was just the day after Halloween. It was also that strange time of year when Thanksgiving and Christmas loomed on the horizon and you have cold nights and warm days. It was as if nature could not decide which way to go.

I had been with the Albany team for about two months or so, and I was doing quite well. Currently, our team was battling for first place with a team from Maine and a Vermont team. I was leading the league in goaltending stats, and my coach, my teammates, and the general manager were all very pleased with my performance. They had paid me a lot of extra dollars to have me sign a contract here, and they had outbid a number of teams for my services. Being very honest, the money was nice, but I had chosen the Albany hockey club for their location as much as any other deciding factor.

I loved upstate New York. I also enjoyed the circuit that we traveled for games, and the bonus for me was that I could be home in a few hours to visit my family and friends. My family, friends, and my best buddy in the entire world, Harry M. Redmond Jr., and his new wife Sky Blu Redmond, were a big part of my life, as was my friend, Ms. Rose Rose. It was always nice, if I had a break in the schedule, and some free time, to leave, check in with them, and hang out in New Jersey for a few days. It was difficult, and very lonely being out on my own, and the strange, sudden breakup of my relationship with my true love, Ms. Binky Hobnobber, had left me in a little bit of a bad way. I was working through it, and hockey was my escape.

The hockey club climbed back in the team bus and we all took a short ride back to the hotel where we were staying. It was a loud and jovial ride back to the hotel, as we all were quite pleased with the hard-fought victory. I could hear the "pop" of cold beer cans being opened on the bus in celebration of the win.

Teammates on a hockey club typically stereotyped the team goaltender, and considered them an eccentric, solitary figure, who generally was a loner. Your teammates expected the goaltender to study shooting angles, geometry, opposition's wrist and slap shots, and other in-depth studies of the intricacies of the game of ice hockey.

I was not that type of goalie. I freewheeled every game.

I enjoyed my teammates, and even though I was new on the Albany Flying Dutchman team this year, I had already made many friends on the hockey club. They joked around with me, teased me about my long-haired, hippie lifestyle, and my very different, hard, northern New Jersey accent.

When we arrived in the hotel lobby, the head coach gave us a short speech on how well we played, cautioned us to stay focused, since it was a long season, and then let us ride for the night.

"Say, Rick, you want to go over with me to that Irish pub we went to last time we were here in Concord?" I asked my best defenseman and buddy on the Flying Dutchman, Rick Tremblay. Rick was a bruiser. He was a tall, strong, lanky defenseman, who was a fearless shot blocker. He had a long reach, and he was one tough guy to beat on the ice. His style of play reminded me very much of my boyhood buddy, Jeff Porter. The three of us, Harry, Jeff, and me, played street hockey together on a dead-end street we named "Geyer Street Gardens" in our hometown a long time ago.

Rick was from Ontario Province in Canada and he was a star on our team. He was also a very funny man, who was a great guy to hang out with and share some good times with. Goaltenders, usually attached to, and were fond of their defensive corps, who played in front of them. Defensemen were your initial protectors on the ice and in a strange way off the ice too. When off the ice and not playing, a goalie would try to keep the defense motivated, and whenever you could, you would hang out with them; buy them some beer, food, and other motivators. It was in your best interest, as they were your guys, much the same as an offensive line protects the quarterback in football.

"Sorry, twenty-seven. I promise that we will go together next time we are in Concord. I am going to eat quickly here in the hotel, and then I have to go up to my room, to have a long, weepy-eyed telephone call with my gal back in Oshawa, because she misses me. I have to make believe that I am very sad and upset too at being away from her for so long. I hope you understand. You know how women are, eh?"

I patted him on the back, smiled, and told him, "I understand, Rick. Hey, whip up a quick set of tears. Maybe think about the pain of blocking that shot in the second period."

"Thanks, Paul. I think that is a good idea!"

I bid him a nice evening and went up to my room to pick up some cash and other items. I was back down to the lobby and out the front door in a flash. The pub was within walking distance of the hotel. Rick and I had stumbled upon it on our first game in Concord earlier in the season. It was just a small, family-owned pub operated by an Irish family. I actually had forgotten the name of the pub and just referred to it as the "Irish pub." However, it did have an actual name. I walked briskly, as I remembered the way to the pub. It was just a few short blocks and some twists and turns from the front door of the hotel in downtown Concord.

There were very few things in life that I enjoyed more than a brisk walk on a cold autumn night in New England. It stirred my soul, lifted my spirits, and made me forget whatever was gnawing at me so deeply these days.

The game that we had just finished playing had been an early game, for some type of giveaway promotion for the New Hampshire team, so it was not very late at night now. I knew that I still had a chance to catch the end of the Boston Bears hockey game on the television at the pub. I grew up a New York Rovers fan, but many rungs up the ladder, the Boston Bears held my contract. I figured I had better start watching the club that within a year or so, I hoped to be a part of, and be the starting goaltender for a long, long time.

It had been a clear day with just a few small puffy clouds, which had engaged in a game of hide and seek with the sun, while the afternoon had whiled away. Now, the clear skies of the day had given way to darkness that seemed, for some reason, to come extra slowly upon Concord today.

The nights in northern New England this time of the year could be very cold, as winter loomed right around the corner, ready to roll in like a freight train with snow, ice, and bitter chills. Before the game had started, I could sense the cold nighttime air creeping in during the day, and now I imagined the locals had agreed with me. They knew this would be one of the coldest nights of the autumn season so far because there was not another person moving around while I walked the streets alone towards the pub.

The wind had now changed around and moved in from the northwest; bringing cold air from high up in the mountains and the Canadian border to sweep around the town. As I walked, I could smell the telltale odor of the smoke of wood fires being set in fireplaces and stoves in the houses that lined the old streets. To me, this was a wonderful smell, which foretold of winter days to come. It filled the nighttime air with puffs of smoke that I could see rising above some housetops.

If Concord had been similar to some of our other recent stops along the hockey circuit, or as it had been in Albany, then a few weeks ago, this city had been ablaze in beautiful, fall foliage colors, framing the landscape in a picture, postcard beauty. What had been a fantastic display of an autumn tapestry of color with the famous New England foliage season, now had given way to bare trees and trunks, with only the stubborn oak trees clinging to dried, brown leaves that shook and rattled a dry cry in the cold night air.

Piles of spent, dried leaves gathered along the street where I was walking. They chased each other into corners and tumbled over one another in an endless game of chase, which would continue on, until the snows of winter appeared to freeze them and stop their journey.

I turned from the main street and walked onto a side street. In front of me was a long row of shops and stores. Most of these were older brick buildings, and I could see that most of them were converted mills and small factories. These types of buildings were distinct leftovers from a bygone era, when manufacturing everything from parts for machines, to gloves, hats, boots, and shoes; drove this area's economy. At one time or another, this area manufactured virtually everything you could ever imagine. Manufacturing built the local economy and now, the old buildings either housed residential apartments or were vacant.

This part of the city was not unlike my own home city of Paterson, New Jersey. The old mills and abandoned factories reminded me of my old neighborhood in Paterson, which was an old city that had at one time harbored a large silk and weaving manufacturing business. That business was the reason that actually brought my mother's side of the family to this country in search of work from England after the big war.

I walked around the last corner and there was the Irish pub right in front of me. I had to guess the pub to be an older building, built in the nineteen forties or so, when this section of the city had been thriving with workers, from one of the now closed down nearby mills. It was constructed of red clay brick, and it had frosted, glass block windows in the front that were all stained and milky from not being cleaned or maintained in many years.

It had a sad, smutty look to it—almost as though it came from some long lost, departed era. The front door was a heavy, old, oak door, with faded paint and lots of chips and dents from many customers and deliveries which had passed through the doors. The front step up from the sidewalk into the pub was steep and much higher in a dimension than an ordinary step. Carved from a large chunk of New Hampshire granite, it now was a reminder of the era of the building of the pub, when construction standards were not worried about, nor were they of any concern.

In one of the front windows was a sad, blinking, neon sign, which slowly blinked, "OPEN" with the letter "N," barely lit. The sign, imprinted with the pub's name, hung on a rusty steel frame directly over the front door. It was a faded metal sign with remnants of a four-leaf clover logo that I could barely read or make out in the darkness. There was a single light bulb that hung on a black iron gooseneck above the sign, but the dimly lit fixture did not help me to read the sign.

As I walked closer, and stood under the sign, I read the name aloud to myself, so that I could remember it for my next visit, "Murphy's Irish Public House." The sign swung in time to the wind and chirped a squeaky melody to the beat of the wind currents.

Those stubborn leaves continued to follow me right up to the front door of the pub, and they chased me right up and into the front door of the establishment.

I reached the front door, stepped up, and covered the large front granite step with one stride, turned the brass doorknob, and walked into the pub. The pub was crowded, and it was loud from the individual conversations going on at the tables. Local folks filled the tables along with what appeared to be relaxed, regular patrons.

The pub was large and wide open. It had a small music stage for bands on my right side, directly inside the front door. There were not any musicians playing now, but a single stool sat in the center of the music stage, with an acoustic guitar leaning up against it. The bar lined the entire back section of the pub, and ran wall to wall, with a mirror mounted on the back wall and the seating areas in front of it.

The hockey game from Boston was playing on the television mounted above the corner of the bar, and a few fans sat at the bar and in tables around the television, while they stared up at the screen, watching the game intently.

I walked up a long center aisle that ran between rows of tables set on each side of the pub. On the far-left side, as I walked towards the bar, were wooden booths that lined one wall from the bar to the front door of the pub.

Quite a few of the patrons and diners turned around

when I walked in and looked my way. Some patrons went back to what they were doing, but a few folks stared at me for a while as I made my way towards the bar. I knew that most of these folks were regular patrons of Murphy's, and I am sure they did not see very many strangers in this small hole in the wall in the corner of the old city. That fact, combined with my long-haired, hippie appearance, my casual attire of a tee shirt with the name of my favorite rock-and-roll band, No Way stamped on it, and my canvas sneakers on my feet, all of which combined to make me a fish out of water.

I did not wear an overcoat, just my vest that I wore on most cold days. I have always disliked heavy overcoats and enjoyed the cold weather. I am sure not many people would have guessed my profession, nor what had brought me to this little city, and I rather enjoyed it that way.

Although I was a social and polite person, I very much enjoyed keeping to myself. I was used to it now.

A few men nodded at me. One chap stared for quite a while, and looked slightly upset at my appearance, which was another common occurrence for me to encounter.

As I approached the bar, there was a table, which had four young ladies seated around it. One of them was a very pretty gal, with long brown hair and a nice smile. She stared at me as I came closer, and she smiled at me. I nodded and smiled back, and she looked a little disappointed when I passed them by, and continued towards the end of the bar, which had a few open stools. I was not getting involved in any female adventures these days.

Not on the road, that was for sure.

I had not dated any women since my girlfriend Binky had decided to end our relationship, and she had taken off for university on the west coast. The opportunity was there, but my motivation was not. I had a next-door neighbor back in Albany, who lived about two or three apartments away from me. She was always circling around and flirting with me. I was polite and friendly to her, but never allowed it to go any farther than sharing a few beers or a cup of coffee on the back porch of our apartment.

I needed to concentrate on my hockey career, and I wanted nothing to do with relationships right now. I also knew in my heart that I was not over Binky. In fact, maybe I never would be.

I sat near the end of the bar, a location close to where it curled around towards the rear-mirrored wall, and I had a good view of the hockey game on the television. Boston was ahead at the end of the second period by a two-to-one margin over Detroit. I settled in on the stool, and I was satisfied. It was a good seat, with no one sitting on either side of me, and a full view of the game, as well as the rest of the pub. The young gal glanced over her shoulder at me and smiled once more, but I just stared ahead and kept my eyes on the screen.

"What will you have there, longhair?" The barkeeper stood in front of me and he startled me as I had been paying attention to the game. "I would not think a guy like you was into hockey," he chuckled a little at his remark, and he wiped his hands on a towel tucked inside of his belt.

I looked up and smiled. Folks are usually nice around these parts, but tonight a few of these chaps had a bit of an edge to them. I could not help but think how, just a few, short years ago, if my best buddy Harry were with me, a comment such as that one could have set up quite a bit of a ruckus.

However, that was now in my mind, an old life, a moment that passed me in time. Simply a memory.

If only the barkeeper knew what I was into, but instead, I asked him politely, "I do not suppose you serve Big Boulder beer around these parts, do you?"

"Big Boulder, nah, sorry. None of that rot gut around

here. With your accent, you must be from New York City. They serve that down that way, in New Jersey, New York, and Connecticut."

"No, sir. I am not from New York City. I am from northern New Jersey. Hey, just pour what is on tap that is local and that you recommend. My old man says that there is really not any bad beer, just those horrible Dingleberries."

"Dingleberry beer, oh man, only had it once. Way too sweet. I will get you a Laconia Pine Street Ale. It is good, not expensive, and produced by a brewery by the big lake in Laconia. It is a small brewery near Paugus Bay on the edge of the lake."

"Sounds good, thanks. Please, pour it in a tall glass if you have them."

He nodded and waved in acknowledgement of my order. I watched the barkeeper pouring the beer out of the tap. He seemed awful young to be a bartender, most of the barkeeps I had run into as of late, were always older, and it seemed funny, but they always had little or no hair. This chap had thick, curly black hair, and I imagined that he could have been of Irish descent. For all I knew, he was a member of the family of owners of the establishment.

He returned and set the ale out in front of me. I had stood up to pull my wallet out of my back pocket and I placed some money down on the bar.

I explained, "I will order some food too, I just need a bit of time to enjoy this ale."

"Whoa! Big guy! You did not look so big seated on the end there." He smiled, waved his hand a little in jest, and said, "I guess that I should have not made that longhair comment."

I sat back down and he took a few dollars off the pile of money. He stopped and placed the dollars back on the pile. He reached out his hand and said, "If you are going to order some food, we can settle up at the end. The name is

Kyle. Kyle Murphy."

Now, this was the Concord, New Hampshire, in which I had become accustomed to on my previous visits!

I took his hand, smiled, and answered, "No offense. I get it all the time. Paul Henson is the name." I squeezed his hand hard, but I did not give him one of my death grips.

"Whoa, boy! Strong guy too." Kyle shook his hand in the air as he asked me, "Say, what brings you to Concord?"

I wanted to avoid any mention of what I did for a living, so I simply said, "Just some traveling business. I spend a lot of time on the road." I shifted gears away from my purposely vague answer.

"Say, in a few minutes, could I please have a plate of the bangers and mash? I had that the last time that I was here back in September and it was very good. It reminded me of my Mum's cooking just a bit."

Kyle Murphy stared at me, and then he wrote the order on his pad. "Sure, no sweat. The bangers are good. You are not Irish though, maybe English, but not Irish. Now, that I look at you, I think I know you. I think you were in here a few months back? Maybe?" Kyle studied my face for a bit, and it seemed as if a memory came to him.

He continued, "I now remember you. I was working the floor that night, but my dad was at the bar. He told me about you when you left. You are a goaltender for the Albany hockey team that is in town today. Big star, too. I read about you in the 'Concord Flyer' sports section. Sure, now I remember . . . a goalie from New Jersey. They had a picture of you in the net, but you could see your hair sticking out from under the mask. That is why you were watching the game." Kyle smiled at me, as he felt that he had worked around my smoke screen after all.

Oh well, the hair gives me away all the time. Folks always seemed to remember a hippie goalie from New Jersey. I took a sip of ale and admitted, "Yeah, yeah, yeah, that is me. I am English, or at least my mother is. A little

Welsh too. My old man, well, he is from New Jersey. I speak some Welsh. Do you know any Gaelic?"

"No, I do not. I love that New Jersey yeah, yeah, yeah, stuff, and your accent. It is wonderful. A New Jersey goalie who speaks Welsh and your mum is English. Quite a combination there, Paul. Say, did we win or did your team?"

"We won. Sorry, Kyle. Three to one, but it was a good game."

He nodded and said, "I will get your order in. I will not tell anyone who you are, Paul. I can tell that you fly quietly."

"Thanks. There might be some Concord fans here, and I do not want to start a hockey brawl!"

I went back to watching the game and sipped my ale. The brew was fresh, and it was very good. On a commercial break in the game, I gazed out at the pub floor and studied some faces of the people seated around the floor of the pub.

I wondered what their individual stories were. What were they all thinking, or doing in their lives right now? Were some of them escaping lost loves, as I was trying hard to do? Were some of them seeking adventures and were far from their own homes, but were feeling lost and empty? I know I was, and despite living out my dream of playing professional ice hockey, I still could not shake the terrible, empty feeling inside of me. Were some, despite the crowd in here, and people all around, lonely, feeling slightly lost, while seeking some kind of direction? If I reached deep within me, that was also a description of me, and how I currently felt.

This had been a hard adjustment in the last three months or so, especially for a young man, whom, except for a short stint in Kansas City, Missouri with a hockey club, had never wandered very far from his home. Now, the adventure was there, but parts of me were missing.

It was all very strange.

I imagined that some folks came to watch the Boston Bears game on the television, but most locals came just out of habit, to have a place of friendly confines to share each other's company and toss a drink or two.

I put my elbow on the bar and tucked my hand under my head. Tonight, was very different, as despite the solid win, and playing a very good game in the net, my mood was melancholy. I could not shake the inner sadness tonight. Perhaps it was the time of the year, the change from the warmth of summer to the colder months. It was as if time ticked on a few notches. But I still was not where I wanted to be.

Past scenes ran through my head, of good times I had with Harry, Rose, and Binky. I could see them now, as I stood in the net, all three of them sitting in a row in the stands watching my hockey game and waving to me. I was smiling under my mask when I spotted them in the crowd, and I waved back to them with my goalie stick. I thought of dates that Binky and I shared as we sat over dinner chatting for hours upon hours. The memories of a warm summer night sitting next to Binky on a park bench for hours, talking about any subject that came into our heads. I could see her hair, her beautiful face, and I could hear her soft voice as she rambled on about her latest efforts researching a long-forgotten subject. I remembered the feel of her soft skin, the glow of her eyes that night, and later on, the unrivaled passion in which we shared. My mind wandered while I wondered where she was right now, what she was doing, and why it all had unraveled as it had. Her memories haunted me and I wondered about all of it, and I had no answers for any of it. I took a long sip of the ale, while thinking that misery loves company, and sometimes, there is nothing like a few sips of some liquid courage, for temporarily enhancing your rather despondent and wandering state of mind.

2

The Stranger

I spotted out of the corner of my eye, the door to the pub open, and inside walked a man. He walked quickly, and he was very large and tall, so he took long strides, and covered ground quickly.

He was dressed all in black, with sharply creased black trousers, a black shirt, and a black leather vest that, despite the cold weather, was unbuttoned except for the last button before his waist. On his head was a black hat with a wide brim which was pulled down close to his ears, but you could still make out some of his facial features, even in the dim lights of the pub.

I could not help but think that although his clothes seemed so expensive and brand new, he appeared as if he was from the past, from some bygone era in time.

Regardless, he was indeed striking in his demeanor and appearance. The man wore a thin, closely trimmed beard that neatly framed his face. On his feet were black, sharp-tipped boots, with a metal clip on the edge that made a distinct clicking noise while he walked along the wooden floor. He walked with an air of confidence as he strode along. You could tell that this was a gentleman that was used to traveling around, and you could easily see that he was comfortable in many types of surroundings.

The man walked over to a coat rack on the side of the pub, removed his hat and vest, and placed them upon a hook on the rack. He then smoothed his hair, tucked in his shirt, and made his way up the center aisle of the pub.

As was the case when I walked in a few minutes earlier, I could guess that this chap was also a stranger, as folks glanced at him and stared his way. Some people nodded, and some even waved, but the stranger did not acknowledge them or even glance their way. He passed the table with the young ladies seated at it, and they all glanced up. One of the ladies pointed at the boots he had on his feet, but they did not speak a word to him. The stranger stopped in front of the bar, looked up and down the bar stools, and then, seeing that there were some open on my end, the stranger walked over towards me.

He looked at me and nodded.

I nodded back.

He then took the seat on the right side next to mine. There remained now, only one open seat left along the entire bar, and that one was between the stranger and the back wall of the pub.

I thought about how this place did some fabulous amount of business; despite the old, worn exterior appearance, it was a gold mine inside!

The second period of the game ended. I leaned back, and finished my ale. It was a good ale; it was not a Big Boulder brand beer around Harry's kitchen table, but not many things in this new life of mine were as enjoyable as that experience was.

I glanced over at the stranger, but I did not say a word. I sensed that he, as I did . . . preferred to be alone. There in the bright light of the bar, you could see that he was about fifty years of age, and with his neatly trimmed, black hair and beard, he was a strikingly handsome man, with piercing brown eyes, which focused dead straight ahead. His weathered face had a few wrinkles around his eyes and along the side of his face.

Kyle came over with his towel and a glass coaster and said, "Hello" to the stranger as he placed the coaster in front of him. The stranger still said not a word, but simply nodded his head just a little in the direction of Kyle Murphy. Kyle took his towel and wiped down the top of the bar in front of the stranger next to me.

He picked up my mug, wiped the counter and said, "Did you like the ale, Paul? Do you want another?"

"Yeah, yeah, yeah, Kyle, it was good. Please, pour me another. Thank you."

"Sure thing. Your food will be out shortly, Paul."

Kyle then turned towards the stranger and he asked him, "What can I get you to drink or eat, sir? Welcome to Murphy's Pub. What brings you in here tonight? I have never seen you in here before."

The stranger looked back at Kyle and answered with a deep, melodious voice, "Please, a glass of your best, top shelf Scotch with ice, and just a little splash of water." He did not answer Kyle's other question. He reached in his vest pocket, took out a fifty-dollar bill, and laid it down in front of him. Kyle looked at him and then at the money.

"Top shelf, eh? The best we have is going to be a twelve-dollar drink."

The stranger looked at Kyle and did not say a word, he just pointed to the fifty-dollar bill. Kyle nodded and went to prepare the drink.

I thought about how the way this guy next to me was dressed, with the fancy clothes and expensive boots; it was easy to see that spending money was not an issue for him. Kyle came back with the drink, placed it on the coaster, and took the cash. He rang up the drink sale at the register and returned with the change.

"There you go," he said as he laid the cash in front of the stranger, who was now slowly sipping his drink while staring straight ahead. The stranger did not acknowledge Kyle, nor did he engage in any additional conversation at all with him or me. I had pegged him correctly. He just wanted to drink and be alone.

That was fine with me.

Kyle brought out my food and placed it in front of me. "Looks good, Paul, piping hot, too. Be careful. Do you need anything else?"

"No, I am good. It does look good. Thank you."

"You're welcome."

I dug in because I was suddenly very hungry. I was not disappointed. It was fantastic. This pub sure was a hidden gem because the food was spectacular. It tasted as if it were a home cooked meal from back home in my dear Mum's kitchen. Oh boy, how I missed some Shepherd's Pie cooked by Mum on a cold day.

The hockey game had returned for the third and final period. The game was still close; therefore, I was eating and keeping my eyes intently on the screen. A few other folks in the pub were also watching. They gave out shouts when the Boston Bears goaltender made some key saves, and when the team from Detroit rallied, they booed terribly. All in all, they were well behaved, and not a raucous bunch of hockey fans at all. Believe me, coming from the leagues that I had played in earlier in my career, and playing in some rinks of which I played in now, I knew raucous hockey fans!

A middle-aged man caught my eyes as he walked up to the bar. He too, must have just come in the front door, then noticed how crowded the pub was, and headed for the bar. He was wavering just a bit, so I immediately got the impression that he was half in the bag already. His eyes were red, his nose was a little puffy, and he had the look of a hard-core drinker.

As he walked by me, I nodded slightly, while he stopped and looked at me to see if he recognized or knew me. Even in a little drunken haze, he realized that I was a stranger; he glanced back and gave me just a slight acknowledgement with a tip of his head. He stopped, looked up at the score of the game, pulled out the last seat left at the bar, and sat down next to the stranger. His clothes were all in disarray, he had some stubble growth on his face from about a two or three-day beard, and his hair was all messy on top of his head.

He turned and looked at the stranger next to him and said, "How ya doing tonight? The Bears are winning . . . I see."

I then determined that he was a regular patron of the pub, as he progressed to the next step with the questions that every single outsider could count upon having a regular ask him or her around here. He looked long and hard at the stranger next to him, and even through slightly drunken eyes, he knew that he was new in town.

The next words out of his mouth were, of course, "Where are you from? What brings you here? I have never seen you in here before."

The stranger did not react. In fact, he did not even move his eyes, which were locked dead ahead. He just raised his glass and took a sip of Scotch.

"What will you have? How about a Mill Pond Ale, there, Mike?" Kyle had wandered over and it was obvious that my supposition of the situation was correct, as Kyle knew this chap. He was a regular, in fact, from the look on his face; he was a very frequent, regular patron.

"Sure Kyle, hey give me a chaser of rye, too, will you?"

"You have cash right, Mike?"

"Ah sure, sure, sorry about that last night, Kyle, here . . . here." The middle-aged man reached into his pocket, took out a pile of rumpled and crumpled dollar bills, and placed them on the bar. He looked over at the stranger sitting next to him, tapped his shirt pocket, and pulled out a pack of cigarettes. His hands shook and trembled as he removed one cigarette from the pack and pulled a book of matches from the same pocket. He grabbed an ashtray sitting in the corner of the bar top and pulled it in front of him.

"Ya mind?" He asked the stranger as he placed the cigarette in his mouth and allowed it to dangle from his lips.

The stranger never answered him. He continued to stare straight ahead.

The middle-aged man assumed that the stranger did not mind. He shrugged his shoulders, and struggled to light the cigarette. His hands trembled and shook. It was difficult to determine if his tremors were alcohol related, or just his nerves. He finally lit the cigarette, took a long drag, and blew the smoke away from us up towards the rear of the bar.

This guy was a mess.

He looked at Kyle and told him, "Take what I stiffed you for yesterday, out of there too."

Kyle nodded, looked at the stranger, saw that he was still working on his drink, and then he checked on me.

"It was good, right? You did not leave a morsel on your plate there, Paul."

"Great, really good. I will have another ale too, Kyle. Thanks."

"Sure thing," Kyle said as he took my plate and mug.

Kyle returned with my drink, as well as the ale and rye whiskey for the man at the end of the bar. The middle-aged man first hurled the shot of rye whiskey down his gullet, tipping his head back. And in an instant, it was gone. Then he moved to the ale, and it did not take him very long to empty his mug of Pine Street's best brew. He downed it about as quickly as I had ever seen anyone drink alcohol. In a flash, he was waving Kyle back over for a refill.

This middle-aged man had some serious issues. I began to feel sorry for him, and I wondered what his story was. I watched him out of the corner of my eye, but no one in our small circle said anything. The stranger just sipped his drink and hardly moved a muscle.

The Bears scored two quick, back-to-back goals and it looked as though they had this game in the bag. All they needed to do was to protect the puck in their own zone, play keep away for five minutes, and this game was over. The locals were happy, and some loud claps filtered through the pub here and there, after the Bears scored the last goal to put the game in the bag. I smiled, as this was hockey country. I felt right at home. Well, in certain ways, I did.

In the short time that it took for the Boston Bears to score a few goals and ice the game, the middle-aged man had gone through even more ales and another shot. I was sure that he was pretty well lit up by now.

When he waved Kyle over for another ale, Kyle asked him, "You are walking right, Mike?"

"Oh sure, Kyle. I do not have a car. My wife still has it. I have not been able to get it back. Now, she will not even answer my phone calls." He snuffed out another cigarette in the ashtray in front of him.

The picture now became a lot clearer. He was drowning his sorrows and numbing himself from the pain. When he had finished the sentence, his eyes went down to the bar, and I saw a level of intense sadness come over him. The drinks had numbed him, but the reality had not left.

His mouth quivered, and his eyes rolled back in his head a little. He had some tears forming in the corners of his eyes, which he pushed away with his hands. He had revealed the source of his pain; which Kyle must have known some of beforehand.

The beer and whiskey must have now been taking full effect, and for some reason, the middle-aged man felt compelled to convey aloud to the stranger all the pain that he was feeling. He turned to the stranger and said, "You know, I just don't know what to do anymore."

The stranger did not move his body, but his eyes moved slightly towards the middle-aged man, and then back to his drink in front of him when the middle-aged man had finished speaking the sentence.

"I cannot find a job, no matter how hard I try. I just can't get it together."

The hockey game ended, and some cheers went up throughout the bar. I even clapped a little; after all, the Bears were in a roundabout way responsible for my paycheck!

Suddenly, the middle-aged man had the words pouring out of him. Whether it was the drink that had loosened his lips, or his own emotions, I could not tell, but for some reason, he felt the need to continue to speak. Even from one seat away, I could hear the conversation clearly. The middle-aged man was speaking directly to the stranger and not to me, but I leaned my head over and listened as I kept my other eye and ear on the wrap-up of the hockey game. I had to admit, I was more than just a bit curious as to what his story was.

"It has been so hard. My wife just would not understand. She just kept yelling and putting more and more pressure on me to find a better job, do something with my life, go make more money. Everything that went wrong was always my fault. I got the blame for everything. No job was ever good enough for her, it was never enough money, and nothing ever worked, or made her happy. It was always something with her. The kids needed clothes. They needed shoes, and toys and this and that. The bills were piling up, and I just could not get through to her about how much pain I was in these days. She just would not help me. She would not even try to understand. One day, a week or so ago, I just took off. I could not take it anymore, and I left."

The middle-aged man picked up his mug and held it in his hand, but did not drink from it, but instead continued to speak to the stranger.

His hand, which was holding the mug, trembled, and I could see the ale moving about in the mug as he spoke, "Now, I feel I should not have left, it was a big mistake, but it eased my pain for a few short days, it was as if I was somehow, set free. I love my wife, despite how she treats me, and what she says to me, and I love my children. It is as if a part of me feels relieved, but my wife tore the other part of me in two. Now, I cannot tell you how lonely I am, and the pain of this loneliness is like nothing that I have ever felt before."

With that, the stranger who up to this point had not said a word or even moved gently shook his head back and forth a little. It seemed that when the middle-aged man had said the word, "lonely," it had sparked something within the stranger. It was apparent that the quiet stranger was now sitting there thinking, almost pondering the word in his mind.

The stranger turned to the middle-aged man, and he finally spoke, "There is actually no loneliness in this world. You will not be lonely, as long as you realize that God or a single person out there in the world cares for you." The stranger's eyes turned towards the ale being held by the man and he continued to speak, "You should have found strength and guidance in your pain, but instead, you are trying to find an answer in the bottom of that mug, but the answer is not there, the answer is in your heart. The loneliness will leave you—once you follow your heart and do what you already know is right." The stranger then turned back to his drink, picked it up, took a sip of it, and he said no more.

Kyle came over and spoke to the stranger, "Would you like another drink, sir?" The stranger did not answer. He simply tapped the money on the bar top and nodded his head.

"I will get it for you," Kyle responded.

The comments from the stranger astounded me, and I could tell that the comments had astounded the middle-aged man too. They had struck a chord in both of us. I had felt the same pain since I had left home, and Binky had left me. I knew very well the feelings of loneliness, which the middle-aged man now felt from leaving his wife and children. It was obvious that he loved his wife and his family, and in utter despair, he had made a bad choice. He had made a knee jerk reaction, instead of doing what the stranger had said, "In following his heart and doing what he already knew was right."

I felt some comfort that I was not actually alone. My religious beliefs were always strong. I knew God, and felt God's presence in my life, but it was something that I very much kept to myself. It was a comfort to know that my beliefs were there for me to lean upon during these days, and I should never forget that. Being on the road now, playing hockey, left little time for attending church or worship services. The team had a team chaplain assigned to us, and I made a mental note to contact him when we arrived back in Albany.

In the hustle and bustle of my new life, perhaps, I too had felt sorry for myself, just a little too much. I had more than just hockey to keep my mind off Binky. I had God, loving friends, and family to turn to these days, and it had been very easy to forget that until now.

This was a timely reminder, and it eased some of my own pain.

The middle-aged man wanted to speak, and he almost started his reply a few times, but the words stalled and they would not come out. I could tell that he badly wanted to have a rebuttal for the stranger, but it seemed as though his mind was blank, and the words would not formulate in his alcohol-altered state of mind.

He looked down at his own appearance; his eyes scanned his messy clothes. He then reached his hand up to the top of his head to feel his messy hair. He rubbed his unshaven face, and then he glanced at his clothes once again. Once more, he looked over at the stranger sitting there. The stranger was shiny, clean, and neat as a pin, all decked out in perfectly tailored clothes that cost more than a person could ever imagine.

Somewhere along the line, it was obvious that the stranger had solved some of these same troubles in his own life. Perhaps, he had confronted some demons along the way, and he had won the battles that all men face at sometime in their lives.

Kyle came over, set the new drink for the stranger, and looked over to the middle-aged man. The middle-aged man took some dollar bills from out of his pocket and laid them across the bar in the direction of Kyle. Kyle did not say a word, but he shrugged his shoulders. I think Kyle was surprised that he was leaving so soon and not ordering another drink.

The middle-aged man did not say another word. He jumped off the bar stool, steadied himself when he landed, and took off towards the center aisle of the pub. He waved to one or two of the locals and hustled up the aisle towards the front of the pub. I watched as he went over to the coat hooks. He searched amongst the clothing for his coat and hat, found them, and put them on. The middle-aged man then turned and looked our way once more. I noticed his face broke out into just the slightest smile. He opened the door and stepped out into the cold night air, and he was gone.

Somehow, someway, in this little exchange, I think he found some answers that he may have been looking for, or perhaps he just woke up. I knew that I did, and I found myself fascinated by the curious stranger and his unique but purposeful behavior.

It was almost as if he had planned it, as though he knew what the man was going to ask him ahead of time.

The stranger picked up his refill and slowly sipped it. But still, his eyes stayed almost straight ahead, and he did not say a single word.

The game wrapped up now and the television station had switched over to a late-night news broadcast. Kyle came over to check on us. I tilted back my mug and finished off the rest of the ale.

"Are you finished, Paul?"

"Yes. Thanks, Kyle. Would you happen to have some tea that you could brew? I could go for a cup to cap off the night."

"Of course, it is not only you Englishmen who enjoy your tea. I will brew a cup for you. Cream and sugar?"

"Just cream. Thanks."

I was very tempted to say, at least, "Hello" to the man next to me, but I resisted. I was going to respect his space and his wish to be alone. For some strange reason, deep inside, I felt that if he wanted to say something to me—then he would.

My eyes scanned the pub floor, and the crowd had thinned just a bit now that the game had ended. I spotted some musicians now gathering around the stage. They were having a few beers and setting up some more instruments. I looked at my watch and saw that it was about nine thirty or so. I was sure that they would begin to play music, around ten o'clock or so, for the late-night crowd. It looked as if from the type of instruments, they had set about, as though they might be an Irish folk band. As much as I enjoyed music, I was not going to stick around for the performance. The team had a midnight curfew on the road for a Saturday night, so I would just finish the tea and head on back to the hotel. I was getting a little tired. We had left Albany early in the morning, and the game was a tough one.

The pretty, young gal from the table close to the bar glanced my way once or twice and our eyes met, but I carefully avoided any projection of any interest in meeting her acquaintance. I did notice, however, a middle-aged lady sitting alone at a table that was one table over from where the young gals were sitting. She had also just finished her meal and now had a full glass of red wine in front of her. I would have guessed her to be in her middle to late forties, and she was one of those types of ladies that you would say was not unattractive, but she was not a ravishing bombshell. She had her own style, and in her own way, she was indeed quite beautiful.

She was well dressed, in a tight black dress with a low-cut neckline. Her hair was short and neatly prepared. She was eyeing the open seat next to the stranger. By following her eyes, I now guessed that she had watched the seat become vacant after the middle-aged man had left, and she was going to try her luck with the handsome stranger. I surmised that she had undoubtedly been watching the stranger since the moment that he walked into the pub. I guess years of watching shooter's eyes in ice hockey to determine their next move had carried over to my "civilian" life.

Sure enough, she picked up her wine, and she slowly made her way to the end of the bar. She signaled her server to carry over her tab.

She then steadied the wine glass in her hand, sauntered over to the bar, grabbed the seat next to the stranger, turned, and asked, "Is this seat being saved for someone? Do you mind if I sit here?"

I could tell by her reaction when she spoke to the stranger and when she saw him up close that he fascinated her with his handsome appearance. She smiled broadly, adjusted her hair, and tugged at her dress just a bit to reveal a touch more of her cleavage. She was clearly thrilled at the empty seat next to the stranger, and the opportunity to engage in a potentially rewarding conversation with him.

This was turning out to be a fascinating evening for me as I studied these interactions from my adjoining bar stool.

The stranger did not answer her, but only slightly nodded and it was hard to say whether he had actually meant yes or no. Predictably, the woman took that to be an approval. She took the seat and immediately tried to start up with a conversation. It was easy to see that she was a gregarious and outgoing person. She had a wonderful smile and a joyful approach.

She even leaned over and around the stranger and said, "Hello there" to me.

I returned her greeting with a welcome and a smile.

This was going to be a good one! A chatterbox next to Mr. Solitude. I remained anxious to see how this scene would unfold.

Kyle brought my tea over. I thanked him and asked him for my check. He leaned close to me as if to make sure that no one else heard what he was going to say, "You know Paul, for a long-haired guy, and a professional ice hockey goalie, you are an awfully polite man."

I smiled and said, "I guess that I do not fit the stereotype. Maybe, I should be doing something else with my life, eh?"

I spotted out of the corner of my eye that the stranger had moved his head slightly; he must have picked up what Kyle had said, despite his lowered voice. I wondered if my profession surprised him or not.

The woman at the end of the bar now jumped in, as she had decided to make her move. Hey, I guess you cannot blame a gal for trying! Being talkative by nature, she picked up with some same lines that Kyle and the middle-aged man had tried, with no success, earlier.

"Where are you from? What brings you here? I have never seen you in here before," and so on and so forth, she went on and on, as she worked hard in an attempt to start a conversation with the stranger.

To her frustration, he would not answer her, and he said not one word. He just sat there, sipping his drink and staring at the back of the bar. Once or twice, he moved his eyes up to the television screen as if he was vaguely interested in what the program might be that came on after the hockey game had ended.

For the most part, though, the stranger was eerily silent.

I had to admire her efforts because the woman did not give up easily. She continued with general attempts at conversation. She tried some comments about the crowd in the pub this evening, how cold it was getting outside, how the game had ended in Boston's favor, and other chitchat. No matter what the chatterbox said, she realized that she was not going to crack what seemed to be an iron fortress of silence around this stranger.

Kyle walked over and asked her if she would like some more red wine.

She thanked him and said, "Yes, just one more glass please, Kyle."

Kyle looked at the stranger and pointed to his glass. He seemed to know by now that the chap was not going to answer, so a simple gesture would suffice for communication. The stranger put up one finger to signal that he was going to have one more. Kyle was off to fill the orders.

I sipped my tea slowly. It was an excellent tea, very well brewed, but it was really hot. I needed to let it cool a bit, or just sip it carefully as not to cook the inside of my mouth.

I could see by the look on the woman's face that she had conceded defeat, and that she now had some growing sadness inside of her. She realized that this conversation was going to go nowhere. She became quieter and more than a little disconcerted.

Kyle came over, placed another red wine down for her, wiped the bar with his rag, dropped the drink for the stranger, and handed me my check. I stood back up off the stool, and I saw the stranger's eyes follow me from the floor to the top of my head. Perhaps he, too, had not realized how tall I was. I took my wallet out and counted out some additional money to pay my check.

The woman took her purse, opened it, and put a few

dollars on the bar. It looked as though she was going to finish her wine and then call it a night. I am sure she felt that she had tried, but she had struck out on this one. Her face and eyes had lost the excitement and the joy that she originally had just a few short minutes ago. I could not help but see some pain and some sadness there. In fact, it was just a little hard to tell, but I thought I could see some tears forming in the corners of her eyes. I think this little failure was somehow the culmination of a situation, the pinnacle of emotions that had led the woman to this point in time.

The woman closed her purse up and she took a longer sip of wine. I could tell that she was trying to finish it to get ready to leave, when both to my utter shock, and the woman's surprise, suddenly, the stranger turned to her and asked, "What kind of wine are you drinking?"

It caught her by surprise—as it did me too!

The stranger had ignored all the previous questions that she had asked, all the words, in which she had previously spoken, had been a futile attempt at inducing a response from the stranger, and now, out of nowhere, he suddenly has asked her what appeared to be a very simple question!

"Oh, oh," her response was clearly flustered, "it is red merlot. I really like the merlot wines, and I enjoy this one. I drink it whenever I come in here."

A glimmer of hope came over her, and it was very obvious to see that her confidence returned. She felt the need to smile broadly at the stranger. It appeared, as if for a second or two, the sadness that was in her eyes might be leaving.

The stranger did not smile back, or say anything. He just looked at her and then at her wine

glass. I watched as the woman's facial expression went flat, and her face changed from a broad smile to a serious look. Perhaps, it was the drink. I had no idea how much wine she had consumed before she joined us at the bar, but she seemed sober to me and spoke clearly. Once more, it was very strange, but not unlike the man before her. The woman also was suddenly compelled to divulge what she was feeling in her heart to this stranger in black. A man she did not even know, but for some reason, she had no concern at all about pouring out her innermost feelings.

"You know, I just have to get out of this old city. I really feel that I need to leave here." So, it began, she turned on her story; she mysteriously poured out of her innermost soul, about her dreams of traveling the world, how long she has been stuck here in Concord, New Hampshire, how boring and horrible it was, and so on and so forth, she carried on with her long list of laments and complaints.

I sipped my tea and waited. This was certainly a most unusual hour or two that I had spent here tonight.

The stranger just listened, and stared at her with his deep set, dark eyes, carefully watching the woman pour out her inner ambitions and dreams, but never saying a word. On and on she went for about five minutes, in a long monologue of a magnificent outpouring of emotional pain, until she ran out of words. Then she stopped as she caught herself, more than just a little embarrassed at her actions and chatterbox ways. She realized that once more she had gone on way too long, and perhaps looked a little foolish to the stranger, by revealing so much of what seemed like her silly dreams of travel and ambitions for no real reason at all.

After all, he had only asked her about her wine, not for her life story! She stopped speaking after she realized that the stranger had not said another word.

She and I both watched him take a long sip of his Scotch. I could tell that this man of very few words was about to say something.

He looked back at the woman and the stranger said, "I have traveled around, in fact, I have been all over this world, and what feels like a few others, I can tell you for certain that there is no, Isle of Avalon. Sometimes, what seems like such a wonderful place to be or to visit is not so wonderful at all. Once the glimmer wears off and shine is gone, you realize that in the end, there are many more people that love and care for you at home, and there are a lot of reasons to stay right where you are. You learn that it is a lot better to be with people who love and care about you, and with what you are comfortable with, then to be uncomfortable in some far off, strange place, chasing some silly dream."

The words he spoke shook me to my very inner being and soul. They tore at me and twisted my insides like a vise. I knew in my heart that my dear Binky had left me and done exactly that. She went off chasing a dream when there were so many people who loved and cared about her at home.

Moreover, I was one of them.

The woman listened, and when the stranger had finished speaking of his experience, she smiled at him. His words seemed as if they were a profound, personal testimony. They were so authoritative and resounding; I could tell that the words had struck a chord deep inside of her, too.

The stranger returned to staring straight ahead, and he spoke no more. It was as if he was looking way past the confines of the bar. Perhaps he was dreaming of a far-off place that he had traveled to a long time ago, or maybe he was dreaming of his home wherever that may have been. It seemed as though, somehow, or someway that he had given the woman a special answer. I suspected it was an answer, which she had been somehow searching for a very long time to find. It also seemed that he had given to her the solution as to why she dreamt all the time, but deep inside, she knew the real reason that she never acted upon those dreams and ambitions.

I watched as she reached in her purse. Her face was

different. She was confident, reassured, and radiant.

She was now an even more beautiful woman, because she shined from the inside as well as the outside.

She placed some more money on the bar and waved to Kyle. She slid out of the bar stool and whispered, "Goodbye and thank you," to the stranger, but the words were barely audible. She nodded and smiled at me as she passed, and I returned the same. She turned and went to the side of the pub wall directly behind us.

There was a pay telephone hanging on the wall, just a few feet away from us. The woman took out some coins from her purse and she dropped them in the slot for the phone. Her hands were shaking as she dialed the number on the old, rotary telephone. I could hear the clicks of the telephone as the dial spun behind me.

I tried not to be obvious, but my curiosity, as well as some other folks in and around the telephone, could not help but watch as the scene unfolded a few feet away from us.

The stranger, however, did not move, but he did take a long, final sip of his drink and placed his glass back on the bar top.

You could overhear that she was speaking to herself as the phone was ringing, as she said aloud, "Please, please, answer the phone," she was repeating over and over. The person on the other end, did apparently answer the phone, and she shouted a loud, "Oh, hello!" She was now unable to conceal her joy when the person had finally answered. You could hear that the two of them had started a conversation, and that her voice was now emotional and excited.

"You know that I have been so stupid, so pigheaded. I now realize that there is no Isle of Avalon. There are no glorious apple trees or grape vineyards that miraculously grow without care or needs, there are no golden bridges, or shiny roads in faraway places. I think I clearly know that you have to go where your heart leads you. I now know that I just want to stay here, and I want to be with you. Is it too late? Can I come over? Can we talk?"

The woman was almost crying into the phone now.

Whoever it was that was on the other end of the line must have told her to come, and to come over quickly, because the woman thanked the person over and over. She explained that she was on her way and ended the conversation with a loud and emphatic, "I love you!"

She hung up the phone and with a smile on her face, she ran up the center aisle of the pub, went to the coat rack, grabbed her coat as quickly as she could, and ran out the front door.

3

Five Leaves

Once more, I have to say that this was certainly one of the strangest few hours that I had experienced in a very long time. I was used to strange and wild encounters in my life, and I had to admit ever since I had met my best buddy's wife, Sky Blu Redmond, I had noticed that I seemed to be tuned into certain unusual aspects of life, which seemed even more peculiar than I had ever noticed before.

Kyle came over, and I gave him the cash for the dinner check. I reached over the bar and shook his hand gently. Kyle then looked at the stranger. The man dressed all in black had slid off the bar stool, pointed at the remaining cash on the bar, and then back to Kyle. He then turned and started to walk away. I heard the click of the metal tips of his boots on the floor as he moved away.

"Hey, thanks for everything, Kyle. I think we will be back in Concord, right after Thanksgiving for another game, so I will be sure to stop in and say hello. I hope I can bring my best buddy on the team, Rick Tremblay next time. He would have come tonight, but he had girlfriend issues."

"Nice to see you, Paul. I will look forward to your next trip into Concord. Say . . . ah . . . that strange guy next to you sure did not say much."

"No, but what he said, sure meant a lot."

I am sure that Kyle did not understand, but he slipped a little piece of paper and a pen to me and smiled, then asked, "Do you mind? In case, you make it to the big league."

"Sure, no sweat." I signed it for him, put number twenty-seven under it, and handed it back to him.

"Hey, thank you there, number twenty-seven. Good luck this year, except when you play the Concord team!"

I waved to him and I was off.

I was walking behind the stranger as we both made our way up the center aisle. As I passed the table with the young ladies, the pretty gal on the end slid out of her chair and stood up in front of me.

She had obviously been waiting for this moment. She smiled as I stopped in front of her in the center aisle. The gal was fairly short and I towered over her. I surmised that she was finally going to make her move.

"Hi there, number twenty-seven, goalie guy. We were at the game today. I knew it was you right away when you walked in. You are an unreal goalie. You shut us down today."

I just smiled and said, "Thanks."

"Handsome, professional, ice hockey goalies, with long hair and beards do not come by here very often. Please call me next time that you are in Concord." She grabbed my hand and placed in my palm, a paper that I am sure had her contact information on it.

I placed the paper in my pocket.

I did smile and as I passed her, I simply added, "Have a nice evening."

I followed behind the stranger who now was almost to the front of the pub when I saw him slip around a table that had about ten or so young men sitting around it. One of the young men was sitting at the end of the table because it was so full; therefore, he was actually sitting out in the middle of the center aisle.

When the stranger passed, he bumped his leg a little on the side of the chair where the young man was sitting. The young man on the end seemed to be loud and more than just a little drunk, and he also seemed as though he was a show off, or the "ringleader" of the rest of the group that was seated there. When he felt the accidental bump, the young man dramatically sprung out of his chair and jumped in front of the stranger.

Oh boy, this could turn bad very quickly. This was not anything that I want to be involved with or be in between. My hockey sense knew when it was going to turn bad very quickly, and I steered clear of these sorts of situations. I could more than handle myself in a little fist-a-cuffs both on the ice and off. I was big, tall, and strong, and even though I was a goalie, I had grown up on the gritty streets of Paterson, and I could tussle with anyone and usually come out ahead.

People who knew me back home as well as on the ice knew that it took a long time to anger me, but you had better steer clear when I did finally crack, because it was not very pretty. Goalies are used to stitches, cuts, and missing teeth, so if you tangle with one, you had better bring your best game, or you are going to lose!

When I was younger, and a lot dumber, and over our many years together, Harry and I had fought our way out of many bars and situations on the ice, and off, but I made a point now of staying out of trouble, away from too much drink, and any wild ladies. I had a professional career at stake, so I just stood there for a minute.

I intended to stay far away from this one.

The ringleader blocked off the main walkway, and he stood there with a stupid, alcohol-induced smirk on his face. His buddies all started to laugh in anticipation of having a little fun with this sharply dressed stranger.

Some patrons in the pub turned to watch as they saw what was going on and wondered what shenanigans this group of want-to-be hooligans was going to try next. I could easily detect that although they thought that they were tough guys; they had no real idea of what tough really was.

The stranger stopped a few feet away from the ringleader; he just stared at him with his piercing dark eyes, and suddenly the ringleader's false bravado faded a little at the sight of the stranger close up. He realized that the stranger was a very large man, in fact, he was immense, and the stranger displayed no fear at all about the situation that the ringleader had foolishly decided to attempt here.

I could tell. I dealt all the time with intimidation, and the testing of men's courage in hockey. It was very plain to see that the stranger had been in a few of these types of confrontations in his past. Turning and running scared was not an option or something that he would do in these types of situations.

Even through his drunken haze, the ringleader knew that he had made a miscalculation in his little attempt to show off for his buddies. The rest of the young men grew quiet at the table as they also realized that the stranger was not the type of man that you tried to provoke or falsely incite.

Now caught, the ringleader looked for an easy way out of his little adventure, without adversely affecting his artificial image as a tough guy. He stammered and tried his best not to look like too much of a fool in front of his drinking pals. Deep in his mind, the sight of this large, tall stranger had invoked true fear in his heart, and he really did not know what to say.

Embarrassed, drunk, and now finding it difficult to stand, he stumbled at his words. And he said the first thing that popped into his intoxicated mind.

He slurred out, "Oh sir, excuse me. I did not see you walking up the aisle. I did not know what direction you were going to go."

I was happy to see that the young man had made a solid choice and not allowed his drunken state of mind to lead him down the wrong path this evening. I sensed a much calmer situation, so I walked up behind the stranger. The stranger looked at the young man for what seemed as if it was a long time. I watched as the stranger's eyes went back and forth from the young man to the table where his buddies all sat.

The stranger said in a low voice, just above a whisper, "Sometimes, the direction you think you are going is not really where you will end up."

When he heard those words, the young ringleader moved out of the aisle, and sunk back down in his chair at the table; he just strangely and abruptly collapsed down into the confines of the chair.

The stranger walked past the table of the young men and strode quickly to the coat rack where he put on his vest and hat and moved to the front door.

I thought how that was such a strange reaction for the young man to have made and wondered where the ringleader was in his life that such a short sentence had made such a profound impact upon him. It was as though those words meant so much more than just a simple statement in reference to walking around someone.

I looked once more at the table with the young man sitting there, and then I walked to the front door. The stranger had opened the door and the cold air rushed into the warm pub. He turned and looked at me. He did not say a word, but he did hold the door open for me.

I said, "Thank you," and stepped up my pace. We both stepped outside and went down the odd-sized front step together. I stood next to him now in the cold darkness. He was tall, but not quite as tall as I was. He adjusted his hat on top of his head, turned to me, and placed his hand upon my shoulder.

I felt a cold chill go down my spine as I looked at him.

"Those words were meant for you too, my long-haired friend."

He then warmly smiled. I could see, even in the dim

reflected light of the pub, a twinkle in his dark eyes. He then spun around to walk away, gave me a little head nod, a tip of his hat, and then a slight wave of his hand.

I stood and watched as he walked briskly away.

I stood there for a long time, pondering his words, and all that had happened during these very strange few hours.

My mind searched my past, and I remembered the words that Sky Blu Redmond had told me on the night when I first met her, "You are very spiritual, you believe in God, and what is right and kind. There is an inner light and fire inside of you Paul, you can feel it, and others can sense it. You would make a great religious leader."

I wondered once more who that man was and why we had met. The fact that this was All Saint's Day made this all so much the stranger. I could hear his boots clicking upon the cold sidewalk as he walked farther away from me. For some reason, I still could not move. I just stood there, watching and listening.

The darkness of this autumn evening was now complete blackness, with only a few street lamps glowing here and there to interrupt the darkness. The clouds now covered up the previous moonlight. An intense cold filled the night air. The kind of cold that would really be more like a winter's night, rather than just an autumn prelude.

The sharp click of the metal tips of the stranger's boots echoed as he walked farther and farther away from the pub. The sounds slowly faded away in the distance . . . until I could no longer hear them.

I looked up when I heard the old metal sign above the front door of the pub squeaking a tune as it waved in the wind. Back and forth the sign swayed, crying for oil to put it out of its misery.

Reaching down into my pocket, I pulled out the little piece of paper with the young lady's information written on it. I glanced at the young lady's name and telephone number scrawled upon it. Who knows, she might just be a wonderful gal. She seemed pleasant, well spoken, and very pretty. She also was a hockey fan!

For some reason, I had also remembered Sky Blu telling me, "People never really go away forever. Even when they die, they return to us, somehow. We remain together forever with the people that we love. She will return to you someday, I can tell."

My voice was just a whisper, "I surely hope so Sky, I surely hope so."

I took the little piece of paper and tore it into the smallest little pieces that I possibly could and I held them up into the wind.

The wind caught the pieces, and then scattered them for all time, while I watched and smiled. Satisfied, I made my way towards the main street and the hotel.

The pile of leaves that had been dancing around on the street in front of the pub continued to follow one another around. The noises that they made as the wind chased them were a sad reminder of their past glory as now, they were simply dried reminders of spring and summer spent wonder. A strong gust of wind blew down the sidewalk while I started to walk up the side street. I looked at my watch and saw that it was just past ten now.

There was plenty of time.

I pulled my old trusty vest up around me as the wind was really whistling now. I watched the piles of leaves, as up and down the road they went, rolling over one another, in between parked cars, and into dark corners of the buildings.

The wind blew strongly, and it actually forced me to bow my head down and face the gust, to prevent debris and dried leaves from the pile from getting into my eyes. When the gust had ended, I stared into the darkness and watched the pile of leaves land right in front of me.

Five of the leaves blew out of the pile, straight up into the air they went, higher and higher, they tumbled over one another, until the momentum was lost, and they slowly drifted back down to the ground, fell in amongst the pile, and mixed in with the rest of the leaves.

THE END

Interlude on an Autumn Afternoon

I struggle against a gust of late October wind.
It pushes me and I bury my head into it.
It twists and turns me, spinning leaves at my feet.
A strong gust forced me backwards.
I bury my head and charge into it.

We never did really end it all.
Never did close the door.
I wonder why.

October winds foretold of November gales.
It was an interlude in my life, and then I moved on.
I often wonder why.

Red, gold, yellow, and brown.
Leaves weave a tapestry of summer heat, memories, and
spring days long since passed.
They tell a story of birth, growth, and death.
They chase around my feet, and the wind pushes them by.
A soft crackle as they tumble in the wind.
Who knows where they end up?
Maybe they never stop.

We never did really end it all.
Never did close the door.
I often wonder why.

October winds foretold of November gales.
It was an interlude in my life, and then I moved on.
I often wonder why.

I pause, stop, and wonder, where did the wind go?
The wind came back, grew stronger, and pushed me back once more.
Where did it come from?
Perhaps the wind in awesome glory,
Really was telling me your story.

Golden autumn days long since passed.
Filtered sunlight, peeking through colored leaves.
Autumns full of laughs, smiles, and some tears.
I see you walking slowly down that sidewalk, kicking the leaves out of your way.

We never did close the door.
I often wonder why.

October cries as November laughs.
It was an interlude in my life, and then I moved on.
Where did you ever go?
I often wonder why.
I often wonder why.

The Hidden Valve

1

The Radiomen

It was just a few short days or so before Halloween in 1991. Mr. Walter P. Thrump sat in front of his ham radio set in the basement of his home at 164 Maple Lane in Jersey City, New Jersey. He hunched over the dials in a very serious manner as he slowly spun the main tuning dial intently and with a purpose. He looked as if he was a safe cracker, listening for the lock tumblers. This was a serious operation, but then again, Walter P. Thrump was a serious man!

He was a byproduct of an era, a throwback to a different time, and a different way of life. A time, when you worked hard, took care of your family, served your country; you always arrived on time or early for work and appointments. You took days off from your job only when you were actually sick or had a vacation that was approved; you married your high school sweetheart, and stayed married, through the good and bad times.

Walter also believed that when you had free time, you played hard, too. He felt after what he had gone through in the Vietnam War; he had earned it, and he was going to live his life to the fullest. Some of his buddies had not been so lucky, and Walter knew that in many situations in the war, he turned out to be the lucky one.

Everything that Walter and his wife owned was old . . . their family car, furniture, house, clothes, everything. They were of the strong belief that you only spent money when you had to, for the things that were important or necessary, and when you wanted something special, you saved your pennies and paid cash for it.

Walter P. Thrump and Mrs. Thrump did not owe any person a single dime, and he was proud of that fact.

Walter was about sixty-five years of age, and he was small. No, in fact, he was tiny. If Walter's height was five feet two, that was a very tall estimate, as five feet, or thereabouts, was a decidedly more accurate dimension. He weighed in at about one hundred and twenty pounds, if he was soaking wet, had on a heavy winter coat, and had a lot of spare change in his pockets.

The little man was, however, one tough, New Jersey guy, who proudly would tell you that he was not afraid of anything or anyone, and truly, the little bulldog was telling the truth.

Walter had about two teeth left in his head. He lived on bologna sandwiches on white bread, with a tiny blob of mustard, cheese puffed snacks, and gallons upon gallons of soda and black coffee.

He enjoyed some beer when he was at home relaxing, but he did not overdo it in the alcohol department. He very seldom drank any hard liquor. In fact, a big boss where he worked had given him a bottle of whiskey for a Christmas present, and Walter, being of a slightly thrifty nature, used it as a mouthwash and rinse! Mrs. Thrump frowned at this practice until Walter showed her the label on the "real" stuff that told of the alcohol content.

Walter P. Thrump never threw away anything that he received for free.

As far as his unusual penchant for consumption of bologna and cheese puffed snacks, everyone who knew him swore that they never saw him eat anything else. No vegetables, no fruits, no other meats, nothing!

He had thick brown hair on his head, without a single strand of grey hair. He wore long, 1970s types of sideburns that framed his craggily face. His hair was amazing! Walter

P. Thrump swore that he did not dye or color it, and for a man of his age, it looked as if he had not lost a single strand of hair in all of his life. He swirled it over to the side as if he was some leftover movie star from the 1950s. His eyes were deep set in his head, and he had a long, pointy nose. One of the first things that strangers noticed was that the little man had keen eyesight and hearing.

He saw everything and missed nothing.

Walter P. Thrump was a sharp little man. Not a bug flew by him that he did not notice.

Walter had lost one lung to cancer from working in a Jersey City glass factory for most of his life. He also knew from his time in the United States Navy that he had inhaled an awful lot of things that he probably should not have inhaled. Walter did not care, he was still alive, and he lived every day, full out, pedal to the metal! Walter P. Thrump, in addition to his fearless nature, was also prideful, tough, reliable, and by the same token, he was caring and kind.

He grew up tough on the streets of Jersey City, New Jersey, and he had picked up his tough guy ways from there. Walter P. Thrump had also served as a radioman in the United States Navy during the Vietnam War. He had seen some rough times in some hot-spots, while assigned to a Marine Corps squadron with Naval Support Activity. You see, Walter P. Thrump was also a hero and a man who stood up and served proudly when his country called his name.

His love of radio began long before his military service. Since he had been a teenager, he was a licensed ham radio operator. His father had been a ham radio operator before him, and Walter had inherited the love of ham radio from his childhood.

On this day, he sat huddled in front of his radios, set in a dark corner of his basement, upon an old desk that he had for longer than he could ever begin to remember. A single, lonely, light bulb, hung by a porcelain socket, suspended from a little zip cord wire above Walter's head.

This was Walter's escape. It was his hobby, but it was also his passion.

His radio set-up had some high frequency gear for tuning long distances; in fact, Walter had contacted other ham radio stations in most of the known countries in the world! He also kept some very high frequency gear, with which he mostly stayed in contact with his local ham radio buddies in Jersey City and the surrounding areas. Surrounding his radios was a little retreat that he had built in the basement of the old house where he and his wife had lived for most of their married lives. Walter had a coffee maker in one corner, and an old black and white television set upon a stand to keep one eye on the New York Bugs baseball games in the summer, or the New York Rovers hockey games in the winter.

Of course, all of his radios were old. Walter bought nothing new. Some of them were leftover military surplus, and his prize rig was a famous American Blabber model X2-4 high frequency rig. It tuned across all the ham bands from eighty meters to ten meters. It still used all vacuum tubes; Walter would have nothing to do with those silly, new solid state, or hybrid rigs! Besides, the glow of the tubes and the heat they gave off kept the little man warm on cold nights down in his basement shack.

Their children were long since married, had their own families, and had moved out on their own. Now, it was just Walter and his wife. Oh yes, and his radios, as well as a maze of wires for his antennas that he had strung on his roof, and between some tall trees that he had in his backyard.

On the walls of his basement radio room were literally hundreds, upon hundreds, of postcards tacked to the walls. They each told a story of the many radio contacts he had made throughout his years of activity in his lifelong hobby. The postcards were confirmation cards called, "QSL

Cards," that are sent between ham radio operators to confirm that each station had actually made a radio connection.

A visitor to the "shack" as Walter P. Thrump called it, even if they did not know a thing about ham radio, would find the exhibition of radio call signs, locations, and faraway, exotic countries displayed upon Walter's walls, very fascinating. Via radio, (and one trip courtesy of Uncle Sam) he had traveled to all four corners of the globe; China, Tibet, Hong Kong, all of Europe, even the Vatican! Australia, Alaska, Russia, Scotland, the list went on and on.

It was fascinating.

It was early on a Saturday afternoon, and Walter was at his Morse code key, pounding out Morse code on twenty meters, trying to make contact with a far-off station in Iceland.

"TF1XYZ DE WA2ASQ."

Walter strained to hear the response by pushing his "cans" as he called them (other folks would simply call them headphones) close to his ears. The faint station had faded away, and alas, he could not make this contact. Walter pulled the cans off his head and sighed. Usually, long distance conditions on the radio bands at the end of October were better than this.

The little, two-meter local range, radio mounted above his desk, crackled, and the speaker came to life, "Whiskey, alpha two alfa, sierra, quebec, this is whiskey bravo two, alfa bravo, charlie calling. Better luck next time, Walt."

Walter smiled at the comment coming over his very high frequency radio. He recognized the voice, and call sign of his friend and co-worker, Mr. Robert Decker. Walter usually called him by his nickname, which was "Deck."

After he had retired from the glass factory, Walter obtained employment in the corporate security business. He now worked as a security officer on the in-house security force, for Substantial Industries at their huge, worldwide, headquarters buildings and campus complex in northern New Jersey. After working there for a very short time, Walter received a promotion to the rank of sergeant of the force. Because of this promotion, all the other security officers reported to him.

Walter P. Thrump loved the job, and he was a perfect fit. The serious little man, now standing and protecting the assets of the worldwide empire known as Substantial Industries.

Other than ham radio, it was what he lived for!

Robert Decker was the manager in charge of the facilities management and maintenance of the large Substantial Industries complex. Deck had also served in the United States Navy, not as a radioman, but in large equipment and boiler maintenance on small and large aircraft carriers. Deck was a little older than Walter was; Deck had served in the Korean War, but the two of them shared many stories together of their times in the United States Navy.

Walter and Deck worked very closely together since the security and the maintenance and management of the facilities worked hand in hand every day. Walter usually worked Monday to Friday, on the late-night graveyard shift, or the four in the afternoon to the midnight shift, with the occasional weekend or holiday fit in there.

On Fridays, when he worked the graveyard shift, he would wait for Deck to arrive at six in the morning, and before Walter went off duty, Deck and Walter would share a cup of coffee together in the boiler room behind the maintenance shop. It was something that Walter greatly looked forward to each day. Deck made the coffee in an old, stainless steel, percolator type coffee maker, with the little clear glass indicator on top of the lid, to show you when the coffee had finished brewing. Deck told Walter that he had that same percolator for many, many years. Walter always thought it was amazing that Deck made such fantastic piping hot coffee in that old percolator.

Walter was thrilled when he first took the security position at Substantial Industries and found out that Deck was also a ham radio operator. The two of them had become close friends, and spoke to one another not only on the very high frequency radio, but they met almost every Saturday night, with some other local hams, on the local eighty-meter band on the higher frequencies.

While Walter had many ham radio friends all over the world, he had very few "actual" friends. Along with another security officer that Walter worked with, named Russell T. Hall, Deck, was the only real friend that Walter P. Thrump had.

Walter grabbed the microphone and keyed the radio. "This is WA2ASQ. So, you were listening in there, huh, Deck? The band dropped out, kind of unusual for the end of October. He was so strong for a few minutes. You should have jumped in there with your beam antenna, and your amplifier. I think you would have worked him."

The speaker crackled with Deck's voice, "This is WB2ABC. Yeah, tough one there, Walter, I think he heard you at first, it just faded so quickly. You know that it's going to be a really unusual situation for me to get on the code key there, Walter. You know Iceland is a nice contact to snag, but I have worked it many times before. You may hear me jump in on code for Bhutan, or something very rare. I would get on the code bands though, if I was operating from some far-off land as a rare one, you know that would be for sure. I would work you first there, Walt. I promise that I would. I would hang out on your favorite spot on twenty meters, Walt. I promise. Right on fourteen zero, three zero. That way, I could hear those long-distance stations calling me, not the other way around. Hey, let me go, I will catch you for the group meeting and net on eighty meters later. The wife is yelling at me to come and eat supper. Seventy-three there, Walt. WB2ABC out."

"Sounds good, hey, seventy-three, Deck. WA2ASQ is

listening." The radios went silent and Walter went back to tuning his big HF radio. He was just reaching for his bag of Big Bob's cheese puffed snacks when he heard the door to the basement open.

"WALTER! TIME TO EAT NOW! I HAVE MADE YOUR BOLOGNA SANDWICH EXTRA THICK TONIGHT! TURN OFF THOSE STUPID RADIOS, AND COME ON UP HERE NOW!" Mrs. Thrump yelled down the stairs at the top of her lungs. She must have thought that Walter could not hear her if he had his cans on his head. Walter flipped the power switch and all of his radios went silent.

"Yeah, yeah, yeah, I hear you!" Walter called back to his wife. "I am never late for anything, honey. Never once in my life, and I am not going to be late for supper, or my name is not, Walter P. Thrump."

He thought as he had yelled back his reply that Deck's wife and Mrs. Thrump must have worked a deal to pull them away from their rigs at the same time. Walter stood up from his chair and made his way to the stairs. He turned off the one little light bulb by turning a little thumb switch on the side of the light fixture. He smiled, because he knew he would be back down after dinner, to talk to Deck and the rest of the gang on the Saturday night roundtable radiotelephone network. Walter, as well as another local group of ham radio operators, along with Deck, met on the radio bands every Saturday night to talk about hot rod cars in the fifties and sixties, their military days, baseball, hockey, football, work, beer, and of course, to complain about their wives.

You know . . . all the important topics!

After the voice net ended, Walter would cruise on down to the code bands and try to find some late-night stations in far-off lands. His wife would watch television and complain the entire time that she could hear Walter's voice and then his Morse code through the television speakers.

He enjoyed getting her a little worked up; it was part of

the fun!

Gertrude W. Thrump was a year younger than her husband, and only an inch shorter, but let me tell you that she was just as tough, if not tougher, than Walter was. You did not mess with Mrs. Walter P. Thrump. She was a no-nonsense type of woman. She wore her hair up straight on top of her head in a beehive type hairdo straight out of a bygone time. She was thin as a rail, even thinner than Walter was. She always wore two little, white, single pearl, dangling type, earrings that hung from her droopy earlobes, and her eyeglasses hung around her neck on a chain. She usually had a scowl upon her face, with most of her hostility directed towards poor Walter.

The Thrumps had been married forever, took each other for granted, and they had reached the point in their relationship where they just sadly tolerated each other. Walter still loved his wife with all of his little heart, but it was really hard to tell what Mrs. Thrump felt.

If the extra slice of bologna on a Saturday night was any indication, then she still had a bit of warmth deep in her heart for the little guy.

After all, he sure was easy to cook for every night!

Walter bounded up the stairs, opened the door, and strode into the kitchen, "Say this looks great, honey!"

Mrs. Thrump whirled around and said in a puzzled, yet stern voice, "It looks great? It is the same thing you always have!"

While shrugging his shoulders, Walter looked down at the table setting, and said, "Yeah, yeah, yeah, I guess, but it looks extra nice."

Mrs. Thrump shook her head and weakly said, "Sit down, Walt."

Walter sat at the table and asked, "Did the mail come today? I am waiting on a QSL card from Shetland Island for that contact I made a few months back. I also am on pins and needles waiting for the results of the Big Bob's food contest that I entered a few weeks back. I just know I am the winner, honey! I can feel it!"

Walter smiled at his wife as he picked up his sandwich and took a big bite.

"Wow, this is great!" He added with a toothless grin as he chomped and gummed the bologna sandwich in his toothless mouth.

Mrs. Thrump dropped her fork and shook her head as she said, "No mail today, Walter. What contest did you enter now? I swear with the money that we spend on stamps for you to enter dumb contests that you never have won one single thing at, we could have bought a new car!"

She felt her husband was an endless dreamer. She had grown tired of his endless contest entries, and fantasy-filled dreams of "Winning the big one!"

Not many things deterred Walter P. Thrump. He always charged forward and kept a positive attitude.

"You remember, dear. I saved up sixty-seven tear tabs off the Big Bob's, extra thick, bologna packages and sent them in with my, completely filled-out, entry form, which I completed in black pen, just as the instructions told me. I talked to a guy at Substantial Industries who won one of these Big Bob's contests. He told me that he was sure he won because he filled the form out really, really, neat with a black pen, just as they tell you on the instruction sheet."

"What did he win, Walt?"

"He won this giant, seven-foot high, inflatable, blow up balloon replica of Big Bob himself, and a jumbo box of Big Bob's black pens! You know the new kind that has those fancy roller tips on them." Walter was very enthusiastic about his associate's hard-earned good fortune.

"You hate new things, Walter. He won a lousy box of pens and a giant, blow up balloon of Big Bob. That is ridiculous."

Walter shook off the negative criticisms, while he took another big bite of his sandwich, "Well, we are in the running for the grand prize! This year, I can just feel that we will win the big one! The food contest's grand prize this year, is an all-expense paid, round trip, for two persons to the American Virgin Islands, a year's supply of whatever your favorite Big Bob's food is, and a new Substantial Industries Zippy model 50 car, or you could just outright win twenty-five, thousand dollars! The second-place trip is a round trip, all-expense paid, one-week vacation to Newington, Connecticut. I think we know someone from there, don't we, honey?" Walter P. Thrump had a big, wide smile on his face as he looked over at his wife.

She shook her head and said, "I never heard of the place."

Walter did not miss a beat, "Of course, there are hundreds of other second, third, fourth and fifth place prizes too!"

"You will not win anything, Walter. You never do. I hope you keep the power down on your radio tonight in your roundtable with the boys. This is the key episode of my El Paso show and I am dying to see if RJ is caught messing around with the other oilman's wife or not. I get tired of the television screen flashing and beeping while you yap away on the radio."

"I will keep it down, honey. Hey, thank you for dinner. I am going back down to the shack to warm up the rig. If it does not warm up long enough before we start the net, it drifts off frequency, you know."

Walter stood up from the table, went over and kissed the top of his wife's forehead, put his dishes in the sink, rinsed out his cup and he was off to the radio shack.

Soon, he was back down in the shack, with his cans on, chatting with Deck and his other radio buddies, about all the good times and interesting things they all did so long ago. Then, he was off bouncing signals across the globe, traveling to far-off lands, and speaking with radiomen who dreamed the same dreams that he did. All of them had escaped the boundaries of their own "radio shacks" and traveled together to the same faraway places.

Occasionally, Mrs. Walter P. Thrump would bang her feet violently on the floor above him, and Walter would glance at the wattmeter bouncing in tune to his transmission.

"Oops," Walter said with a smile on his face as he reached over and turned the transmission power output down a little on his rig.

Monday came quickly, and just the same as all weekends seem to do, this one evaporated rather quickly. The upcoming schedule for Walter required him to work the entire week on the late-night graveyard shift. He did not mind, he loved to work, and the graveyard shift was fine with him, as it gave him more time to wander the hallways and nooks of the giant Substantial Industries complex.

Walter's main security assignment was to the largest building in the complex, which was also the corporate headquarters. Deck had come to count upon Walter and his keen observation skills during his building rounds, to check everything and identify things that his maintenance crew missed or selectively chose to ignore.

Walter P. Thrump missed nothing, not even a single burnt out light bulb, or the smallest drip on a valve-packing faucet nut escaped the keen eyes of Walter P. Thrump. He would write detailed reports to his radio buddy and leave it on Deck's desk. The two of them made a good team.

Both Deck and Walter reported to the same manager at Substantial; a middle-aged man named Arnold Plank. Mr. Plank was the Director of Corporate Operations at Substantial Industries, and he had been there since the completion of the construction of the corporate headquarters. He was a very tall, thin man who was a nervous wreck. He chain-smoked cigarettes, had beady little eyes, a baldhead, and a thin moustache that he trimmed into a neat line about his mouth. Although he was very soft spoken, he was always on edge, and nervous about everything. You could understand at times why Mr. Plank would be so nervous. It was a huge responsibility, to make sure the corporate headquarters of one of the world's largest companies ran the same as a finely tuned watch!

Mr. Plank came to rely on the team of Deck and Walt to assist him in his duties. The two of them, along with a long-time employee named Joe Clarke, who ran the mailroom and package delivery operations, were Mr. Plank's key employees.

Deck was a mechanical and electrical genius, who easily solved what appeared to be complex and potential disasters and malfunctions with the infrastructure of the complex buildings. His time in the United States Navy at sea during the war in difficult situations had taught him how to deal with such troubles quickly and efficiently. Deck knew the location of every valve, switch, pipe, compressor, and wire within the sprawling chain of facilities and buildings. He taught his buddy Walter where many of these items were, and although Walter was not part of the maintenance or mechanical team at Substantial Industries, Deck considered Walter a quasi-maintenance mechanic for his fantastic all-around knowledge.

Deck was comfortable when Walter worked the graveyard shift because that is when his two least knowledgeable workers on his maintenance staff also worked. They were two young men who had very little experience and no real skills. Deck had received a lot of pressure to give them jobs, since one of the men was the son of one of the higher up executives of the sales division at Substantial Industries, and the other, was a nephew of a director in the human resource's department.

The first maintenance mechanic hired and who at least possessed rudimentary trade skills was Johnny Cantrelli.

Johnny was a nice, polite young man who tried very hard, but seemed to always fall a little short.

The other mechanic, Rodney Brigham, was a total disaster. His father was one of the most powerful and successful sales executives in the automotive division of Substantial Industries, and he had put severe pressure on Deck to make sure his son had some kind of job at Substantial. Rodney was lazy and unmotivated. He was difficult to deal with at times, and had zero skills. You could tell he had grown up with a silver spoon in his mouth, and his lack of motivation came from the fact that he never wanted for anything in his entire life.

Despite Deck's best efforts to teach them, as well as to pair the young mechanics with more skilled and experienced crew members, they learned very little. In reality, Deck had told Walter they both were knuckleheads and incompetent bums, who he could only allocate the simplest of tasks to and try hard to keep them from making a mess of something.

Deck mostly assigned them simple tasks of making building rounds and recording data, and told them for the most part, other than changing light bulbs, never to touch tools or equipment.

They even had a difficult time putting up the yearly Christmas and holiday decorations when one of them fell off a ladder while decorating the large tree in the lobby of Substantial's main building.

In self-defense, about six months ago, and in the secret hope that they would tire of working the graveyard shift, and quit their positions, Deck had stuck these two bumblers on the late shift. Walter's presence gave Deck the comfort of keeping a close eye on them, and Walter did his best to steer them out of trouble whenever he could.

Walter always rose at the same time whenever he worked the late shift; his body had little trouble adjusting to the shift changes. Since he seemed to have a built-in alarm clock, he was up at six in the early evening and ready to go. After checking the mail, and overcoming the profound disappointment of not receiving his QSL card from Shetland Island, or his Big Bob's food contest results, Walter made his way towards the kitchen. His wife had left him a note, as she had to run to the corner store for some supplies, so Walter dug into his bologna sandwich, cheese puffed snacks, and a glass of soda eagerly. He had plenty of time, but he wanted to relax, read the newspaper, chat with Mrs. Thrump in between pauses when she was yelling at him for something, and tune around on his ham radios for just a little while before he had to go off to work.

Walter finished his lunch, and within a few minutes, he was down on the radio. Looking at his kitchen clock, he knew that it was time to catch Deck on the VHF radio and see what was going on today.

He grabbed the microphone, listened, and then keyed the radio, "Whiskey bravo two, alfa, bravo, charlie, this is whiskey, alpha two, alfa, sierra, quebec."

Walter un-keyed the microphone and listened as the repeater held the transmission for a little while then went silent.

"Hmm? That is not like Deck to miss being on the air at this time." Walter looked at his rig with a puzzled look on his face. Walter double-checked the clock above his rig, picked the microphone back up, and gave out an identical call to Deck. Walter waited and waited, but there was silence on the other end. Deck did not answer, and the repeater went silent.

"He must have had something to do. I hope he is not stuck at work with some kind of trouble, but that is still unusual for him not to call me back," Walter said to himself as he rose from his chair.

He heard the back door open and close, and Walter decided to go and see what Mrs. Thrump had been up to at the food store. He walked up the stairs and into the kitchen, when the telephone on the wall of the kitchen started to ring.

Mrs. Thrump looked over at her husband and said with her usual abruptness, "Can you get that, Walter? You can see that my hands are full."

Walter had already intended on picking up the telephone as he pulled it out of the cradle and announced, "Hello. This is, Walter P. Thrump."

"Walter," there was a long pause on the other end; "this is Mr. Plank."

Walter was surprised, since Mr. Plank was the last person who he ever expected to be on the other end of the telephone. He paused for a moment or two, then he came alive, "Oh . . . hello, Mr. Plank. How are you?"

"Walter, I am sorry to bother you at home, but this is a very difficult telephone call for me to have to make. I have to say this will not be a pleasant telephone call for both of us. I have to tell you that Robert Decker has . . . well," there was another long pause, "he passed away this afternoon, very suddenly and tragically, Walter."

Walter P. Thrump was stunned. He felt his body shake and quiver as the words resounded directly through to his soul. He could not find the strength to respond or to say a word.

"I am very sorry, Walter. I know how close you two men were. Not only with the both of you guys working together, but also with your ham radio hobby. I felt that I needed to call you, and tell you myself, when I heard the news. He was an outstanding man and a great worker. I am very upset. I do not know how you replace a person such as Deck, both in work and in life."

Walter had finally recovered enough to say, "How? I mean . . . what happened? I just spoke to him on the radio last night, Mr. Plank."

"He came into work early today, but he left early. I did not speak to him, I was in a meeting, and he left me a message saying that he was going home because he was feeling very ill. I have never known Deck to be ill or to miss even a single day of work. In fact, I cannot ever recall him missing a day of work in all of these years. Then later this afternoon, I received a call from his son, telling me that he had gone to the hospital and suffered a massive heart attack. They could not save him. I am sure they tried everything, but it was not to be. I am very sorry, Walter. His son asked that I call you and tell you the news."

Mrs. Thrump now knew that something was seriously wrong. She came over and stood next to Walter while studying his reaction. She was puzzled as to what was the cause of her husband's distress.

"I will understand, if you need to take tonight off, Walter, I can call in another. . .."

"No!" Walter shouted. "That would be the last thing that Deck would have wanted. I will be in, Mr. Plank. I will be in. I will not be late either, I will be there at eleven forty tonight, or my name is not, Walter P. Thrump."

"Thank you for your dedication, Walter. I will keep you posted as I am sure Mrs. Decker or her son will too. I think the funeral will be on Wednesday on Halloween. I am sorry, Walter. I will have Deck's supervisor, Tommy Mckee, run the department until I can sort this all out. Goodbye, please call me if you feel the need to speak."

Walter P. Thrump could not even muster up enough strength to say another word. He hung the telephone up slowly and secured it back into the cradle. He walked to the table as his wife watched him, and he sank into his chair at the kitchen table.

"What is it, Walter? What has happened to Deck?" Mrs. Thrump was working hard to piece the conversation together from some of what she had been able to surmise from afar. She knew that whatever it was, it had been terrible news that had affected Walter greatly. She came over and placed her hand on Walter's shoulder as he sat at the table.

He looked up at his wife and said very quietly, "He has passed away, honey. My friend has passed away. Ham radio station, WB2ABC is a silent key, the air waves will never be the same." Walter looked at his wife with tears running down his cheeks.

Mrs. Thrump felt terrible. She held her husband's hand while she whispered, "I am sorry, Walter. I am very sorry. I know that he was your best friend."

True to his word, at exactly eleven forty that night, a long trail of blue smoke appeared behind an old, rusty, 1974 Whizzer station wagon, pulling into the main driveway, in front of the Substantial Industries Worldwide Corporate Headquarters Building.

The driver of the station wagon was Walter P. Thrump.

He rolled the old bomb into a parking space, and he shut off the ignition switch. The car spit, choked, and coughed up a big cloud of smoke as the engine rattled to a stop. He rolled down the driver's door window, reached his hand and arm out to pull the door open (the inside handle had been broken for years) and he climbed out of the car. Walter rolled the window back up, grabbed his trusty old lunch pail, and adjusted his uniform. He then made sure that he proudly displayed his brass whistle and badge on his chest. He put his security hat on top of his head and turned to walk into the lobby front door. Just before he entered the front door, Walter P. Thrump stopped, looked at the huge clock hanging on the side of the tower that loomed above Substantial Industries main facility, and confirmed the time.

He then spoke softly to himself, "Seventy-three Deck, seventy-three. Sergeant Walter P. Thrump is reporting for duty. It is eleven forty or my name is not Walter P. Thrump."

Yes, indeed, Mr. Walter P. Thrump was a serious man.

2

A Halloween Night

Halloween arrived, and it was a cold, but sunny day. Mr. and Mrs. Walter P. Thrump attended the solemn funeral for Mr. Robert Decker, WB2ABC. On this sad day, Walter dug out a suit that smelled like strong mothballs and did not really fit him so well anymore. After all, he had kept the same suit for more than thirty years now. He had grown a little skinnier than even he had been years ago, and the suit hung on his small frame like a tent.

Mrs. Thrump wore a black dress, which she wore very seldom, but it still fit her well. Unlike Walter, Mrs. Thrump had stayed about the same weight and frame size for most of her sixty-three years.

It was quite the glorious funeral service, because Deck had many friends both at work and in his life. A small contingent of a color guard attended the service from the military organization that Robert Decker had been a long-time member of in his hometown. They presented the colors, and paid a stirring tribute to Deck, in honor of his naval service to his country. Walter choked back tears as he spoke a few words, as did some other members of the local ham radio club that Deck, Walter, and other local amateur radio operators belonged to for many years.

It was a sad, but heartfelt tribute to their mutual ham radio friend. Walter spoke of how his friend had been a radioman to the very end. There were many things that Deck was, but to a bunch of ham radio operators gathered here today, he was first and foremost . . . WB2ABC.

Substantial Industries had a large group that attended the service, and Mr. Plank, as well as two or three other executives, provided short speeches on Deck's dedicated and outstanding service to the company.

The graveside service was touching, as the pastor from the Lutheran church that Deck was a member of conducted a moving and stirring service that was a fitting religious tribute to a great man.

The Decker family held a brunch get-together at a local restaurant after the services, and Walter and Mrs. Thrump had the pleasure of meeting all of Deck's family, even if it was under such tragic circumstances. Robert Decker's son asked Walter to come by the Decker house, once the dust had settled next week, to help him sort out all the radio gear. He told Walter that his father had written in his last will and testament that some of his radio gear should go to the radio club, but also some of it his father wanted Walter to have for his own radio shack. The little man was very touched, and he fought back tears a number of times while listening to how much his friend thought about him. Walter and Mrs. Thrump left the restaurant, with the promise to assist the Decker family in any way that they could, to help them through this difficult period.

For Walter P. Thrump, this had not been an easy day to deal with and he already missed his friend more than he could describe. Both his workday, and his radio hobby, would never be the same.

In true Walter P. Thrump fashion, he refused to miss a day at work, even under these very difficult circumstances. It was just not what Walter was going to do, and he felt that Deck would never have wanted or allowed it.

As usual, Walter pulled up in his rust bucket vehicle, right on time, and of course, he was not one minute late. Walter strode into the lobby of Substantial Industries with his trusty lunch pail, his uniform neat as a pin, and his badge and whistle proudly displayed. He relieved the security officer, who was on duty before him, signed into the logging system, and at the stroke of midnight, Sergeant Walter P. Thrump was on duty.

Substantial Industries was never in better hands.

On his first building tour of his shift, up into the north tower on one of the upper floors, he ran into the two young maintenance mechanics that Deck had exiled to the graveyard shift.

"Hey Walter, it sure is sad about, Deck," Johnny Cantrelli said, as he met Walter in the main hallway of the twenty-seventh floor, holding a stepladder in his hands. Johnny was with his nighttime sidekick, Rodney Brigham, and it appeared that the two men were changing light bulbs in the hallways.

"Yes, it sure is there, Johnny. It sure is," Walter answered while confirming what work the two men could be getting into tonight. "Are youse guys working on a list of work that Tommy Mckee gave you?"

Rodney nodded his head in agreement and answered Walter, "Yup, that's right. Tommy gave us a list for tonight, and the first assignment was for us guys to re-lamp these hallway lights. Then, we have one roll towel dispenser to hang on the wall in the executive suite men's restroom."

He pointed at a drill that was on a tool cart, with some screws and a dispenser that was still in the box. Walter scanned the tools for trouble, but it all seemed harmless enough that even these two geniuses could not get into too much trouble with.

Walter noticed that there were small screws on the cart and some larger ones, too.

"Say, what are those big, lag bolts for? They are awfully big to hang some, little, towel dispensers on the wall, aren't they?"

"Oh yeah, yeah, yeah, Walt. Those are for another job," Johnny reassured Walter, while picking up the bolts and checking them out.

"Deck sure was a great guy. We are going to miss him around here, that is for sure," Rodney said while staring at Walter. Rodney then added, "I am a little spooked that his funeral was today on Halloween. It is a little spooky to be here, and go in the shop, see his desk, and his tools. You know what I mean there, Sergeant Thrump. Do you find it creepy too?"

The little man tugged at his security uniform belt, felt his hip for his two-way radio, and dug his feet into the hallway floor.

"Nah, I do not find it creepy at all there, men. I am not afraid of anything or anyone, or my name is not, Walter P. Thrump. Well, carry on, men, and please just work smart tonight. None of us need any adventures."

The two young men assured Walter that they would stay out of trouble and that it would be a quiet night. Walter felt confident that the work assignments were harmless, so Walter once more went on his way to finish his building tours.

As his nighttime tour progressed, Walter continued on his way, checking doors, calling in on his radio to the other security officers stationed in the other buildings, checking door locks, and shutting down lights, which were accidentally left on.

He finally made his way down to the bottom floor of the main tower, and he slowly walked towards the back of the main hallway on the first floor, where the door to the maintenance shop wing was located. Walter opened the door to the wing, and there in front of him was Tommy McKee's office. The next office over was Deck's office.

Walter walked up and he touched the wall plaque on the outside of the door that was stamped, "Robert T. Decker." Walter felt a cold shiver go down his spine. The little security officer spun around and checked all around him as he realized that it was just a little case of nerves fueled by the day's activities.

"Stay cool . . . there, Thrump," Walter warned himself aloud. "Just that comment about Halloween that has you a little spooked. There is no reason to be jumpy." Walter turned the key in the door of Deck's office and turned the light switch on. He stuck his head in and scanned the office. Nothing had changed . . . it was the same as it was when Walter had last seen it. Deck's file cabinet stood in the corner, with all the file drawers neatly closed. His desk was untouched, just as if he would be in at the crack of dawn, with even his chair neatly tucked under the desk. Nothing was out of place, his pads on his desk, his pencils and pens, his two-way radio sitting in the desk charger with a little red light glowing on top of it.

Walter sighed; it was all so very sad. He really missed his friend and was having a hard time accepting that he was actually gone. Walter shut off the light switch and closed the door.

Walter made his way into the maintenance shop, which was right next to Deck's office. He passed the rows of workbenches and tools lined up neatly on the walls. A motor and a fan blade from an air-conditioning unit sat on a workbench. No doubt, this was a repair underway by the daytime crew, Walter surmised as he studied the parts strewn across the bench. Walter made his way past the locker room, where the men dressed in their uniforms and kept some of their own personal gear.

He opened the door to the boiler room and scanned the lights on the wall that indicated the present state of the boilers. There was a watchman's key station to punch here in this room, but Walter never just made a quick punch, and exited a room. He was always looking for troubles that required his intervention.

One boiler was on high fire and the remaining two boilers were cruising, waiting for the call. Everything was clear, but with those two misfits on duty tonight, Walter knew that he better check for any boiler flame issues or other troubles. He was sure those two dummies on duty tonight did not even know what to look for on a boiler until it was too late! It was a cold night out there, and he did not desire for any troubles to occur with the heating plant tonight.

Walter P. Thrump missed nothing, not one single item. Walter's eyes went up and down the boiler room. He spotted the old coffee percolator sitting on the workbench in the far corner of the boiler room. Another sad reminder of his now departed friend. How sad that he would no longer share a hot cup of coffee with his old buddy.

Walter felt strongly that no one should use the old coffee percolator ever again, and he decided to speak with Mr. Plank about it. In honor and a tribute to his buddy, Walter would ask if he could take it home. He would then retire it forever more and never make another pot of coffee with the machine again. Reaching up, Walter punched his watchman's time clock with the key on the wall in the boiler room, shut off the light switch, and closed the door.

Soon, Walter was back in the main lobby, sitting at the main security desk, completing all the details of his building tour. He called in the results of his tour, to his back up officer, who was on duty in the building across the street from the corporate headquarters, "Sergeant Walter P. Thrump clear of the building tour and back on duty at the main lobby desk. A negative for trouble on the tour and the time of completion is fourteen hundred hours." Walter just loved the radio part of his job!

The two-way radio crackled with the voice of Officer Mendez in the other building. "Roger, Sergeant Thrump. Everything is clear here too. I will begin my building tours now. I am rolling my lobby telephone to your location and extension, sir."

Walter smiled as he looked at his desk clock, and he confirmed the finely tuned security machine that he ran here at Substantial Industries. He had planned and staggered the building rounds, so that a security officer was always on duty in the lobbies at one time or another for telephone emergencies. His plan worked to perfection.

Walter was busy filling out the logbook with his usual meticulous details, when the two-way radio broke the squelch with the frantic voice of Johnny Cantrelli, "Come in, Sergeant Thrump! This is maintenance twelve. We have an emergency here in the executive suite!" Walter jumped into action as soon as he heard the word, "emergency."

Walter P. Thrump lived for emergencies!

He grabbed his radio and keyed the microphone, "This is, Sergeant Walter P. Thrump, go ahead, maintenance twelve."

"Sergeant Thrump, we have a major trouble in the restroom here in the executive suite. Rodney was drilling the holes for the towel dispenser into the wall and well . . . well, I think. . .."

There was a very long pause, and Walter could swear that he could hear water rushing in the background of the radio.

"I think that we hit a pipe with the screws! Now, the room is flooding from the water rushing through the wall. I sure hope you know where the shutoff valve is! The water is pouring out all over the place and the room is getting pretty messy!"

Walter held the radio to his ear, and his immediate reaction was that those two guys were a bunch of jerks, but that was not going to help this situation.

He keyed the microphone and answered, "This is, Sergeant Walter P. Thrump. I am on the way!" Then in a display of his best United States Navy training, and in a tribute to Deck, he keyed the radio and added, "In the meantime, control the water as best you can, start the bilge pumps, and bail, men! Come in, Officer Mendez, this is, Sergeant Thrump!" Walter was now very excited, but his training as a radioman was working hard towards forcing him to remain cool.

"This is, Officer Mendez. I heard the radio call. I am heading back to the lobby and suspending my tour. I will stand by for assistance."

Walter was very satisfied at the reaction of Officer Mendez, who had obviously heard the call on the radio and anticipated the situation.

"Roger!" Walter called out on his two-way radio as he made his way to the staircase.

If there was a security rule in the rule book, then Walter P. Thrump knew what it was and could recite them all from his memory. Utilizing the elevators in the case of an emergency was strictly against the security rule book. A trapped security officer, who was stuck inside a malfunctioning elevator during an emergency situation, was not a useful security officer. The executive suite was an extremely long trip from the main lobby security station. Poor Walter, with his one lung, was going to have to suck it up and make it. The rule forced Walter into taking the stairs.

Walter P. Thrump followed the rules!

After what seemed like a climb to the other end of the world, poor Walter finally made it to the executive suite. He rushed as best he could, while huffing, puffing, and quite literally gasping for air, towards the men's executive restroom. Sure enough, the description the two maintenance men had given Walter was right on target. The water was pouring out of the wall as the two hapless, fraudulent, maintenance men tried their best to minimize the ongoing damage to the room from the errant screw, which had struck the pipe inside the wall.

"What happened?" Walter shouted his question above the roar of the water.

Johnny and Rodney looked at Walter, and then they both glanced towards the tool cart as they tried to catch the water pouring out of the wall into a five-gallon bucket that they held up to the hole where the water was pouring out.

Johnny shouted back to Walter, "The first screws did not hold, so Rodney used those bigger ones, and all of a sudden the water started to pour out! We hit a big pipe, Walter! We do not know where the shutoff valve is! We checked all over!"

Walter thought about the big screws that he had seen on the cart and rolled his eyes. He was tempted to say; how stupid could you be to use a screw that could hold up half of the building to secure a towel dispenser? However, Walter knew that statement would not serve any purpose at all, except to delay the situation.

There was a large hole now in the wall where the two dopes had bashed the tile away, to see where the water was coming from. The water was shooting straight out under extreme pressure and the maintenance mechanics were soaked to the skin from their vain efforts to shut off the water.

Walter peered into the hole, but all he could see was a large copper pipe with a stream of water shooting out of the side of it. The trick now was to find a shutoff valve, and stop the water. The water did not seem to be hot, but Walter needed to confirm which line was broken.

Walter yelled back at Rodney and Johnny while asking, "Is it cold water or the hot side?"

"Cold water, so at least we are not getting burned!" Johnny answered.

Well, that was a plus. Walter could see where the two buffoons had taken a ladder and looked in the restroom ceiling to no avail, so Walter ran out into the hallway and scanned it up and down. To tell the truth, he was gasping for air, his pants were falling off his little waist, and he had no idea at all of what to do to shut off this water.

He stood in the hallway spinning around, looking in every direction, without a clue where to look for help.

He thought for a moment to call Tommy Mckee, but that

would only delay the situation even more.

In desperation, Walter spoke aloud, hoping that somehow, a thought would come into his mind, 'Where do I look, Deck? What would you do?'

Despite the two men doing their best at controlling the water leak inside the restroom, Walter could see the water coming out from under the door of the restroom, and making the way down the hallway into the expensive carpet that lined the ultra-exclusive, executive suite of Substantial Industries.

Suddenly, it was very strange, but it was as if a little voice had spoken inside of Walter's head. Walter then remembered Deck telling him one day that he kept a chart in his file cabinet in his office, of the location of emergency water shut-off valves. Walter could not explain it, but he had this thought suddenly pop in his mind, and he was off as quickly as his little legs could carry him.

Down the stairs, the little security officer went, floor after floor, until the poor man finally reached the bottom level. Still gasping for air, he made it to the door of Deck's office, and after fumbling for the master key; he unlocked the door and turned the lights on. Walter was surprised to see that the third file cabinet drawer was open, and a file was sticking straight up into the air.

He looked at the manila folder that was sticking out and saw that the label on the folder was indicating, "Valve locations, executive suite."

"Funny, I swear this drawer was closed, when I did my rounds before. Those two idiots must have been in here," Walter said between gasps for air. He grabbed the folder, opened it, and there, dead in the middle of the folder, was a large diagram with a big, red arrow. The arrow pointed to a valve located in the ceiling of the main hallway about halfway down the executive wing. Next to the arrow, a label in the diagram proclaimed in block letters, "COLD WATER SHUT-OFF VALVE FOR ALL MEN'S

RESTROOMS EXECUTIVE LEVEL."

Walter closed the folder and placed it back in the drawer. He was off as fast as his little legs and his one lung could take him. Despite the pain and the agony, Walter P. Thrump was not going to break a single rule or regulation, and the little man gallantly tackled the stairs once more.

He fought and struggled his way back up the twenty or so flights of stairs to the executive suite. And somehow, by a miracle, or by the grace and mercy of God . . . Sergeant Walter P. Thrump made it!

His two-way radio was crackling with Officer Mendez calling for a status update, but poor Walter did not have the breath, or the strength, to answer his calls. He opened the door at the top of the stairs and looked up and down the hallway. Disoriented from the lack of oxygen, Walter realized that he was ready to collapse. He bent over at the waist and gasped for air. When he recovered a little, he looked up and down the main hallway, and he spotted a little door open in the ceiling and the lid swinging in the center of the main hallway.

"Those two jerks must have already found the valve," he spoke aloud.

Walter had recovered some of his bearings, and his breathing was somewhat under control, so he ran towards the restroom and swung the door to the room open. The room was a mess with deeper water now, and Johnny and Rodney were still fighting to control the flow of water.

Apparently, they had not found the valve!

Puzzled, Walter yelled to them with the last bit of air that he had left in his lungs, "Grab that ladder! I know where the valve is!"

Johnny grabbed the ladder, followed Walter to the hallway, and set the ladder under the little door that was open. Johnny climbed up and looked inside the compartment in the ceiling as Walter heard him turning a valve handle that was making an awful lot of noise.

"Please hold, please hold," Walter was saying over and over, as Johnny spun the valve handle.

Johnny looked down from the ladder and poked his head out from above the ceiling as he reported, "The valve is closed now, Walter!"

A few seconds later, Rodney came running out of the restroom, "The water has stopped! Youse guys shut it off with that valve!"

"Oh, thank goodness!" Walter grabbed his radio, and while he took one long breath of air, he keyed the radio, and called out, "This is, Sergeant Walter P. Thrump, come in, Officer Mendez."

"Go ahead, Sergeant Trump."

"Situation is under control, thank you for standing by."

"Roger. You had me worried when you did not answer. Let me know when you are back at the lobby desk, Sergeant Thrump."

"Roger, thank you, Officer Mendez. This is, Sergeant Walter P. Thrump out!"

Walter bent over, then sat down on the floor in the hallway and leaned up against the wall. He still was breathing very heavily, and his legs were shaking from the repeated long climbs up and down the stairs.

Johnny came over and leaned over the top of the little man. He was dripping with water, and a few drops rolled off his long hair and fell onto Walter as Johnny asked him, "Are you all right there, Walter? We are really sorry about this. Rodney and I will get the wet vacuum to suck up the water and clean it all up. We had better leave fixing the hole in the pipe for Tommy and the day crew though, I am afraid that we will just make more of a mess. Thanks for finding the valve. I think we would have been in a real mess if you did not find that shutoff!"

"Yeah, yeah, yeah, do not touch anything else, will you!" Walter shouted back at Johnny, between gasps for air. When Walter heard the mere suggestion that these two nitwits would attempt to use tools once more, his mind had swirled with thoughts of additional disasters.

"Just clean it all up, and hopefully, we can get the water back on when the early maintenance crew comes in. I will leave Tommy a note on his desk. He gets into the shop in another few hours, so they might be able to have it all fixed, before most of the executives come in. The hole in the tile wall. Well, I guess, they will need to deal with that within a few days, but at least the water will be back on. I cannot even imagine how a simple job such as hanging a dispenser on the wall turned into such an adventure!"

Walter slowly tried to stand back up onto his feet, and Rodney joined Johnny, and they each grabbed Walter by his shoulders, and helped him the rest of the way.

"We did not mean to cause such troubles, Sergeant Thrump," Rodney said, as he looked at Walter with forlorn eyes and a down-frowned mouth.

Walter looked back at them as he hobbled into the main hallway, and he suddenly felt sorry for the two men. He felt they needed a little boost to their now shattered confidence, so he told them, "I know, I know, you did not mean to cause the troubles, but at least youse guys found the door in the hallway, and looked in Deck's files for the shutoff location. That was good thinking on your part, there guys. Plus, somehow, you two guys did manage to keep the water from flooding the whole, entire hallway."

Rodney looked at Johnny and shrugged his shoulders.

Johnny's head was shaking back and forth, and he spoke up with a puzzled look on his face, "We did not find the door in the hallway, Walt. We thought you found it. Now that I come to think of it . . . how did you open it without a ladder? You came and got our ladder out of the restroom!"

Johnny shifted uneasily on his feet, and Rodney leaned in with his eyes open wide. "What file with shutoff valves, are you talking about, Walter? I have not been in Deck's files and neither has Rodney. We never left the room. All we were working hard to do was to push the water to the floor drains to stop the whole executive suite from being underwater!"

Walter was stunned while he recounted the events in his head. The little man, who was not afraid of anything, suddenly found his spine tingling. Walter's eyes darted back and forth in his head and his mouth opened widely.

The first thought in his head was that the two dummies were playing with him, and he smiled as he stammered back at them at the thought of the joke, "Ah, youse guys, you are kidding me! That was a good one. It has been a long night, so I guess we deserve to. . .." Walter's voice trailed off as he saw the reaction on Rodney's face and then on Johnny's face.

"Walter, I swear, we never left the restroom. Think about it . . . no offense, but we would have easily beaten you back here, and had it shut down by the time that you made it back! There is no one else working tonight, just the three of us! Officer Mendez did not come over. We all know that!"

Johnny became excited, and his eyes were wide.

Rodney grabbed the top of his head as he paced in a nervous little circle and wrung his hands together, "I told youse guys! Tonight, has me spooked out! Halloween night! Deck . . . gone . . . an open, secret door showing us some hidden valve! This whole thing is giving me the creeps. Youse guys . . . what happened here?"

Walter stepped back, and he reeled a little. He looked once more at the two young men and shook his head back and forth. His legs felt weak; surely, it was from all of that running and climbing during the emergency! Walter looked back at the hallway wall; he then sat back down in the hallway and leaned his back up against the wall.

"I have overextended myself tonight, men. I need to—I need to—sit here for a minute."

Rodney and Johnny came over and placed their hands

onto Walter's shoulders as the three men stared at the little door still hanging open from the middle of the hallway ceiling. A door which had concealed a hidden valve. A valve that very few people would have even known to be located there, in such an obscure location.

It was a hidden valve that the three of them were positively sure that Robert "Deck" Decker would have been the only person who would have known where it was located.

After resting, Walter asked the two young men to clean up, and he made his way back down to the security post. He would need to leave an incident report in his security log, detailing the events and emergency of the late-night shift for Tommy Mckee and Mr. Plank.

Walter settled back in at the main security post and began to write all the details of the incident in his logbook. He called into Officer Mendez and left a telephone message for Tommy Mckee to check the security notes when he came in for his shift.

Walter was exhausted and his legs ached, but the determined little man never would let anyone know it! He looked at his desk clock, and it was now close to five in the morning. He sighed, as he sure would like this long shift to be over soon.

It had been a very strange Halloween night and a long day. Walter was tired, and he was working hard to prevent jumping to any conclusions as to what exactly had transpired here tonight.

Back in the maintenance shop, Tommy Mckee, who was now the acting manager of the entire maintenance department, reported for his day of work, he turned his key in his office door, took his hat and coat off, and hung them on the hook in his office. He let loose a long sigh; it sure was not going to be the same around here without Deck. They had worked together for about five years, and he knew he would miss the guidance and mentoring of the old hand. Deck was a good guy and Tommy Mckee missed him already. Tommy wanted to do a good job, and make Deck proud of him, so he was in extra early to make sure that all was well in the complex.

He also knew that the two weakest links of the department were on duty last night, and you never knew what Rodney and Johnny could get into. He did also feel some comfort in the knowledge that Walter P. Thrump was on duty last night, and with Walter around, those two bumblers could only get into so much trouble before old Walter would be on them!

He noticed that the message light was lit up on the telephone, but after checking some papers on his desk, he decided to check the boilers first before listening to his messages.

It had been a cold night and making sure the heat was in good shape was the first thing that Tommy felt that he had to do. He walked over to the shop and into the boiler room. After flipping on the lights, he checked the board for any alarms and for the status of the boilers. He was relieved to see that all was well with the heating plant. He checked the boiler temperatures and pressures, filled out the logbooks, blew down the drains, and checked all the safeties on them.

Tommy was about to leave when he noticed that the old coffee percolator of Deck's was set up on the workbench. The electric plug for the coffee percolator was in the wall, and the little glass on top was full of steaming hot coffee. Tommy walked over to it, and he thought how it sure smells good. The machine was making those little, "popping" sounds that the percolator made to indicate that the coffee had completed brewing, and was now ready to drink.

Tommy grabbed his mug from under the workbench and he poured the freshly brewed coffee into his cup. This was going to taste good.

"That is strange. I wonder who would have made a pot

of coffee with Deck's percolator. I guess old Walter pulled it out for one last time in honor of Deck. That was nice of him."

Tommy was speaking his thoughts to no one as he leaned into the piping hot coffee.

Yes, indeed, it surely tasted good.

"Boy oh boy, Deck taught Walter well. This coffee tastes just like Deck made it himself!"

Tommy McKee was satisfied that all was well. He smiled, and he walked out of the boiler room, shut off the light switch, and he closed the door behind him.

3

Early Morning Static

The old 1974 Whizzer station wagon pulled in front of 164 Maple Lane in Jersey City, New Jersey. Walter P. Thrump rolled down the window, opened his door latch, and climbed out of the wagon. He then rolled the window back up and slammed the car door. He grabbed his trusty old lunch pail, his security cap, and made his way slowly to the front door of his home.

Walter was still a little shaky on his legs, and he was exhausted from the whirlwind activities that he had been through during his work shift. He certainly could not explain all that had happened, but he was too tired to think about it now. Despite his outward appearance and his fearless reputation, the entire episode had left him shaken, and more than a little puzzled. It was indeed more than just a little strange. Maybe it was one of those events that would forever remain a mystery. After all, Johnny and Rodney had no explanation for the events, either.

As Walter slowly walked up the porch steps, he looked down at the jack-o'-lantern pumpkin sitting on the top step of the porch, and he was reminded that last night was indeed Halloween. He then reached into his pocket for the door key and he noticed a medium size box sitting on the front porch. The local package delivery truck must have already been through the neighborhood. His keen little eyes looked down at the label, and he spotted that the front of the box had the stamp of the official Big Bob's famous logo!

"Oh, boy!" Walter shouted as he reached down to pick up the box, "I am a prize winner! I knew it. I could feel it this time!" Walter carefully spun the key in the door, and he was careful to contain his excitement, as not to wake Mrs. Thrump, who must have been still sleeping from staying up all night, watching reruns of her favorite episodes of, "El Paso."

When he walked into the house, he glanced at the clock on the living room wall, and noted the time with a smile as he spoke to himself, "Eight forty-seven in the morning. Right on time or my name is not Walter P. Thrump. I may still have time to tune twenty meters quick and see if there is an opening to Australia or New Zealand!"

Walter closed the door behind him, carefully rushed into the kitchen, and placed his gear and the box on the table. Sure enough, the box had ink stamps all over it declaring that the recipient was a lucky, "Official Big Bob's prize winner!"

Walter took out his pocket knife and carefully sliced through the tape holding the flaps of the box together. He folded it open and reached inside the box. There inside, he spotted a large, multicolored, printed letter and a handsomely, printed certificate carefully laid on top of the shredded packing material.

Walter picked up the paper and read it aloud, "Congratulations to Mr. Walter P. Thrump of 164 Maple Lane in Jersey City, New Jersey, for being a prize winner in this year's Big Bob's Food Contest! While you did not win the grand prize, you were a winner of one of our special, twenty-seventh place prizes, as well as, a proud holder of a suitable for framing, official, Big Bob's Food Contest Entry Certificate! Thank you for your support of Big Bob and his food empire."

Walter was thrilled. "Wow, a certificate too!"

Walter stared at a fantastic certificate that was certainly suitable for framing, and proudly declared his lofty status within the massive Big Bob's organization. He then turned his attention to the prize, and he eagerly dug around in the box to find the contents. After some probing, and making a mess all over the kitchen with the shredded packing material, Walter pulled out one smaller box, and then one larger box.

"Wow! Two boxes!" Walter exclaimed, as he was now astounded at his good fortune. He flipped them out of the original shipping box, and held both of them up in order to read the labels. The first box had a label, which had printed upon it in large block letters, "One box of Big Bob's Custom, Whiz Bang, Roller Tip, Black Pens."

Walter then looked at the side of the other box, which was larger, and the label there declared that the contents were, "One seven-foot, inflatable, Big Bob replica balloon."

"Well, it sure was not the trip to the American Virgin Islands or Newington, Connecticut, but at least, I am a winner. I guess an awful lot of folks must win the balloon and the pens. I cannot wait to tell, Gertrude!"

Nothing deterred the forever-positive Walter P. Thrump. Nothing . . . not even twenty-seventh place prizes, not weird things that go bump on Halloween nights, not crabby wives, not anything.

He cleaned up the mess and the boxes, tucked his prizes, letters, and the certificate under his arm, and down into the radio shack, he went. After flipping on the power switch, and waiting for the rigs to warm up, Walter P. Thrump carefully placed his cans over his ears, and settled in front of his beloved American Blabber model X2-4 high frequency rig.

Walter tuned the dial slowly across the twenty-meter band and listened with a keen ear to the Morse code signals. There was not too much going on, so Walter decided to drum up some activity and see if he could entice a station to call him. He selected his favorite frequency of 14.030, grabbed his code key, and pounded out an invitation to call his radio station: CQ CQ CQ CQ DE WA2ASQ WA2ASQ AR K.

He stopped the transmission and listened carefully, and he thought he did hear a very weak signal that was replying to his call.

When Walter heard the very weak signal, he pushed the cans to his head, fiddled with his filters, and closed his eyes as he tried to pick up the code rhythms. The signal was very weak, but he thought he picked up the Morse letter, "A" and then the Morse letter "C," but the signals had faded in static.

The station may have been from a faraway land or some type of exotic DX!

Walter grabbed the code key and pounded out a clarification call to see if the signals would improve. QRZ? QRZ? DE WA2ASQ, WA2ASQ AR K.

He stopped transmitting, but the band had faded out, and all that Walter heard now was static. Walter was disappointed that he may have missed a good one.

Terrible, early morning static, he thought.

He grabbed the code key and tapped out a message that told the world and beyond that, he was going off the air: WA2ASQ CL 73 AR SK.

Walter pulled his cans off his head and flipped off the power switch. He closed the light switch and made his way towards the stairs. His leg muscles still ached from his long night of running around, but it was nothing that a nice, warm bath of Epsom salts would not cure.

Sometimes, we are better off not knowing certain things in this life, and it really is best if we save learning about life's strangest mysteries for another time or another place.

You see, Walter P. Thrump had given up just a little too early on the radio call. If he had stayed on the air, and waited for the band to shift, he might have heard that way down deep in the static, a very faint signal had responded to Walter's Morse code call signaling to the world and beyond that, he was pulling the power switch.

A ham operator with the call sign, G3ZZZ listening to the activity, in front of his radio set on the other side of the big pond in England, had heard Walter's call, and he was just reaching for his key to call WA2ASQ, when he realized that Walter had indicated that he was going off the air. He leaned back and was about to tune to find another station when he heard a faint station tap out a reply to Walter P. Thrump's closing call. The English ham grabbed his pen, copied the very weak, and barely readable Morse code signals onto his pad, "WA2ASQ DE WB2ABC, CUL 73 WALT AR CL SK."

The English ham operator placed his pen down on the pad, and said to himself, "Hmm, must be a chap that he knows, it is a shame that he missed him."

He then tuned his frequency dial away, and went tuning up the band, seeking another station to call.

Yes, it was a shame that he missed him.

A real shame, indeed. . ..

THE END

Red Wine and Autumn Memories

I have always felt that I have an awful lot to be thankful for in my life. I think that God granted me a full time of it in this world. I will repeat just a tad more emphatically that I have an awful lot to be *very* thankful for in my life. I have experienced more things in my life than most people could ever have dreamed of experiencing. I have met such an array of wonderful and fascinating people over my lifetime that I truly feel blessed.

Now, I do admit; I have had an unusual combination of careers that have contributed to where I am now in my thoughts, but nonetheless, I have still been very lucky to be where I am right now.

First off, playing professional ice hockey early on in my life brought me to visit places that I had only ever heard of in schoolbooks, or I had spotted on maps. I started out on the gritty streets in good old Paterson and then Haledon, New Jersey, shooting sawed off ends of Christmas trees that were acting as hockey pucks, around on Geyer Street with my best friends, Harry M. Redmond Junior and Jeffrey Porter. I then made my way to the outskirts of Canada, and then wandered around New England, the southeastern United States, and even the Midwest.

Playing professional ice hockey, then afterwards, becoming a Lutheran pastor, sure made this apple roll far from the tree!

That statement brings me to clichés and idioms. I for one do not find them annoying or contrite. I use them in my sermons and my writings all the time. Oftentimes, I wonder why some people frown upon them and discourage their use. I feel another one coming on, as the old, "you cannot judge a book by its cover," has come to mind for me this afternoon. Then again, my writings never follow proper rules of grammar or structure. In true Harry and Paul tradition, I would not have it any other way.

My mind wandered back once more to the past, on this clear, wonderful, autumn afternoon, and it alerted my memory banks to turn on and dial up a few old memories. It never does take too much to flip me back in time these days. A word, a commonly spoken phrase, a sunset, or a cold day, and the ghosts of the past, which I believe that until the end of my time will always follow me around, come roaring back into my mind.

On this perfect autumn afternoon, it was my wonderful wife, who triggered the memory.

My wife, Binky, and our two children, Heather Sarah and Paul William, were off on a mission to pick up some supplies for school projects. That left me alone to handle some household chores. I planned to rake up the leaves in the entire front yard of the parsonage this late October Saturday afternoon, gather, and then bag up all the leaves.

It was a perfect October day. It was the kind of October day, where the world is on fire in a once a year, colorful and awe-inspiring display. Where the hillsides, the roadsides, and in this case, our own backyard, exploded in colors that reminded us that God is indeed the greatest artist of us all.

I love the autumn weather, and this cold and wonderfully crisp afternoon was the perfect day to tackle the project. It was a golden day here in northern New Jersey. The sun filtered down through the leaves, and the wind gently shook some more leaves from the branches above my head. The spent leaves fluttered to the ground like rain in front of me. The front lawn of the parsonage of

Reunion Lutheran Church was a carpet of spent, dried leaves and I was determined to clean them all up. Besides, not only was it great to be outside, but also raking leaves was a great exercise too!

As I was leaning on the rake, waving goodbye to my family, watching them pull out of our driveway, my wife set off the memory trigger.

We were planning to have our best friends, Harry and Rose Redmond, and their little girl, Blue Cloud; over to our house for dinner tonight, and as Binky pulled out of the driveway, she stuck her head out of the jeep and asked me, "Should I pick up some red wine for tonight for Rose? Rose has been drinking wine as of late, instead of her usual Purple Pirate beers. I think that we may be out of red wine, twenty-seven!"

I thought about it for a moment and answered her, "I think you are correct, please go ahead and pick some up on your way home." Binky had nodded, waved, and they were off.

That was it. I was off to another time and place, as I leaned on my rake, and thought about red wine, not judging books by covers, and apples rolling far away from trees, or something like that.

"Great game, twenty-seven. You played great. That glove save on that shot during the power play in the third period was something special. Were you screened just a little, or what?"

"Hey, Coach Davis. Thanks for the kind words, I got lucky on that save, the screen just moved in time."

Coach Davis shook his head in disagreement of my statement. He looked at me, while I finished dressing into my civilian clothes, in the locker room of the Albany Flying Dutchman in Albany, New York, in October 1980.

"I don't think so there, Paulie. I think that luck had very little to do with it. You are quite a goalie and as the head coach here, I sure am happy that we managed to sign you for this season. You will not be here for long. You will be in the big time soon, number twenty-seven. I can tell. I have been around this game for more than thirty-five years."

I nodded my head and said, "Thank you," as I reached down to tie the laces on my shoes.

Coach Davis sat down on the bench next to me. He was from Ontario Province in Canada. He was about fifty years old, with a thick head of hair and a torn-up face. When I describe his face as torn up, I really mean it! He wore the scars of a lifetime of hockey without helmets, face shields, and mouthpieces.

He had made it to the big time, he played in the big league for about ten years with the Boston Bears, and the word was that he had a reputation as a tough defenseman with a fearless approach to the game. He was one big, strong, tough player, and looking at him now, he looked as though he could still play. I knew from practices that he could still skate well, and his slap shot was a rocket from the point.

I had a few bruises to prove it.

I could also tell that he was a hard drinker, and he had lived a rough life, but deep down he loved hockey, and working with the young players, more than he did anything else. I had only been on the Albany team for about a month or so, but I really liked him, as well as respected him. He knew the game, and although he was tough on his players, he was fair.

"You know, twenty-seven, I cannot quite figure it out, but for a nice, polite, young man who actually looks like a hippie . . . you have an edge. You are fearless, and play at times so hard, I swear you are going to eat that puck! I cannot even recall knowing more than a handful of persons from New Jersey, let alone a professional goalie from there. In retrospect, you know, I have to admit, when I first saw a picture of you, I chuckled."

Coach Davis leaned his head back on the wall of the

locker room and smiled as if he remembered his comical reaction and shock at my appearance.

Coach Davis continued, "Some, long-haired hippie kid, with a beard, and all that facial hair, I thought to myself, this is a joke, eh. This kid is a hippie, not a goalie, eh! The scout who was showing me the film clips of your play, had told me to laugh now, but once I saw the film, then he assured me that I would stop laughing. He was right, Henson, he was right. I have seen a lot of goalies, but at your age, I cannot think of one who was better." Coach Davis continued as he then asked me, "Say, Henson, if you do not have any plans, can I buy you dinner and a few beers? We can talk a little strategy, but we can just, well, you know, talk. We can walk to that little bar and grille close to the arena here. Hopefully, not very many people recognize us and we can eat and drink in peace, eh?"

"I would enjoy that, Coach Davis. Thank you," I said as I stood up and shook his hand.

Coach Davis whistled, and he commented while shaking his right hand in the air, "I often forget how tall and strong you are. Big chap, for a goalie too. Man, you are one strong, young man."

We left the arena and walked together to the bar, which was a short distance from the hockey arena. Downtown Albany, New York, was very pleasant. It was a very clean city, with well laid out city streets. For a smaller city, it really had everything that you could ever need, or want, without being overwhelming. I really was growing accustomed to the city, and I was certainly enjoying my time here. The bar was crowded, and a few patrons who were Albany Flying Dutchman fans recognized the two of us right away.

We greeted them, signed some autographs, and thanked them for being fans. After the fanfare died down, the two of us settled down at the bar and ordered a few beers. Coach Davis joked with the barkeeper, who did not know a thing about hockey, but he turned out to be a good sport about the situation.

It turned out that I was correct in my analysis of Coach Davis and his drinking habits. He chugged the first beer, ordered a shot of whiskey, and by the time that it took me to finish one beer; he had already downed two more.

We chatted about hockey, my skills, things that I needed to do better, things the team needed to improve upon, and a myriad of other hockey related subjects. I had the feeling that this was a threefold mission to teach me some things, get to know me better, but also to pass some moments in time for Coach Davis.

Deep down, he seemed to harbor some inner sadness, some kind of painful loneliness. Those were feelings that I also knew so well, and I shared.

As we sat there downing our beers, a young, and very pretty woman walked over and sat down a few bar stools away from us. She had selected a stool close to my right side, and while she sat down, she made a point of smiling and winking her right eye at me. She had shoulder-length brown hair, wide green eyes, and a wonderful smile. She had a perfect figure, and she was dressed in a white pullover sweater, with tight, blue jean dungarees on.

She was indeed gorgeous.

She was only sitting there for a minute or two when the barkeeper came right over and took her order. He smiled at the young woman and made small talk; it was obvious that he was not going to allow such a pretty young woman to fly under his radar for very long!

Coach Davis had watched the scene unfold, and he leaned over to me and spoke in a low voice, "Nice-looking young woman there, twenty-seven, eh? She sure has her eye on you, eh? It must be all that hair, and that beard. I imagine you could have your pick of them, Paulie. I like how you decide to stay away from all of that romance and allure, even though these young women are drooling over you all night long in every stop we make. This is admirable, Paul, but I cannot help but think there is more to it than that, eh? Is there a woman back home? I never hear you mention that there is."

Coach Davis seemed as though he was looking for an answer, and I was sure the drinks were finally affecting him, because he was rambling a bit in the conversation, and he then leaned in close to me for an answer.

I was suddenly uncomfortable, because I didn't really want to share with my head coach my true inner feelings, and the fact that the love of my life, Ms. Binky Hobnobber, had up and left me, and without any notice, suddenly and abruptly ended our relationship. Her sudden departure had sent me into a tailspin, a downward spiral of emotions, filled with pain and loneliness that I did not want to face, or even to admit.

Hockey was my release, my comfort. I hid behind my goalie mask, where it was safe, and not one single person knew the real Paul John Henson. I could hide there and Coach Davis was correct. I did have a hard edge since Binky left me, and it was in the playing of my position that it manifested the most.

I loved playing the position of goaltender; it was so unique. I could be the hero, and the bad guy at the same time, and it perfectly fit my present state of mind.

I was sure that I could have struck up many relationships with all the attractive gals that came along, smiled, winked, and flirted, and even took it to the next level. But the trouble was that I could never forget, Binky. She was in my heart and mind forever, and there was no escape.

I decided to stall and whip up a little smokescreen, "Well, she sure is pretty, Coach Davis, but I want to keep my mind on hockey. I need to stay focused."

As soon as the words came out of my mouth, I could detect that Coach Davis knew that they were insincere. I took a long swig of beer and I could feel some numbness from the alcohol creeping in now. We had ordered some sandwiches, and the barkeeper came over, set them in front of us, and brought us both another round of beer. Coach Davis did not answer me, but he stared as the barkeeper sat a long, stemmed glass, filled with red wine in front of the gorgeous woman.

The woman crossed her legs, glanced over in our direction, smiled at me, flipped her hair, and took a slow, seductive sip of the wine, while she coyly watched me over the rim of the wine glass.

She was a classy woman, and she knew how to work her assets well.

Coach Davis sighed, and I could see him lean back on his stool. His mind suddenly seemed to be far away, perhaps, to another time or place. It was then that I knew the smoke screen had not worked, as he said to me in his thick Canadian accent, "Lost a young love along the way eh, Henson?"

I did not answer him, but I intently stared right back at his face and eyes. I had not fooled anyone, and certainly, I had not fooled this very intuitive, sharp, and perceptive man.

"Is she as pretty as that gal there drinking that glass of red wine, twenty-seven?"

Perhaps it was the beer or the emotions, but it all was coming back to me now, and I no longer held back, "A lot prettier, Coach Davis."

I spoke softly, and the tone of my voice was sad, almost forlorn. Would be a more accurate description.

"Really? What color is her hair, the same as this gal?"

"No, she has blonde hair. It is long, down past her shoulders. She has blue eyes that sparkle like little stars when the light hits them. I still see them in my mind every day, Coach Davis. Every single day, I see her eyes, hear her voice, feel her gentle touch on my body, and I remember every kiss and incredible moment of passion that we ever shared. Every, single, day, I am haunted by her, Coach Davis."

Coach Davis nodded as if he understood. He took a big bite of his sandwich, and so did I. We sat in silence for a few minutes while enjoying our meal and we chased the bites down with sips of our beer.

Suddenly, Coach Davis leaned back on his stool, folded his arms across his chest and said softly, "Me too, twenty-seven. I lost a woman along the way. It was a long time ago. She was from Toronto, and I was from a little town out in the pucker brush that no one ever heard of. She was a big city woman, how would you say, a sophisticate, or a socialite, eh? She traveled in fancy and wealthy circles."

Coach Davis smiled and he took a long sip of his beer. He folded up his napkin, tossed it on top of his empty plate, and pushed the plate away. The drinks had set in heavily now on Coach Davis, and he now must have been feeling the same as I had just felt because his guard was down.

Who knew?

Here was this rugged, tough, former professional hockey player, now turned coach, who was now full of emotions and sadness as he became lost in his romantic past.

He was a book whose cover certainly did not match.

He looked straight at me with bloodshot and watery eyes and spoke once more, "I was not always this carved up, stitched up, ugly mug. Before I played hockey for so many years, I actually was a good-looking chap, and she was, for some unknown reason, smitten with me. We met at a hockey game that was so long ago that I could not remember or even guess what the name of the team was, or who I was even playing for. Nonetheless, tell you where it was. She was special, with long, brown hair down to her waist, brown eyes, perfect face, a perfect figure, and features. Her smile was something that I will never forget. It was like a golden ray of warm sun, and her voice was soft and kind. Like your beautiful woman, she was even prettier than this young woman next to us is."

Coach Davis looked away from me for a minute. Then he stared back, and his eyes had a far-away look upon them. He had traveled back in time to face the ghosts that also followed him around.

"We met at this time of the year, Paulie. In the autumn, when the leaves were turning golden yellows, reds, and beginning to fall, when the cold air would whip down out of Alberta and Manitoba, and Toronto began to turn cold. The autumn of the year is very special, eh? It is when you say goodbye to the heat of the summer, and the world changes into a maze of color and refreshment. Changes of the seasons are so profound, it is as if another page in your life has passed, and you have turned another corner. We would sit on gorgeous autumn afternoons in those wonderful, street-side seats and tables at the outdoor bars and cafes on Yonge Street in downtown Toronto. You have been there. Have you not, Paulie? You know how special it is there on Yonge Street, eh?"

I had been listening very carefully, and I was amazed at the depth of his emotion, the profound descriptions, and the range of this tough man's insight and personality.

I nodded and replied, "I have, Coach Davis, and I agree that it really is very special. Our first road trip was there, and the guys on the team who know downtown Toronto, took me around when we had spare time."

Coach Davis nodded and finished off the last of his beer. He signaled the barkeeper to take our plates away and bring us another round.

"We would sit at those outdoor tables and talk for hours upon hours on those, wonderful, autumn afternoons, with the colors ablaze in the trees above our heads, and the cool breeze would blow wisps of her hair all around her. She elegantly drank red wine out of long-stemmed glasses, just like that young woman here tonight does. She wore pullover sweaters just as she is wearing tonight, too. Strange, eh? It is sometimes very strange, how life is really one big circle and memories come roaring back in your mind, from such simple situations. Then, she was gone, I cannot tell you why or how, but the last memory that I have of her is her walking down a sidewalk on a late October afternoon, kicking the dried leaves out of the way, her smile as wide and as beautiful as anything on God's good creation. Our love was real, and then it all disappeared. It is funny, twenty-seven, but as hard as I try to remember the reason that she left, I still cannot. It is very strange, but I am just not sure to this very day, why it all ended."

Coach Davis paused a long time, and he fiddled with his beer mug. He was obviously in pain and searching for an answer. An answer that had never come to him, despite the many years that had passed.

I stared at the man, and then out of respect, and to take some pressure off, I grabbed my mug and took a long sip of the beer.

He then turned to me as his mind must have settled on a thought and he said, "Red wine and autumn memories, eh, twenty-seven. That is all I have left of her."

The barkeeper set the new beers down in front of us. We both took long sips and stared straight ahead.

Coach Davis leaned back on his stool once more and his eyes rolled back in his head a bit. He then leaned forward and hunched over his mug.

I could see in the dim light of the bar, some tears in the edges of his eyes, as he turned to speak to me, "I wonder where she is now, Paulie? Perhaps, somewhere in Canada. I guess. I wonder if she ever married, if she had children, what our lives would have been like. Maybe someday, I will find out."

He looked at me while remaining hunched over his mug, and he spoke very quietly, "Maybe someday, your lovely woman will come back to you too. That big circle of life may roll back for both of us twenty-seven, you never know, eh?"

"I hope so, Coach Davis, I hope so," was all I could manage to say without choking up. We both were the same. We were both hiding in our hockey worlds and trying in vain to purge the memories from our hearts and minds. The two of us sat in silence the rest of the time, both of us lost in a stupor of beer and booze, and dreaming of our women so far away.

The common trouble was that we did not even know where they both were.

"Well, I think it is time, twenty-seven. Thank you for the time and the chat." Coach Davis motioned for me to keep my wallet in my back pocket; he reached into his wallet and plunked down a wad of bills on the bar top.

He leaned over to me as we both landed on our feet; we teetered and tottered a bit from the influence of our drinks until both of us caught our direction.

Coach Davis then spoke low, so no one else could hear us. He was enjoying this moment, as he said with a big smile, "That young woman is about to be very disappointed. She had her sights set on you, Paul, and all of her hard work is about to go to waste. A woman who looks as she does, she is not used to rejection, Paul, but I guess we both have our red wine and autumn memories, eh?" Coach Davis put his arm around me and gave me a playful shove.

"We sure do, Coach Davis. We sure do."

We walked out of the bar, out onto the main street, and headed back to the hotel, pulling our light jackets around us as the cold wind whipped down the city streets. I remember that we walked most of the way together in silence, and enjoyed the cold, autumn night air in Albany,

New York.

A gust of wind blew, and it unleashed a barrage of leaves from the trees above my head. I stopped leaning upon my rake, and came back to reality, as I watched the leaves fly through the air towards me. The leaves blew all around and chased one another into a pile that stopped at the base of a hedgerow on the side of the parsonage's front yard.

I grabbed the rake and started to gather up the carpet of leaves.

As I worked the rake, I thought about where Coach Davis was right now. I received a Christmas card from him last year. He wrote that he had finally retired from the Boston Bears organization, and was living on a lake up near Orillia, Ontario. Lake Couchiching, if I remembered correctly, or maybe it was Lake Simcoe. I could not remember now which one it was.

He had invited me up to go fishing with him and talk about the old times. He had also paid me a warm compliment in a note that he had written inside that card, which meant an awful lot to me.

He had written inside the card that, "Paul John Henson was still the best goalie that I have ever seen. None better ever, then the long-haired hippie from New Jersey, who wore number twenty-seven."

Those were special words, especially coming from a man who had spent a lifetime in ice hockey. Let me tell you that they were something very special.

I stopped raking the leaves again, and I leaned upon the rake once more. I stared out at the trees that lined the property of Reunion Lutheran Church and smiled. It was such a gorgeous autumn afternoon. The colors of the leaves provided a display of a once-a-year testimony to nature's beauty.

I never asked if he ever found her, and he never asked me the same question. I had this dream that he somehow, or someway, did find the woman with the golden smile. I hoped and imagined that, right now, he was sitting with her in some chairs lined up on the edge of the lake, while enjoying this amazing afternoon. They were relaxing together, watching the sunset over the lake, and admiring the fantastic tapestry of autumn colors in the mountains that lined the water's edge.

I bet you that they both are sipping red wine from long-stemmed glasses, and talking about autumn memories, eh?

THE END

Love in a Pumpkin

"Now, now, twenty-seven! My dear Paul, do not become all engrossed in the hockey game this afternoon. According to my research, you still have seventy-one games remaining in the season, for you to watch." Binky, my lovely, yet forceful wife, was putting the clamps on me for sitting down to watch the New York Rovers game on the television on this October afternoon.

I felt a slight protest was in order, which I knew would be in vain, nonetheless, I needed to muster up a last gasp attempt.

"But, Binky, they are playing the Comets this afternoon in a matinee game from the garden, and the young goalie, Shambley is in the net!"

Binky stood watching me while I stood in front of the television fiddling with a blasted, new-fangled, cable box, of which I never could work correctly.

Binky dug her left foot in the carpet, and tapped her finger on top of the television, as she was about to make a forceful point, "Well, first off, I know you will need to call your seven-year-old son to come and help you tune the cable box to the correct channel. Second, the last time that Shambley played in the goal, all you did was stand in the living room and scream for him to stand up on his skates, and cut down the angles. I cannot believe that you would enjoy spending a fabulous autumn afternoon locked here in our house screaming at the television. The last and most important reason, Pastor Paul John Henson, is that your two children are already outside waiting for you to take them to pick out Halloween pumpkins, just as you had promised us this week Wednesday, after work at around seven o'clock in the early evening. I am sure you have not forgotten your promise to your children and your wife, now have you, dear Paul?"

Binky folded her arms across her chest and zoomed in for a famous Binky Hobnobber Henson stare as I stopped fiddling with the cable box. I was in trouble, when Binky used my full name, and my "pastor" title in a sentence addressed directly to me, then I was in some very serious trouble.

Oh, oh! It was time to fudge my way through this one. I clicked off the television and smiled at my wife as I said, "Nah, nah, nah, of course, I have not forgotten. Well, dear Binky, I was just about to say, how there are so many more games to watch this season and Shambley is a bum, anyway."

Binky fluffed her hair and smiled back as she quickly moved into action.

My wife was intense now as she barked out the afternoon instructions, "Oh very good, twenty-seven! Now, please take your heavier zipper jacket, and leave your favorite light vest in the closet. I am very glad that you are dressed in your No Way tee shirt and your canvas sneakers rather than your pastor's collar. I do want this afternoon to be a special family outing. Therefore, although I am aware of your obligations, just for today, I prefer not to interact with someone who requires some type of pastoral care, as tends to happen quite often, when you venture out in public wearing your collar. I must also continually remind you that with the approach of the cold weather that you need to stay warmer, dear Paul. I must also remind you that despite your fondness for the colder temperatures, you are no longer twenty years old anymore. I will meet you out in the driveway. I am so excited!"

Binky stood up on her toes and gave me a kiss on my cheek while I weakly nodded in agreement to all of her orders. She smiled and out the door, she scampered off to gather up our children.

My, oh my, she is still quite the whirlwind.

I had narrowly escaped that time since I was almost in some serious trouble, as I *had* forgotten my promise. It had been a tough week at the church office with many boring and slightly unproductive meetings, and time had run away from me.

I wanted to relax and watch the hockey game.

I knew that was a poor excuse because I did promise my children a traditional trip to the garden center for them to pick out some pumpkins for Halloween.

I was about to learn my lesson as to why these types of moments in our lives should never be forgotten.

Our son, Paul William, was already seven years old, and he had grown tall and strong already. He wore his blonde hair long as I still did. His mother would never entertain any such foolishness as to think that he should cut it all off. He loved sports, and hockey was his first love. Much to his mother's chagrin, he played goaltender, as his father did, and he had started to skate this past winter. As he was growing up, he had taken on more of my appearance, as well as some of my personality. He was quiet, smart, athletic, insightful, and slightly introverted. In the quiet way that he now stood back and studied situations, but did not say much, I could see more and more of Paul John Henson in Paul William Henson these days!

Our daughter was quite the opposite of her brother. Heather Sarah was about five years old now and she was a fireball! She was so much like Binky in her personality that there would never be any question at all that she was Binky Hobnobber Henson's little girl!

Heather Sarah's beauty was indescribable; she was just as captivating at five years old as Binky was stunning at any age. Heather Sarah had long, curly red hair, perfect features, and a dynamic personality. Just as her mother did, Heather Sarah asked a million questions, checked and dissected every angle of life into the smallest detail, and the little girl was as sharp as a tack. It was actually frightening as to how smart she was! She was a chip off the old research block for sure, and Binky was happily teaching her everything that she knew.

My wife, Binky Henson, was in my opinion, the most perfect woman in the world. I found it amazing that she had grown even more beautiful and gorgeous, as the years had passed, than she ever was. I had no qualms in saying that she was a woman who was my dream; she was my soul mate, and my love. She still researched everything in life down to the finest details and never missed a trick. It drove many people crazy as she analyzed everything, but to me, it just made me love her more! It was one of the most fascinating aspects of her quirky and wonderful personality that I loved, along with her penchant for being cute, coy, and captivating, whenever she wanted to be. Binky was one of a kind, and she was my lovely wife.

I was indeed a very lucky man.

I grabbed my jacket and the keys to my old jeep, locked the door to our house, and met Binky and the children in the jeep.

"Dear Father, you really were not going to watch the hockey game this afternoon, now, were you?" Heather Sarah zoomed in for an answer. She had inherited the staring gene from her mother and she had put me on-the-spot right away.

I started the jeep, put it in gear and said, "Well I have to be. . .."

"Shambley is a bum in the net, dear Father. He flops down too much," Paul William proclaimed as he had saved me from the wrath of our five-year-old little girl.

"I want a big pumpkin! I want one that is round and fat!

Can we find a round and fat one?" Heather Sarah had shifted gears as I pulled the jeep out onto the main road and we headed for the garden center.

"Sure, sure, sure, you guys can pick out whatever you want this year. You and Paul William can each get a pumpkin and we will get one for the family. We can put them all on the front porch."

"Now, twenty-seven, you promised us that you would show us how to carve the pumpkins this year. Grandpa Henson's method seems far superior to Popo Hobnobber's ideas. I must admit that I found the entire process disgusting as a young girl, and my brother and I would much rather to have painted the outside of our pumpkins. The juice and mushy pulp inside, used to mess my nails up for weeks, and the odors associated with the practice, were atrocious. My dear father would become frustrated with Uncle Tinky and me when we would run away when he carved the pumpkin. Dear Father would throw the carved pumpkin away and just paint faces on some new ones for us."

I laughed at the thought of my wife and my brother-in-law running away in horror at the carving of a pumpkin.

My father-in-law, Senator William T. Hobnobber, was quite the character, and famous for his absolute lack of patience that was for sure. The thought had struck our two children, funny too. They were laughing at the description that Binky had provided of the repulsive pumpkin, "mush."

As we approached the garden center, Heather Sarah asked me, "Dear Father, why did God make pumpkins?"

"Well, for food, I would think, Heather Sarah. You can make some wonderful pies from pumpkins."

I looked in the rearview mirror to see her and Paul William both shaking their heads in adamant disagreement with my answer.

"We had pumpkin pie at Grandma Henson's house last

year and it is yucky," Paul William declared and his sister agreed. "Why else? You are a pastor, dear Father, and you know all about God and these things," now my son was putting me on the spot.

"Well . . . maybe for the seeds . . . yeah, yeah, yeah, they are good. We can scoop them out, bake them, and put some salt on them. They taste good, and they are good for you too," I was happy with my answer, until I saw them both shaking their heads again.

"Uncle Harry gave us a pack of them last year. They stuck in our teeth and dear Mother yelled at him. It took her a long time to pick them out," Paul William told us. He was always hanging around my best buddy, Harry M. Redmond Jr., and in very much the same manner as I had encountered all these years; you sometimes ended up guilty by association when you hung around with Harry.

"Why, dear Father? Why? Are pumpkins in the Bible?" Heather Sarah was still digging, and even though she was in the backseat of the jeep, I could picture her staring at me with an intense gaze. "Fritzie and I need to know for sure!" She held up her stuffed doggie, Fritzie, who went everywhere with us, and pushed him into the back of my head.

Binky was chuckling now, and she leaned over and grabbed my hand, as she whispered, "On the spot dear Paul, oh thou, whose knowledge of the Bible runs so deep, huh?"

"I think I need some more time, kids. Let me think about it. Right now, we are here, so let's go pick out some nice pumpkins," I said, as I gently tapped my wife's hand in reassurance.

The arrival into the garden center parking lot saved me from any further impossible questions. We parked the jeep, the kids jumped out, and they were hopping about with excitement as they eagerly pleaded with us to hurry up to begin the search for the pumpkins.

I followed behind Binky and the children while they made their way towards rows upon rows of pumpkins set upon the ground and some wooden stands for display. There were many other shoppers and families doing the same since Halloween was just a few days away now.

It was a lovely autumn day, and the fresh clean air, set upon the backdrop of the colors in the trees, made for a wonderful setting for this type of event.

I had forgotten all about the hockey game now while we wandered in and amongst the rows of pumpkins. I watched my wife and children, as they studied every angle of the pumpkins and worked hard, to select the perfect ones they wanted for their Halloween fun.

A middle-aged man was working the garden center in the rows where Binky and the children had settled. He had spotted Binky and the children looking at the pumpkins and made his way towards them. I had bent down to study a few larger ones on the ground and my family had walked ahead of me when the man came over. I could tell by the look in his eyes and his face that he was coming over to assist Binky and the children, rather than the multitude of other shoppers, because my wife's beauty had caught his eye.

I saw his eyes go up and down on Binky as he studied my wife.

Binky was dressed in a form-fitting dress, which displayed her curves and female features in a conservative, but outstanding manner. Binky's figure was amazing, even after bearing two children and approaching middle age. She was a woman of rare and striking beauty, and she had caught this man's eye.

He hustled over as he said, "Well, hi there, pretty lady and youse kiddies. Shopping for the perfect pumpkin, I see," he smiled widely as Binky looked up at him.

Binky knew the drill.

I smiled, as I knew that the worker was about to meet

his match.

"Now sir, my children, and I are searching for the exact pumpkin for our Halloween celebration this year. Can you tell me if these are Connecticut Field Pumpkins, Big Max, or Magic Hybrids? My research this week indicated that all of those varieties, I have mentioned are the optimum varieties for carving and display," Binky finished and she zoomed in wide-eyed for his response. The children also zoomed in close with the same stare they had inherited from their mother and waited for the answer.

The worker's sudden eagerness to serve the beautiful woman in which he had spotted shopping for pumpkins had faded a bit, and he stopped and rubbed the top of his head.

"Well, lady . . . I do not really know. . .."

"You are employed here, and you do not know what type of products you sell or their origins?"

"Well, I ah can't say. Do you really research pumpkins, lady?"

All three of them, Binky, Heather, Sarah, and Paul William, stood in unison, and nodded their heads rapidly to indicate that was indeed the case. The poor worker was astounded, as he watched the nodding display, and his formerly bouncing hormones had now decided to go into full retreat mode.

I chuckled at how quickly Binky Henson neutralized the man and his ambitions to serve her.

Binky finally stopped nodding. She turned towards me and pointed, while she told the garden center worker, "Well, my husband will know. You see, he is very smart on a wide variety of subjects. I am sure that he will be able to pick out the best variety for our use."

The three of them started to nod once more as the worker looked up and saw me approaching. Now that he knew Binky was married, and she was, how should we say, "a bit of an educated shopper," and there was no "opportunity" here, he was off to plan his escape.

"I will go check for you, lady," he said, as off he quickly scampered.

"Ha! I see that you chased him off, dear Binky."

I reached over, put my arm around her as she smiled at me.

"He was most inefficient, twenty-seven. Now, do you see the perfect pumpkins? We are going to rely upon your knowledge and expertise here, you know. You will need to carve them, and show us all how it is done, while the children and I take notes."

Only Binky Henson could make Halloween pumpkin carving into a research project!

"I think that I have some in mind over here. You need the pumpkins to be round but have a flat bottom so they stand up and do not roll around. I also like to find ones that have a good-sized stem intact, so you can grab a hold of them and lift the top off easily to put the candles inside."

"Well, lead on, dear Paul. The afternoon is waning and we need to leave enough time to carve them all for our display before dark."

We wandered around a bit more, picked out three nice pumpkins as I explained the ins and outs of the world of pumpkins to Binky and the children.

We marked them all with each person's name with a small marker that Binky had in her purse, so we did not mix them up. I did not want to cause a dispute amongst the kiddies as to whose pumpkin may be whose! I remembered a few of those battles I had with my own sister.

My old man had taught me all too well.

I was surprised, when after we had picked out one pumpkin for the family, one for Heather Sarah, and one for Paul William, that my wife wandered into a row and she picked one out too.

She held it up, studied it, and she smiled.

I heard her say, "Perfect," under her breath.

"Twenty-seven, could you please get me one of those carts to carry all of these on? They are quite dirty, and I would rather not get my dress, hands, and nails dirty here."

I nodded and pulled a cart over. We placed all the pumpkins upon it and wheeled the load to a checkout register set up in the middle of the pumpkin display. Binky also grabbed some dried-out corn stalks that had caught her eye, and she thought they would look nice for the front of our porch for a nice autumn display. We paid for the merchandise and made our way back to the jeep.

The children were beside themselves with excitement as we loaded the pumpkins and cornstalks. They were asking a million questions, and I did my best to answer them all as patiently as I could.

As we drove away, I gave them each something to think about, "Now you two kiddies need to think about what types of faces that you would like me to carve on your pumpkins. Do you want scary, happy, sad, or just regular, old, jack-o'-lanterns?"

While the kids were pondering that for a moment, I asked Binky, "Say, what was the pumpkin that you picked out for, dear?"

She smiled and simply said, "Oh . . . it is mine. I wanted one too." Binky's answer was vague, which was rather unusual for her.

We arrived home, and Binky scooted into the house to bake some homemade chocolate chip cookies, a batch of my favorite peanut butter cookies, and to pour us each a glass of some apple cider, which she had bought during the week.

I set up a carving station on the picnic table in the yard and laid out some newspapers on top of the table for protection. We gathered the pumpkins together as Heather Sarah and Paul William told me what the faces should look like for each of their pumpkins.

"Fritzie and I want a happy pumpkin!" Heather Sarah instructed me.

"I want one who is scared, Father!" Paul told me as he even drew on a piece of paper what he wanted it to look like.

I drew the faces on the pumpkins with a crayon and once the children approved the designs, I went to work carving them up. Binky arrived with the snacks and as this wonderful autumn afternoon waned, I carved up the pumpkins.

Binky studied my every move, and she even took notes as to how I was carving the pumpkins. I explained, step-by-step, as I cut the top, scooped the pulp out onto the newspaper, and the kids ran away from the smell of it.

"YUCK! YUCK! YUCK!"

The two of them screamed as they ran away. Even Binky screwed her face up at the smell and appearance of the pumpkin pulp.

Paul William finally became brave enough to put his hand in the "mush" as he sorted out the seeds to give the baking idea another try.

"Paul William, ask your mother if you can get the strainer from the kitchen, and you can drop the seeds in there now, in order to make it easier to wash them off," I told our son. He nodded and once Binky approved; he ran off.

Binky smiled at me as I explained how Grandpa Henson had taught me to carve pumpkins so long ago. I could tell that my wife was enjoying this family time together. Soon enough, I completed carving the pumpkins, and I dare to say, I had done a very good job at the carving.

We all decided to make the family pumpkin, a traditional jack-o'-lantern, and it turned out rather nicely. I explained how carving the teeth inside of the mouth is always the most difficult part.

The pumpkins were perfect, and we set them on the

front porch, all together on the top step. Binky bundled her cornstalks. She tied them to a post on the porch, and we had a wonderful display on our family home for the holiday. I explained that we would find some candles to put inside and light them up tonight once it was dark. The children were thrilled, and I had to admit, it was a magical time.

We had shared a wonderful autumn afternoon together, and it certainly was a day in which I would never forget. I felt bad about my previous behavior, and I said a little prayer for forgiveness that I would have considered a hockey game to be more important than a day such as this one had been. Even Lutheran clergymen act as if we are knuckleheads, and on occasion, we need reminders as to God's plan for families.

"Come along, everyone. It is time to eat now. I have made some homemade pizza for us to enjoy," Binky waved us into the house as the display had now been finished.

"Be sure to wash your hands! Maybe later, we will cook the pumpkin seeds."

"Fritzie and I love pizza," Heather Sarah barreled into the house a million miles per hour screaming about pizza the entire way.

"Twenty-seven, do you want a Dingleberry beer or a Big Boulder beer with your pizza?"

"A Big Boulder, please dear Binky, those Dingleberries are way too sweet."

We ate, and it seemed unusual to me, but after we had finished dinner, Binky coaxed me to sit down in my easy chair. She suggested that I watch the news on television, and she was able to arouse my curiosity enough to find out who won the game today and see how Shambley had performed in the net. She told me that she did not need any help in the kitchen with the dishes and chased me away.

It almost seemed as if she wanted to get rid of me.

I heard some rustling in the kitchen, spotted Binky

gathering newspapers, while wearing an apron over the top of her dress, her long hair tied back, and she was wearing rubber gloves.

I almost got up out of my chair to see what she was doing, but the sports news came on, and I became lost in the telecast.

Paul William was now sitting on the floor watching the broadcast with me, and we both moaned and groaned as the announcer told us the Rovers had been plastered and lost the hockey game by the score of five goals to one. We were lost in the film clips and highlights of the game for quite a while.

Shambley was a bum!

"I bet he flopped all over the ice, dear Father!" Paul William told me.

"I think you're right, Paul William. He is a bum. Oh, how I wish I could get back in the net one more time! I would show them!"

Binky appeared with her coat and hat on, with Heather Sarah holding Fritzie and standing next to her. They were both dressed to go outside.

Binky told us, "Now, my dear Paul, no more talk of a comeback. Please, both of you will need to put your coats and hats on and meet us on the front porch. It is dark, and we shall see how wonderful our Halloween display is now. I have found some candles and while you two hockey pucks were proclaiming sad laments over Shambley's ineptness in the net today, Heather Sarah and I have lit the pumpkins. Now, come along. Come along, you two!"

Heather Sarah bounced along happily, and she yelled out into the cold night air, "You have to see! Happy Halloween!"

Paul William and I put our coats and hats on, and both of us followed Binky and Heather Sarah out the front door and down the steps. I could see the flickering of the lit pumpkins in the darkness, and we all stood in front of them on the front walkway to see how they looked. I could hear Heather Sarah giggling, and Binky waving at her to be quiet as we viewed them. They looked fantastic . . . one happy one, one scared one, the traditional jack-o'-lantern, and one more, all lined up on the front porch in order.

Wait!

One more?

Hello, what is this?

I smiled as Binky came over and put her arm through mine. Paul William and Heather Sarah laughed and giggled at the sight of the last pumpkin.

There on the porch was Binky's pumpkin, and it was lit up and carved with a large, "I LUV 27."

Binky looked up at me, while the lights from the candles flickered in the autumn night and reflected in her eyes, as she whispered, "And I mean it too. I hope you appreciate how hard it was for me to endure that yucky, mushy, stuff."

The kiddies moaned and groaned at first, as Binky and I started kissing, and then they giggled at our behavior.

Heather Sarah came over and she tugged at my pants as we were kissing and she said, "Dear Father, you never did answer my question, but now you do not have to. I now know why God made pumpkins."

We both looked down at her as she smiled and said, "So that Mommies could tell Daddies that they love them. I bet you now are going to say some words in Welsh that you think Paul William and I do not understand, but we know it means that you love each other. You then will put 'Dinky the Orange Teddy Bear' cartoon on the television for us, and you will giggle, and sneak upstairs to your bedroom, when you think Paul William and I are not watching."

I marveled at this little girl that our love and God's grace had given us. I scooped her up in my arms and kissed her, as I felt some very rare tears running down my cheeks.

"You know something, little girl, you are way too smart

for your age, so I am going to say to you all aloud here, Rwy'n dy garu di wastad ac am byth."

As Paul William arrived to hug us all together, Heather Sarah laughed and said, "We will love you forever too, dear Father."

We stood there hugging in the cold autumn air for a few minutes as the flickering candles cast a warm glow upon all of us.

Binky yelled out to the children, "Come along, it is now time to watch Dinky on the television, kids. We will blow the candles out for now. We can light them again tomorrow night."

She then turned towards me, fluffed her hair, and winked at me, as she whispered, "I would not want our daughter to be wrong, you know, twenty-seven."

As life marches on, we create memories in so many simple ways. I think we just have to open our hearts and minds to them and put them away for safekeeping. The best memories seem to come from the times when you least expected them to appear. Oftentimes, you do not have to shell out some large amounts of money, or travel off to some distant, far-off land, or plan some elaborate gatherings for you to create special memories.

In our lives, it is the simple times, the quiet times that mean the most. They embed in your mind forever more, now, and until the end of time.

Binky held out her hand for my hand. I grasped it, and we went back into the house.

I thought about how I was sure glad that I skipped that hockey game.

THE END

Flickering Light on an Autumn Night

Flickering light inside of a carved orange canvas.
Dancing in the wind inside of a hollowed-out smile.
Deep-set eyes and a perfect grin.
Deep cuts in a tough skin that grew all summer.
You will not give in easily, no not you.

And you laugh at me and the drippy contents upon a newspaper.
Smile; wink at me as you stand, with green eyes glowing.
Pull your sweater around you on a cold October night.
Your beauty is beyond compare.
My love for you is not even measured.
Not in this time, not on this earth.
Flickering light on an autumn night.

The wind blows the candle out.
I relight it.
Dancing in the wind upon a porch so long ago.
A precursor to a lifetime together.
Dancing in the wind teasing our very souls.

And you laugh at me and the drippy contents upon a newspaper.
Smile; wink at me as you stand, with green eyes glowing in the night.
Pull your sweater around you on a cold October night.
Your beauty is beyond compare
My love for you is not even measured.
Not in this time, not on this earth
Flickering light on an autumn night.

The night wanes and the frost settles in.
The pumpkin grows cold, it shrivels, and the candle struggles.
Struggling to remain lit against the wind, on a cold October night.
A telltale sign of November gales and crisp days ahead.
The little orange head hangs in, smiling in the night.

And you laugh at me and the drippy contents upon a newspaper.
Smile; wink at me as you stand, with green eyes glowing.
Pull your sweater around you on a cold October night.
Your beauty is beyond compare.
My love for you is not even measured.
Not in this time, not on this earth.
Flickering light on an autumn night.

Wander in the nights of Octobers long since in the past.
Old memories of a time so long ago.
A light in the night, a memory of a time when we were so happy.
A cold, old, carved pumpkin, upon a porch so long ago.
The light remains lit.
I think by our love alone.

And you laugh at me and the drippy contents upon a newspaper.
Smile; wink at me as you stand, with green eyes glowing.
Pull your sweater around you on a cold October night.
Your beauty is beyond compare.
My love for you is not even measured.
Not in this time, not on this earth.
Flickering light on an autumn night.
Flickering light on an autumn night.

Epilogue

If I could bottle up all the seasons into a glass bottle, then screw the lid on tightly, and release them when I wanted to, what a wonderful world I could have.

I could let a little winter cold out, along with just a little snow, when I wanted it. I would let escape a touch of heat from August whenever I might need it. Not too much now!

I could let out a deep, earthy smell of spring warmth on an April morning, with some rain in the afternoon, to make the flowers bloom and the grasses grow.

However, in my little glass bottle, I think that I would let a bit more autumn out as opposed to the other seasons. The colors, the wind, the cold nights, and the warm days.

Autumn; it is when the world comes alive after stifling summer heat, when the warm sun reminds us that it is still there, and the cold winds foretell of the winter and snow to come.

I stood on my porch on this cold November morning, took a deep breath, and sucked all the autumn season into my soul.

It felt good. It really felt good.

ABOUT THE AUTHOR

If you ask Paul John Hausleben, he will tell you that he is not an author, he is just a storyteller. His mission is to continue to write and tell stories to warm your heart, make you laugh, and sometimes make you cry, just a little. Most of all, he deals in memories, and helps you to remember the good times of your own life, and the special people who touched you along the way. Paul was born and raised in Paterson, and then nearby Haledon, New Jersey, and began writing at an early age. He revisited a writing career later in his life, and he now is the author of a number of novels, compilations, short stories and audio and video works. Most of his work touches upon nostalgic remembrances of simpler times, and tells the stories of heartfelt, humorous, and special human relationships. Other than writing, among many careers both paid and unpaid, he is a former semi-professional hockey goaltender, a music fan and music reviewer, an avid sports fan, photographer and amateur radio operator. He now resides in Somewhere, U.S.A., but his heart always remains along Belmont Avenue in good old Paterson, and Haledon, New Jersey.

Titles by the same author that you also may enjoy:

The Time Bomb in The Cupboard and Other Adventures of Harry and Paul.

The Night Always Comes, Another story from the Adventures of Harry and Paul.

Reunion, A sequel to the Night Always Comes and Another story from the Adventures of Harry and Paul

The Christmas Tree and Other Christmas Stories. Tales for a Christmas Evening

Crows on a High Wire

The Miracle Tree, Another story from the Adventures of Harry and Paul

The Summer Collection

And many others

Coming Soon?

You may contact us via email at ctte27@gmail.com

www.ingramcontent.com/pod-product-compliance
Lightning Source LLC
LaVergne TN
LVHW091049080826
845145LV00002B/678

9780988633636